A Deal to Die for

an Al Pennyback mystery

Charles Ray

Uhuru Press

North Potomac, MD

For information about this and other works of this author, contact the author at charlesray.author@gmail.com.

Printed in the United States of America

Cover created with Cover Genie Pro

Cover art by the author

ISBN: 0692066039
ISBN-13: 978-0692066034

DEDICATION

To the men and women who serve as first responders in emergencies,
natural and manmade, and a special shout out to the law enforcement,
federal and local, who run forward when danger threatens..

Chapter One

The moment I laid eyes on her, I decided that I didn't like her.

I'm not sure exactly what it was that caused that reaction. Maybe it was the way she looked down her nose at Heather, my partner, as she pushed through the door into my office. Or, it could've been the look of superiority on her porcelain face as she looked across the room at me. She wore a form fitting dress that hugged curves that, on any other woman, might have caused me to look at her in appreciation, but my eyes didn't go to her small, pert breasts, or the smooth curve of hips below a tiny waist. They kept going, instead, to the cold disdain I could see in her ice-blue eyes. The diamonds she wore at strategic locations on her body, her ears, around her neck, and at her wrist, added to the sense of coldness I detected coming from her. Of course, the guy who pushed in behind her didn't help my opinion either.

An inch taller than her five-seven or so, with narrow shoulders and a bit of a pot belly, draped in a charcoal gray suit that looked like it cost as much as my entire wardrobe, and carrying a brown, alligator hide attaché case clutched against his sunken chest, with his slicked back brown hair, thin on top and sides, with a hairline that started close to the top of his egg-shaped skull, and small, brown eyes that darted from the woman to me like a rat trying to decide between a hunk of cheese and a stale chunk of bread, he had the look of an ambulance-chasing lawyer of the ilk you see on the TV commercials, offering to help you get the maximum payout from exposure to some harmful substance at your place of work.

The look on Heather's face as she ushered them in vacillated between frustration and fury. Her lips were pinched tight, and there were red circles on her cheeks. She stood behind them, her hand on the edge of the door, and her eyes half-closed. Her body was so tense, I could almost see vibrations in the blue pantsuit she wore.

"Al," she said, her voice as tight as the muscles in her arms. "You have visitors. They *say* they have important business that can only be discussed with you."

I debated standing, something my grandmother taught me to always do whenever a lady entered the room, then reminded myself that she didn't fit my definition of a lady, so to hell with it. I looked up, glanced at her, and slid my gaze off her to Heather.

"What kind of business, partner?"

There, take that. Heather smiled. I'd guessed that the ice queen and her minion had assumed Heather, being a woman, a young, good looking woman, was my secretary. Okay, she *had* started out as a combination secretary-administrative assistant, but Heather Bunche, who I called Honey Bunch sometimes when

6

no one else was around, over the more than a decade we'd worked together, become an integral part of A.E. Pennyback, Confidential Enquiries. I'd helped her get her private investigator's licenses in the District of Columbia, Maryland, and Virginia, and then made her full partner. A whiz with computers, and possessing a rolodex with more names, phone numbers and addresses than Ma Bell, she took care of a lot of the inside research, while I, who had only recently learned to use my laptop computer for more than reading email and playing computer chess, but at six feet and just under two hundred pounds, with twenty years of special operations experience in the army before retiring and getting my own PI license, did the street work. We had a pretty good deal going, what with the ten grand a month retainer from the law firm of Holcombe, Stein and Chang that we were paid to do investigative work—mostly serving papers and tracking down deadbeat clients—thanks to my old army buddy, Quincy Chang, a former army JAG officer I'd served with at Fort Bragg, North Carolina, and the occasional over-the-transom case, we paid all the bills and had a decent hunk of change left over each month.

So, I don't sit idly by when I sense someone's showing my partner disrespect. And, when that somebody's a spoiled, rich brat like the one standing in front of my desk, looking at me like I was a gardener who'd forgotten to trim the front hedge, it totally pisses me off, and I'm not shy about showing it.

The way the ice queen's jaws tightened told me my remark had hit home.

"They didn't wish to share it with me," Heather said.

I locked gaze with ice queen. "And, why would you refuse to tell my partner why you want to see me?"

The question seemed to confuse her. She blinked I didn't. I can keep my eyes open for up to three minutes without blinking. I do that sometimes when

I'm questioning someone, or when I have need to intimidate without making threats. An unblinking stare drives most people bonkers, so you damn betcha they blink first.

The ambulance chaser pushed forward, his immaculately manicured hand thrust forward.

"Apologies on behalf of my client, Mr. Pennyback," he said. "We didn't know that Ms. Bunche was a partner in the firm . . . the name, you see. I am Merriwether Baldridge, attorney-at-law, and my client is Loretta Palmer. We, uh, she, that is, has need of your particular expertise."

I didn't want to stand up, but refusing to shake his hand went beyond rude, which I also didn't want to be. As much as I dislike rich people and certain types of lawyers—the overly slick, expensively dressed, ass-kissing kind like the one shoving his hand at me head that list—I dislike people who are gratuitously rude even more, even if that someone is me. So, I stood and took his hand. As I expected, his handshake was limp, and his hands felt damp.

After a slight squeeze and two pumps, I let go; resisting the urge to wipe my hand on my trousers.

"Have a seat," I said, pointing at the two straight back chairs, one on either side of my desk. "Heather, go get a chair for yourself."

That earned me a sharp look from the ice queen, so I ignored her and focused on Baldridge, giving him my best 'what the hell do you want with me' glare. It worked, too. He squirmed and clutched his case tighter against his chest.

I let the silence hover in the office until Heather returned with one of the visitors' chairs she keeps beside her desk. She placed it directly in front of the desk, halfway between our two visitors, sat, and crossed one shapely leg over the other, her hands demurely in her lap, and ignored them both.

"Okay," I said, just as the tension seemed to be

reaching the point of explosion; ice queen's cheeks were turning red, and Baldridge's knees were bouncing up and down. "What can *we* do for you?" I addressed my question to Baldridge. Out of the corner of my eye I saw the circles of red on Palmer's cheeks get darker.

Good. I was getting to her. That, I thought, should teach her to mess around on my turf. Heather smiled.

Baldridge, on the other hand, didn't seem to notice.

"My client, Ms. Palmer," he said. "Has need of your . . . expertise."

That told me a lot . . . of nothing. I have a wide array of skills, many acquired during my twenty or so years in uniform, being sent on special operations assignments in some of the less savory locations in the world, and dealing with some *really* unsavory characters. Somehow, though, I didn't think a slick lawyer in an expensive suit was referring to my martial skills. I've worked as a private investigator for well over ten years, maybe closer to twenty years, actually, since I got my PI license when I was thirty-eight, and was now pushing fifty-five, so I assumed it was my investigative skills that interested him. Retained by my buddy Quincy's law firm, like I said, we mostly serve papers and track down people. On occasion, the cases that come in 'over the transom' as it were require a few of my military skills, like conducting reconnaissance, or going head-to-head with bad guys, but, thankfully, not often. Oh, and despite being qualified with most weapons short of the Bradley fighting vehicle or a Sherman tank, I do not carry a weapon in my work. I don't even *own* one. Unlike the private eyes you see on TV or the big screen, I don't go around with a handgun at my waist, under my arm, or on my ankle. I have black belts in taekwondo, karate, and ju-jitsu, and if that's not enough to handle a bad guy, I run like hell.

So, anyway, I just sat there, a blank expression on my face, and looked at Baldridge. Heather broke the silence.

"And, just which aspect of our expertise does your client require?" she asked.

They both switched their gazes from me to her. The ice queen looked at her down her nose, while Baldridge gave her the once over a second time, as if maybe he'd not noticed upon arriving that she's really quite stunning. She ignored Palmer, and returned Baldridge's ogling gaze with a look that could freeze ethanol. He blinked, and looked down at his shiny wing tips.

"Uh, well, I was told that he, er, you, uh, I mean, your firm, is pretty good at finding people," he said.

"We have been known to find people who didn't want to be found," Heather said, nodding. "Who do you wish to be found?"

She had Baldridge's complete attention. Ice queen, on the other hand, had a resentful look on a face that would've looked better without it. I think I had her number. She was accustomed to being the queen bee in any gathering, and Heather was stealing the limelight. It didn't seem to make her feel any better that Heather, with her slightly curly blonde hair, cut to just below her ear lobes and down on her forehead, just short of her arched eyebrows, was better looking. Ice queen's looks, for the most part, looked like they'd come from an expensive salon visit and even more expensive cosmetics, while, except for a little blush, and a tinge of lipstick, Heather's was pure DNA.

"Uh," Baldridge said. "It's not exactly someone, but something my client wants you to find." He put his attaché case on his lap, and folded his hands atop it.

"Just what is this *thing* you want us to find?" I cut in, shooting an unfriendly look at Baldridge.

Baldridge didn't seem to be affected by my look. He cleared his throat. "Perhaps, it would help if I gave you some background information first," he said. "Ms. Palmer was recently convinced to make a substantial investment in a real estate venture. We have since learned that the venture was not genuine, and Ms. Palmer would like to avail herself of your services to get her money back."

I had to clench my teeth to keep from laughing.

"Listen, Mr. Baldridge. Sounds to me like your client got herself scammed, conned, taken for a ride. Getting her money back's probably not an option if I understand how these things work, but if there is a chance to do it, it'll have to be through the courts. We don't usually take lost property cases, but even if we did, money lost to a con man's not really the kind of lost property we deal with. Besides, the con artist who took her has probably already spent it."

His gaze dropped to his hands, and he began tapping his fingertips together. "Uh, we have it on fairly good authority that he didn't spend the money," he said.

"So, why don't you ask him for it, or if he refuses, take him to court?"

"Well, we can't exactly do that."

"Why not?"

I was beginning to lose interest in the conversation.

"Because," Loretta Palmer said, a slight accent in her voice I hadn't noticed before. "the shithead who conned me is dead."

"Oh," I said. "I can see how that might be a bit complicated."

"What's worse," she continued. "The police think I killed him."

Charles Ray

Chapter Two

Now, I *really* didn't like Loretta Palmer. I mean, hell, she could've led with that little piece of information, right?

"Why do the cops think you killed this . . . person?" I asked.

She looked at me, really looked at me, as in made direct eye contact with that icy glare of hers.

"Well," she said. "It's probably because I threatened to cut his heart out if he didn't give me my money back."

"Oh, I see. Were there any witnesses to this threat?"

She shrugged. "About fifty, I think."

This woman was as cold as an ice floe in the Arctic. None of what she was saying, which was beginning to give me a minor case of heartburn, seemed to phase her at all.

"Uh, I think some explanation is in order," Baldridge said.

I gave him a look that was only a few degrees

13

warmer than the look Palmer was shooting my way. "You think so?"

"Perhaps," he said. "If Ms. Palmer gave you some background, you would understand the situation better."

"That usually helps," I said. I was on a roll. When my sarcasm generator is turned on, it often goes on auto pilot. I shifted my glacial gaze to Palmer. "Okay, why don't you tell me what motivated you to threaten to cut someone's heart out?"

She crossed her legs, causing her dress to slide up displaying an expanse of ivory-colored thigh, her eyes on me to see if I was looking. I locked eyes with her, which caused her to frown. I folded my arms across my chest and sat back in my chair.

"The little rat who stole my money is named Sydney Simpson," she said.

"Ahem, Loretta, perhaps it would be best if you did not include such colorful descriptions, and just stuck to the facts," Baldridge said.

She flashed him a venomous look. "Put a sock in it, Merriwether. It's my damn story, and I'll tell it any way I please." She turned back to me, the venom gone from her gaze, but the iciness was still there. "Now, where was I?"

"Sydney Simpson stole your money," I prompted.

"Yeah, right. Okay, here's how it happened." She uncrossed and re-crossed her legs, treating me to a view of the other thigh, watching me out of the corner of her eye as she did. When I kept my eyes on her face, she frowned and pulled the hem of her dress down toward her knees. "Sydney started this real estate club, and got me to join."

I must have looked confused—mainly, because I had no idea what she was talking about. I looked at Heather.

"A real estate club," Heather said. "Is where a group of people all pool their money and buy property, which they hold until the price goes up, or they renovate and flip it for a profit."

See, she knows this stuff. That's why she's such a good partner.

"Okay," I said to Palmer. "Go on with your story. You joined this real estate club?"

"That's right. The buy-in at first was just fifteen hundred bucks, and there were twenty of us. Sydney used the thirty thousand we put in to buy a run-down apartment building near the waterfront in the District . . . not far from here. Three months later, he sold it to some developer who is looking to gentrify the neighborhood or something. Anyway, we each made five hundred off the deal."

I'd heard of people doing that, buying distressed properties in low-income neighborhoods slated to be demolished and replaced by expensive condos and shops, and then 'flipping' or selling them for sometimes as much as twice the purchase price. This, though, was the first time I'd heard of real estate clubs. I rank property speculators, especially those who participate in schemes that drive poor people out of their neighborhoods in favor of yuppies and their yogurt bars and exercise clubs, even lower than ambulance-chasing lawyers who talk people into joining expensive class-action lawsuits, which, when they win, most of the settlement goes in their pockets instead of the plaintiffs'. Now, I had a new category to dislike—clubs of people who engage in such endeavors.

"Sounds to me like you were making money," I said. "Invest fifteen hundred, sit back, and collect two thousand for doing absolutely nothing. What's the problem?"

"The problem is, it was a pyramid scheme. We weren't the first group of suckers that Sydney had conned into joining this little enterprise. There were at least forty other people before us, and more after us, and he used the money he'd collected from the group after us to pay us for the first deal, and the money he collected from us to pay the ones he'd conned before us."

"I'm familiar with how pyramid schemes work," I said. Of course, I'd never realized that the real estate market could work that way as well.

"I was just giving you the background." She snorted through her narrow, haughty nose. "Anyway, with the returns we got on that first investment, he had us hooked. That's when he came up with this idea for this block of rural land north of Germantown, west of I-270. Said we could buy up a bunch of farms and soon we'd be able to sell the land to the tech and medical companies building in the I-270 tech corridor. It seemed like a good idea at the time. You see all the new companies going up around Rockville and Gaithersburg. I mean, it's just a matter of time until they spread up past Germantown."

"I'm still not seeing how this worked. How were you cheated?"

She took an expensive looking silk handkerchief from the small purse she carried, and dabbed at her lips and cheeks. "This was a big one, limited, he said, to a few select investors. The catch was, though, that each investor had to put up five hundred thousand. There were ten of us, and he estimated the return on investment would be in the neighborhood of sixty percent."

I did some quick math in my head. Ten suckers at half a mil each, meant that this Simpson dude raked in five million. Five million tax-free dollars. Heather and I were in the wrong line of work.

"So, he absconded with your five hundred thou? I take it there *was* no land purchase."

She shook her head. "No, there *was* land, several parcels in fact. But, when a few of us approached him to ask when we would begin to see some return on our investment, he gave us the run around. About that time, another group showed up. They turned out to be the suckers behind us, the ones he would pay off with some of the money he got from us. Then, he'd get more money from them, and use part of that to pay off the next bunch, and so on."

She dabbed at her lips again.

"Well, when I tumbled to what was going on, I blew it. I demanded my money back then and there. He tried giving me some song and dance about the need to be patient, and how he had a couple of real live purchase prospects line up, but I wasn't buying it. I'm afraid, I blew my stack. I threatened him."

"That's when you threatened to cut his heart out?"

"Yeah, I told him he had twenty-four hours to return my money, or I would cut his fucking heart out—my exact words—then, I stormed out and went back home."

"And, there were, what, ten or fifteen witnesses?"

"More like twenty."

"What happened next?"

"I went to his place in Rockville the next afternoon. I rang and rang his bell, but he didn't answer, so I figured he'd skipped town. I mean, his car wasn't in the driveway. So, I went back home."

"Did you try calling him, or anything?"

"Duh! Of course, I tried calling, but he wasn't picking up his cell. Why do you think I went to his place?"

"Well, just asking," I said. "How else am I supposed to learn?"

She cocked her head to the side and looked at me like you'd look at a suspicious-smelling spot on the bottom of your shoe.

"Was that supposed to be a joke?" she asked.

"No, I was quite serious."

"That's good, because it definitely was not funny. Now, are you going to help me or not?"

I shrugged. "I don't see how I *can* help you, Ms. . . . Palmer. It's hardly likely this Simpson guy put it in a bank account that you could access, or a shoebox under his bed. I guess what I'm saying, is that it's not likely you're gonna get your money back, since, as you've said, Mr. Simpson is currently deceased, and can't be taken to court."

"I don't think he moved the money out of the country," she said. "And, while it's too much to fit into a single shoebox, I think he did hide the cash somewhere. I just need you to find it."

Right. A con man stashes five million cash somewhere, who the hell knows where, and yours truly just waltzes in and finds it. Finding a needle in a haystack's a piece of cake by comparison. This would be like finding a snowball in a snowstorm, while hanging by your ankles from the side of a cliff over a bottomless pit. And, just in case, like the blind squirrel who occasionally stumbles across a nut, I did happen to find the money, a whole bunch of official agencies, like the local cops, the FBI, the IRS, and for all I knew, the SEC, would want to know where the hell I found it, and they'd probably be asking me those questions from the free side of steel bars.

"Our specialty is finding people, sometimes we can even find documents. We've never tried to find money before. I'm not sure we can help you."

She sat back in her chair and pouted like a four-year-old who'd just been told she can't watch any more cartoons. Then, she glared at Baldridge. "What the hey, Merriwether? I thought you said this guy was the best in the business."

"We are the best," Heather said. "At what we do. It's just that we don't normally take cases like this."

Palmer gave her a dismissive glance.

"Ms. Palmer," I said. "You say you went to his house. If it was the money he took from you that you were interested in, why didn't you go to his office?"

"Because, he worked mostly from his—" And, then, she snapped her mouth shut and studied her well-manicured nails. I think she realized that she'd said more than she intended.

"He worked mostly from home? That seems a strange thing for a con man to do. I would think he'd want to keep his marks from knowing where he lived."

Her cheeks sported two red blossoms. I was getting the feeling that there was more, much more, to this than meets the eye.

"What aren't you telling us, Ms. Palmer?" I tried to be gentle with the question, but she flinched as if I'd slapped her.

"Uh, well, you see, the other members of the club *didn't* know where he lived." She still refused to make eye contact with me.

"And, why is it that you did?"

I knew the answer, but I wanted to hear it from her.

"I've been to his house a few times." That said so quietly, I had to lean forward to hear it.

"In other words," Heather said. "Your relationship with Mr. Simpson was a bit more than just business?"

I like the delicate way she phrased it; far better than I would have.

"Well," Palmer said. "Yes. Not that that matters."

Like hell it didn't matter. If she and the victim were having an affair, there was a good chance she'd left DNA or fingerprint evidence all over his place—and, I was assuming here that his home was where he'd been murdered. I decided to drop that little bomb on her, just to see how she'd react.

"Assuming he was killed at his home, Ms. Palmer," I said. "I would imagine the cops have turned up plenty evidence to place you at the scene, which probably explains why they think you might have killed him. And, given that he took you for so much money, you also have motive. That takes care of two of the three things they need to establish probably cause, motive and opportunity. All they need is to establish means, and they'll probably be coming for you."

Her porcelain face went pale, the color of a fish's belly, and her eyes lost the glacial stare. They went all round and kind of out of focus.

"I'm afraid, Mr. Pennyback," Baldridge said in that unctuous voice of his. "They probably have means as well."

"Explain," I said.

"Mr. Simpson was killed by a single stab to the heart with a nine-inch letter opener. That letter opener belongs, belonged to Ms. Palmer."

"How the hell did *her* letter opener end up in this guy's chest?"

"I, uh, gave it to him," she said. "He saw it once when he . . . spent the night at my place, and he liked it so much, I just gave it to him. I hardly ever used it anyway."

I shook my head. "Well, that puts a whole different spin on this case. Instead of worrying about getting your money back, you probably ought to be worried about staying out of jail."

I didn't think she get any paler, but I was wrong. Her face went deathly white. She hadn't thought about that. The rich are like that. Until life walks up and slaps them in the face, they never think the bad things the rest of us know all too well can happen to them. She'd probably been thinking that being considered a suspect in Simpson's murder was just a nuisance. Certainly, someone of her socio-economic background didn't have to worry about anything so crass as actually being arrested. Now, thanks to yours truly, that prospect had been made abundantly clear to her, and her poor mind was having trouble processing it.

Her lawyer, on the other hand, had been thinking along those lines.

"You're absolutely right, Mr. Pennyback," he said. "Which is why I'd like to hire you."

"Huh? You haven't been listening. I've already told you, we're not in the business of finding money."

"No, but you have, in the past, come to the rescue of people who were wrongly accused of crime by the system. That's really what we need you for; to prove my client did not kill this Simpson person."

My gut reaction was to say, no. I'm not fond of the privileged classes. I don't like to see injustice, but they all have so much, it seems to me only fair that they sometimes feel what life's like for those they consider to be lesser beings. Heather, though, is made of better stuff than me. She's never one to let her personal feelings stand in the way of doing the right thing.

"It's the kind of case we're good at," she said. "I think we should take it."

Three pairs of eyes turned to her, none with a more shocked expression than mine. She looked at Baldridge.

"You have to understand, though," she said. "That if the evidence indicates your client is in fact guilty, we will have to turn it over to the police."

Baldridge swallowed hard, and blinked. "Of course, but I assure you, she is innocent."

"In that case," Heather said. "As long as you're okay with our fee of one thousand dollars a day plus expenses, with a five-thousand-dollar up-front deposit, we'll take the case."

Oh, and did I mention that, in addition to being a whiz with a computer and Rolodex™, Heather is also one hell of a sharp business person?

Baldridge smiled and regarded Heather with a look of total respect; one shark to another.

"That is perfectly reasonable," he said.

"Well, my partner will draw up a contract," I said. "And, we'll get started right away. We'll need names and addresses of everyone involved in this real estate deal, and some way to reach both of you in case of emergency."

As Heather escorted them back to her office in front, I noticed that Palmer was looking at her differently. It wasn't exactly friendly, but I sensed a grudging respect. I resolved to let Heather handle her.

Chapter Three

The next day was hump day, that day when every drone working in a sterile, impersonal cubicle in one of the alphabet soup of government agencies, federal, state, and local, in the Washington, DC area, has his or her mind on the upcoming weekend.

For two categories of workers, though, Wednesday was just another day. One category included private investigators like Heather and me, for whom one day seemed to just merge into the next with no noticeable difference. We went where our active cases took us. A hot lead didn't care whether it was Friday or Sunday. The other category was the region's first responders. The firemen, EMT's and cops, who had to be available 24/7, every day of the year. Crime and emergencies, paid no attention to calendars or holiday schedules, except as good times to crop up.

It was for that reason that, when I called my old pal, Detective Buster Mayweather, of the Washington

Metropolitan Police Department, neither of us sounded all that chirpy on the phone—that it, until I invited him to join me for lunch at our favorite place, Mom's, a soul food joint in Sixteenth Street, not far from U Street in Shaw District. This part of DC's Northwest quadrant had been devastated in the riots following Martin Luther King, Jr.'s assassination in the 1960s, but was slowly being rebuilt and converted into a kind of trendy arts and intellectual area, with book stores and coffee shops replacing a lot of the pawn shops that had been there. Mom's, however, survived the smashing and burning, and continued to represent the older history of the area with the fat-laden, fried food of the south popularly known as soul food—another way of describing the food that poor black people were forced to eat in the forties and fifties, but that had been popularized and named by yuppies in the late sixties and seventies. Mom, who must have weighed somewhere in the neighborhood of three hundred pounds, and in the northern part of that neighborhood at that, had ruled the roost for as long as anyone could remember, and over the ten years that Buster and I had been dropping in about three or four times a month, had adopted us as the prodigal sons she'd never had.

Since the Palmer case was our only ongoing case—Quincy Chang's law firm hadn't sent work our way for over ten days, which was fine with me, since they deposited the ten-grand retainer in our account every month whether they'd used our services or not—and I needed to consult with Buster before deciding how to handle it, I decided an early lunch was in order. Heather was happy with that, because it gave her the opportunity to do some computer research on everyone involved, and educate herself on real estate scams, and Buster was happy for any excuse to get out from behind his desk at the precinct. So, we agreed to meet at 11:00.

As usual, he beat me there. He occupied our usual table in the right corner, sitting so that he could watch the street through the big plate glass window, and keep an eye on the interior at the same time, with another chair in the corner for me—I don't like sitting in a public place with my back exposed—his big hands cupping a mug of steaming coffee.

"What took you so long?" he asked.

I looked at the Bulova on my left wrist, a gift from Sandra, my significant, but still unmarried, other for my fifty-fourth birthday the previous July. It was 11:01, and considering that I'd stopped a few seconds to say hello to Moms, perched on a stool near the cash register, meant I'd entered the place right on time, meant that he was being sarcastic. I decided to ignore him, and turned my attention to Mom. She'd followed me to the table.

"You want coffee, Al honey?" she asked in a girlish voice that was totally out of character with her generous frame.

"Yeah," I said. "And, what's good today?"

"Everything, child. But, I got somethin' special in mind for you two. I'll go get your coffee and let you enjoy it while I gets your dinner ready."

Like a lot of southerners, and Mom came from somewhere way in the deep south—I could never remember, and she didn't often talk about it—her three meals were breakfast, dinner and supper. For her, lunch was something you carried to work in a tin pail. She's also a lot like the stereotypical Italian restaurant owner; she decides what you want to eat, and you don't argue with her. So, I didn't. I just smiled and nodded, while she waddled off to get my coffee.

"Okay," Buster said. "What you want from me?"

"What makes you think I want something? Couldn't I just be wanting to have lunch with my best friend?"

"Hell no, not on a Wednesday. Our usual day's Friday, and I ain't lettin' you off the hook this Friday neither, just so's you know. So, spill, pardner, what you want?"

"Okay, amigo, you got me. I'm working on a new case, and I need some background information."

"Like what?"

"What do you know about real estate scams?"

His cup, halfway to his lips, stopped in midair, and he looked at me over the rim.

"Since when have you been interested in stuff like that? You got a client that got conned?"

I nodded, and then gave him the background on Loretta Palmer's situation, leaving out the part about the murder of the con man and her being a suspect. That, though, was a wasted effort on my part. Buster sometimes used street argot when he talks, but he's far from dumb; in fact, he's a lot smarter than I am about a lot of things, and while he plays the role of a street-smart DC cop, he's tied in to most of what happens in the greater DC metro area, an essential skill for a cop in a city that has almost as many police agencies as food trucks.

"I've heard of this guy, Simpson," he said. "He was based in Rockville, but we've got a sheet on him here in the District. His street moniker was Slick, and he specialized in pyramid schemes."

"Why do you keep referring to him in past tense?" I asked.

"I use past tense, 'cause he ain't scamming nobody no more. Somebody shoved a letter opened into his schemin' heart a few days ago."

I tried to look surprised. "Really? Did he get killed here in the District?"

"Nah, somebody did him at his house in Rockville. I saw the report in the precinct, though, 'cause they think it might've been one of his victims who did him, and many of 'em are residents of DC." He paused, his eyes nearly closed. "In fact, I seem to remember seein' the name Loretta Palmer on the list of his . . . clients.

Is this the same Loretta Palmer you're workin' for?"

Now, I don't like sharing details of an investigation outside the immediate circle of Heather and myself, especially at the start, but Buster's been my best friend for nearly two decades, and he's risked his job *and* his life for me on more than one occasion, and one thing I do not do is lie to a friend without a pretty darn good reason. At that moment, I couldn't think of a reason to lie.

"Yeah, as a matter of fact, one and the same," I said.

"Aw, man, don't tell me she's hired you to prove she didn't do it?"

"Okay, I won't tell you."

Charles Ray

Chapter Four

Buster and I, as I've said, go way back. I met him nearly twenty years ago, when I was still in the army, a young colonel working at the Pentagon as a special operations planning officer, and living with my wife, Sarah, and our six-year-old son, Ethan, in a converted brownstone townhouse on the fringes of the Georgetown area in the District.

I still remembered the day he and I met, one neither of us is likely to forget. I'd put in a few extra hours in my office in the basement of the A Ring of the world's biggest office building, across the Potomac River from DC, between Arlington and Alexandria, bordered on the north by Arlington National Cemetery. It wasn't unusual for me to arrive home late. There was always some emergency somewhere in the world to cause us drones in the Pentagon to be chained to our desks for up to eighteen hours a day. Sarah, the daughter of a Philippine general I'd worked with during deployments to the islands, was a trooper about it, and seldom complained. On that particular day, though, she'd been a little peeved, because Ethan's school soccer team was playing a team in Arlington, and I'd been scheduled to drive them to and from the game. When I called to tell her I'd be late, and couldn't make it, she informed me that she'd drive in my place, and I could hear the disappointment in her voice; not because of having to drive, but, because I would miss yet another of my son's games.

The house was empty at 8:30 when I arrived, but I knew the game was scheduled to end at 6:00, and after probably stopping somewhere to buy ice cream for Ethan and his teammates, she'd be arriving any time, so I shucked my uniform jacket and began preparing supper, planning to surprise them—and, hopefully, getting back in their good graces. By 9:00, they still hadn't returned, and I began to worry a bit. I was just about to put on my jacket and head over to Arlington, when the doorbell rang.

It was Buster, then a beat cop, with two uniformed officers from the Arlington County Police Department. As soon as I saw the expressions on their faces, I felt cold all over and an ache in my gut like I'd been sucker punched. I'd done enough casualty notification duty to know that look.

They were professional, but the tension in their voices and expressions showed how much they disliked such duty. The Arlington guys let Buster do the talking, and his steady, deep voice, was probably the only thing that kept me from completely losing it.

Sarah had been driving east on Arlington Boulevard with Ethan and his team crammed into our 1990 Ford Econoline van, when, just west of Fort Myer, a truck driver driving north on one of the cross streets had run the stop sign and t-boned the van. The speed of the truck completely caved in the right side of the van, and pushed it completely across Arlington Boulevard, before it was stopped by a utility pole, which then collapsed the left side. The driver of the truck escaped with minor cuts and bruises, but there were no survivors in the van.

When Buster got to that part of the story, I did freak out for a moment, but he managed to calm me down. He took me in his cruiser, and we followed the county cops to the Arlington morgue, where, along with the parents of the other boys, we were taken in one by one to formally identify the 'deceased.' I was like a zombie when I saw those two still forms on those sterile steel trays, covered with green sheets. Everything was a blur. But, through it all, Buster never left my side.

He stayed with me while I signed the required forms; took me home and stayed at the house that night, while I sat at the kitchen table staring at the wall; and was there with me over the next few days as I made final arrangements. Tragedy brought us together, but it was the strength of his character that created what became a friendship.

With the two people who meant the most to me suddenly gone, I felt I had nothing to live for, but Buster helped keep me sane. He also helped set me on the course my life eventually took.

I took leave from my Pentagon job to plan the funeral, and then extended that leave afterwards, and did nothing but hang around the house. After the sixth week, I finally went back to work just long enough to put in my retirement papers, and then returned home, where I sat around and moped some more.

Buster let me mope for a full two months, before hooking up with Quincy Chang, an old Judge Advocate General friend from my Fort Bragg days who'd left the army and gone into private practice in the DC area, eventually becoming a full partner in the firm of Holcombe, Stein, and Chang, and holding what has now become known as an intervention, but was then known as friends slapping some sense into another friend's head, and the two of them browbeat me into coming out of my shell and getting my shit together.

After a few hours of cajoling, cursing, and comforting, they convinced me that I needed to get back to work, and after some more conversation, decided that I might be good at private investigation, since I was a bit too old to apply for a job as a cop. Quincy sweetened the pot by arranging for his firm to put me on retainer to serve papers, find people, do background checks, and the like.

And, that's how A.E. Pennyback, Confidential Enquiries was born. Yeah, that's me, A.E. Pennyback, or, on my birth certificate, Alfred Einstein Pennyback. The first and middle name thanks to my mother who had a thing for the German scientist, and hoped that I'd grow up and follow in his footsteps. I disappointed her by joining the army right out of high school, something my dad was kind of proud of, but would never say so in her presence. They both perished in a hurricane that hit the coast of Texas while they were visiting a cousin in Garrison who had a house on the beach. The entire house was swept away in a storm surge, and no bodies were ever recovered. I was stationed overseas at the time, but the army gave me compassionate leave to attend a memorial service for them back in our East Texas home town, a town a never went back to. With no bodies in graves to visit, it never seemed to make any sense.

Anyway, back to the PI business. I opened shop on the second floor of a building on Fourth Street Southwest, just north of the army's Fort Lesley J. McNair, and almost within sight of the Washington Channel and the Potomac during the winter when the leaves had fallen and I could get glimpses between the towering condos behind my building. My building looked a little like some of those motels you find on back roads in the south, with names like 'Dew Drop Inn,' or 'Rebel Inn.'

It didn't take me long after hanging up my shingle—

actually, after having the firm's name painted on the door—for me to realize that there was one aspect of the private eye business that I needed help with; the paperwork. You'd be amazed at the amount of paperwork even a one-person business has to do, and paperwork is not my strong suit. I got lucky in that regard. Heather Bunche, had just graduated from secretarial school and needed a job. A tiny, perky-faced blonde, she quickly demonstrated that she was an expert with a computer, had secretarial and administrative contacts all over the area, thanks to her secretarial school, and was almost anal-retentive in her organizational skills. After ten years of being my office manager and assistant, I helped her get her PI license, and made her a partner. I wanted to change the name of the firm to reflect that, but she talked me out of it, explaining that people knew us by that name, so it made sense to keep it.

You now know the names of my first three friends in the area, and my true best friends. They're also people who come in handy when I get saddled with a tough case.

A recent addition to my list of friends is Carlton 'Blood' Raine, an octogenarian retired CIA agent, one of the first black men to be a full-fledged field agent in the agency, who got his nickname, not from the old slang term for blacks, but from some of the operations he was on during his long career. I'd met Blood through Quincy, who'd never explained how they knew each other, and we'd hit it off. He still had agency contacts, and was occasionally given some of their new gadgets to evaluate. He, too, is on my list of people I call friend, along with Elizabeth Sung, his now live-in girlfriend. Elizabeth has her own law firm in DC's Chinatown, where she serves the region's large Chinese community.

The final person in my life, Sandra Winter, holds a special place in my mind and heart. She's a friend—

and more. A teacher at Carter High School, one of the District's inner-city schools, I met her when I was asked to investigate the shooting of one of her students. The cops had basically written it off as just another gang-related killing, but the kid's grandmother disagreed. Turned out she was right, and, with Sandra's help, I'd caught the real killer, an art thief who lived next door to her that the boy, visiting his teacher, had seen moving contraband. We got off to a rocky start, finally decided that we really liked each other, and she moved her stuff, rented her house in Takoma Park, and moved into my farm house off River Road, west of Potomac Village, in Montgomery County, Maryland.

In addition to these, I count Buster's wife, Alma, as a friend—she and Sandra were once kidnapped by a West Virginia militia group to coerce Buster not to testify in a murder case they'd been involved in, and had developed a close bond. Furthermore, Sandra and I were god parents to their twins, little Albert and Sandra.

And, there you have it; the people who count in my life. For them I would do almost anything, and I try and withhold nothing from them. So, I don't think that telling Buster everything I knew about the case really violated client confidentiality.

He promised to look into it and get back to me.

That's what friends are for.

Chapter Five

My next stop after lunch was Quincy's office on K Street. High up in a gleaming office building of glass, steel and concrete, Quincy's corner office has a view of the White House and Washington Monument to the south. The firm has the entire floor, and as a senior partner, a quarter of the space is his, along with six associates to help him with paperwork and case preparation, and a blue-haired administrative assistant of indeterminate age who shamelessly flirted with me every time I visited.

After extricating myself from what would've meant a trip to HR if I'd been the one doing it, I finally closed the door to Quincy's office, with the blue-haired menace on the opposite side.

Quincy, his jacket hanging on a rack in the corner, and his mauve shirt's sleeves rolled up to the elbow, sat behind his desk, with a knowing smile on his face. Sometimes, I suspected he put the siren at the front desk up to her hi-jinks just to try and get a rise out of me.

"So, Al," he said. "To what do I owe this unannounced visit? I don't think we have any cases for you at the moment."

I plopped down in the chair at the right of his desk and crossed my legs. "I'm not here about work, Quince, well, at least, not about the work I do for you guys. I need some background information for another case I'm working on."

His brow wrinkled as he looked at the inch-thick stack of papers in the center of his desk.

"Wel-l-l, I suppose I could give you a few minutes. What do you want to know?"

"Tell me what you know about real estate fraud," I said.

He went back in his chair, his hands up in surrender. "Whoa, compadre, I said a few minutes. It'd take me a week to fill you in on even the basics of real estate fraud. I mean, you have foreclosure rescue, mortgage elimination, home improvement scams, illegal flipping, land fraud, rental fraud, and that's just off the top of my head. Fraud's present in the real estate industry just like any other, and since the real estate bubble started contracting last year, it's been on the rise. Hell, I don't think the government even knows how many billions, yeah, I said billions, of dollars con artists bilk people of each year."

"Oh," was all I could say. I really had no idea it was that bad, but Quincy's not one to exaggerate. If he says it's bad, brother, it's bad. I needed to refine my question a bit.

"Okay, what can you tell me about real estate investment clubs?"

"Okay, that's a little more manageable," he said. "First, you have to understand, stuff like this has always been happening, but lately, it's on the rise." I gave him my single-brow raised look. "Seriously, it has. The big banks don't always advertise it because it'd expose their risky loan behavior, and a lot of the victims don't report it because they're embarrassed, but, we're talking about billions annually."

The eyebrow went down. "Holy shit. That's rivaling the drug trade."

"Probably. Frankly, we have better statistics about the drug trade. Anyway, you wanted to know about real estate clubs. I'll try to give it to you without legal terms. Basically, it's when a group of people pool funds to buy property for investment purposes that the individuals probably wouldn't have been able to buy on their own. The way con men use it varies." He picked up a gold Mont Blanc pen and a yellow legal pad and began making notes. "Sometimes, the person running the scam will have legitimate property, which he or she either promises will either be sold at a high markup from the purchase price, or will start to generate profitable income in a short period of time. Needless to say, neither outcome is realized."

"So," I said. "The con man pockets the investors' money and runs?"

"Sometimes. The real sophisticated con artists, though, construct pyramid schemes and pocket real money from them."

I looked confused again. "Okay, buddy," I said. "I'm only sort of familiar with pyramid schemes. How do they work in this case?"

"Just like they do in any other field. Money from new investors is used to pay old investors, which often gets them to invest more. Eventually, though, no one gets a payoff, but by then, the con man has pocketed the funds and is in the wind. Oh, another thing about these big real estate scams; they're often used to launder money."

"Whoa, buddy, you lost me there. How does that work?"

He made a few notes. "Remember when you bought your farm; all the fees you had to pay at closing? Well, in a big commercial transaction, you can multiply the fees, both the number and amounts, by a whole lot. And, the sad thing is, that while banks are required to report suspicious deposits or fund transfers, realtors are not."

"Don't tell me the drug cartels are using real estate to launder their dirty money."

"Sorry, bud, but they are," he said. "So is organized crime and international terrorist networks. And, believe it or not, despite the blowback of 9/11, it's easier to do here in the good old US of A than almost anywhere else in the world."

All I could think was, 'oh, shit.' He'd said the magic word, terrorist. Since the planes hit the twin towers in New York and the Pentagon, the military, police, and security agencies had terrorism on the brain, and were seeing terrorists behind every bush. Air travel, which had for a long time been getting more and more uncomfortable, became geometrically worse, with long lines for security checks, limitations on what could be carried on flights, and surly TSA agents acting like little emperors at airports all over the country. I don't fly all that much, preferring to jump out of planes rather than land in them, and I liked it even less since that day. Of course, like all bureaucracies, the security measures were bothersome, but not always that effective. The real estate and money laundering loop hole was a case in point. The government was screwing with banking operations to interfere with terrorist funding, but not real estate transactions. I suppose it was like the attitude they had about using planes as weapons before a bunch of fanatics did it—it can't happen, because no one would do something like that. Well, they did, and if the guys responsible for predicting such things hadn't had their heads in rectal defilade, they wouldn't have been so surprised. Ever hear of kamikaze bombers in World War II? Yeah, not only do American bureaucrats not know foreign languages or cultures, but they're also ignorant of American history.

"I guess they don't think terrorists would be interested in buying land," I said.

"Who the hell knows." He had a disgusted look on his face. "I just know that getting congress to even think about passing some kind of legislation to look at it is like trying to pass a kidney stone the size of a softball—painful as hell, and ultimately unsuccessful. Why this sudden interest in real estate fraud?"

I gave him the background on the case, leaving out my decidedly mixed feelings about my client.

"So," he said when I'd finished. "She wants you to retrieve her money and prove she didn't kill the guy. How do you plan to do that?"

"Do which?" I asked. "I don't think I have a snowball's chance in hell of getting her money back. As for proving she's not the murderer, that'll mean finding out who really did it, now won't it?"

"You confident she didn't do it? After all, he did bilk her for a lot of money. People have killed for less. And, from what you told me, she had means and opportunity in addition to motive."

That was a good question. The truth was, I wasn't sure. Heather, on the other hand, who disliked Loretta Palmer even more than I did, seemed pretty certain she was innocent. My gut wasn't telling me anything one way or another, so I was going with Heather's gut. Hell, she had a pretty good track record.

"Heather thinks she's innocent," I said. "So, I'm going with that. She's rich, spoiled, and frankly, not too bright, but I didn't get a killer vibe from her."

"Just asking. Do you need anything else from me?"

I stood, and smiled. "Nah, but if I do, I know where you live."

Charles Ray

Chapter Six

I left Quincy's building, swung by the office and filled Heather in on what I'd learned from him and Buster, and headed home, arriving at my farmhouse off River Road at 6:30 pm.

Sandra was already there, sitting on the sofa facing the door, dressed and ready for our evening out. She wore a lime green blouse with sleeves that ended at her elbows, open at the neck just enough to show a shadow where her cleavage began, and dark green pants that hugged a slender waist, flaring hips, and athletic legs.

The nice thing about being a teacher is that when she doesn't have parent-teacher conferences or after-school activity, she's home before 5:00 every day. And, she's such an understanding person, she rarely gets upset when I'm late getting home on days when we have evening activities planned.

Today was no exception.

When I walked through the door, she jumped up from the sofa and we collided midway between door and furniture. She adhered her body to mine, breast to mid-thigh, threw her arms around my waist and pulled me close, and we did a lip-lock that sent little tingles up and down my arms, legs, and other extremities.

After a long and satisfying kiss, she pulled away, but kept her arms around my waist. She's almost my height, so she doesn't have to look up to look into my eyes.

"Tough day?" she asked.

"Not so much tough as complex," I responded.

"Oh, do tell."

I disentangled and put my hands on her shoulders. "Yeah, let me grab a shower and change, and I'll tell you all about it at the restaurant."

Thanks to my army conditioning, the shower and change routine only took fifteen minutes, and we were in my green Volkswagen classic bug by 7:00, heading for Little River Turnpike in Annandale, Virginia, an area just inside the I-495 Beltway, southwest of Alexandria, that has the highest concentration of Koreans in the DC metro area. From the I-395 expressway south to the beltway, the turnpike looks like a foreign country, with the majority of the business signs in the angular Korean alphabet known as *han-gul*. Everything from restaurants to real estate agents to video shops. The only thing they haven't done is redo the street signs in Korean, but the area is still known as Little Korea by most locals.

The drive, River Road to the beltway, and around the outer loop to Little River Turnpike off-ramp, then north east to Seoul Garden Restaurant, took forty minutes.

Seoul Garden was a one-story, box-like building with brown, faux wood siding and green slate roof, sitting in the middle of a macadam parking lot at the south end of a block that contained a strip mall, a gas station, a Korean bakery, and two pawn shops. Eating out is what people do in the area, and at nearly 8:00 pm, the parking lot was crowded. We found a space for the bug adjacent to the sidewalk, as far as you could be from the building and not be in the adjacent business's parking lot.

Inside was just as crowded, but thankfully, we didn't have to wait for a table. The waitress, a tiny Korean woman with a horrific overbite, gave us a table in the back corner near the door to the kitchen. Not the best table in the place, what with the smell of cooking grease coming from the kitchen, and the constant flow of waitresses and busboys, which explained its availability, but it beat waiting.

I ordered two large bottles of OB, a traditional Korean beer, and got the menu to look over while the waitress went for the drinks. The menu, a large fourteen by twenty-inch card, plastic coated on both sides, listed all the place's offerings, complete with color pictures, and labels in English and Korean.

By the time the waitress was back with two frosted brown bottles and two glasses, we'd decided what we wanted.

Most foreigners, when they eat at Korean restaurants, go for the *bulgogi*, which is thinly sliced beef that's been marinated in soy sauce for several hours, and then cooked over a fire right at the table. While it's great, the *kalbi*, either beef or pork, cut up into small rectangles, and a bit thicker than the barbecued beef, not marinated, but still cooked right at the table, is even better. Better yet, is the way you eat it. After the meat is cooked, you put it on a lettuce leaf, with bean paste, a bit of rice, sliced garlic, and *kimchi*, or pickled vegetables; then, you roll it up into a ball, about the size of a tennis ball, and cram it into your mouth, chewing as you cram. It looks like a gross way to eat, but talk about fun. Along with the kalbi, we ordered *mae-un-tang,* a spicy seafood soup. With just those two dishes ordered, we still ended up with a table laden with food, because a Korean meal comes with extra rice, and at least six side dishes of *kimchi,* ranging from the pungent radish with garlic and red pepper to pickled crab bits to chopped turnip in water with a touch of salt.

All of this food is placed around the grill in the center of the table, and diners are given chopsticks and spoons, and engage in communal eating.

Dinner conversation during a Korean meal is minimal, until the food is done, and the after-dinner drinking begins. A group of local Korean businessmen, their jackets draped over the backs of their chairs, sleeves rolled up, and faces already crimson, seated near us, were already well into the drinking portion of the evening, laughing and telling jokes in Korean; in loud voices. In any other restaurant, this would have earned them dirty looks from fellow diners, but here, it was just a sign that they'd enjoyed the meal. Sandra and I hardly noticed as we tucked into the mound of meat on the grill.

Once our appetites were sated, we ordered our second beers, and sat back, rubbing our stomachs.

"I feel guilty doing this," she said. "After chastising my students for their table manners in the cafeteria, to eat with my hands the way we did tonight seems hypocritical."

"Hey, if Carter's cafeteria served Korean food, you wouldn't have to," I said.

She took a long swallow of her second beer. "Okay," she said, as she put her glass down. "Tell me about your new case."

"This one's a doozy." I gave her the quick summary.

"So, this rich woman let herself get conned out of a ton of money, and the con man ended up dead, and she's the prime suspect." She caught on quickly.

"I don't have all the details, just her side of the

story," I said. "But that's essentially it."

"You know you don't have any hope of actually getting her money back, don't you?"

"Of course, I know that, and I've tried to make it clear to her. I'm not sure she was listening to me when I said it, though. Anyway, I'm focusing my efforts on trying to find out who killed the guy. At least, that way I will have earned our fee."

Her brow wrinkled and she pursed her lips. "You're going to be stepping on some toes on this one, Al, but you know that already. Wouldn't it be better to let the authorities handle this?"

In a perfect world it would be, but, unfortunately, we don't live in a perfect world. We live in a world where, if things can go wrong, they will go awfully wrong, at the wrong time.

"You're right, babe," I said. "I'm gonna be stepping on toes, and since the murder happened in Montgomery County, I won't have Buster to run interference. But, I'll just have to deal with that. As for letting them handle it, if they focus on my client as the prime suspect, confirmation bias will tend to have them ignoring any evidence that doesn't support that theory."

Her expression was pained. She was more than familiar with that situation. It was how we met. The police had assumed that her young student, a black male teen who lived in a low-income neighborhood, gunned down in the street, had to be involved with street gangs. As a result, they hadn't put the resources into investigating his death that might have been put in if he'd come from a middle-class neighborhood. And, it's not that the authorities don't care. Resources are scarce, and they have to put those resources where they think they have the most impact, or chance of success. Sadly, many of the low-income neighborhoods with the highest crime rates don't trust, and therefore, don't cooperate with the police, making the police reluctant to put too much effort into areas where they believe they will get no cooperation—a vicious circle that no one seems able to break.

"From what you've said, though, your client is rich. With her money, she should be able to high enough high-powered legal help to create enough doubt, making it difficult to convict her unless there's evidence putting her at the scene at the time of the murder—and, I assume that if the police had that, she'd be in jail already."

There was that, of course. But, it didn't mean they wouldn't get enough evidence to support a circumstantial case—hell, there've been cases where they got a conviction without a body. But, Sandra was right. With her money Loretta Palmer could tie the prosecution in knots, unlike the average shmuck who would get plowed under by the system. As far as I was concerned, though, no one should have to do that, and it didn't matter what I thought of my client personally; if she was innocent, she shouldn't have to spend an hour in a courtroom, much less in a cell. And, if I had anything to say about it, she wouldn't.

"In the meantime, though, the real killer is walking free. I can't stand by and let that happen."

She knew me well enough not to argue.

Chapter Seven

I arrived at the office the next morning at 8:15, and, as usual, Heather was already there, a cup of jasmine tea in her hand, and her eyes focused on her laptop screen. She mumbled something unintelligible as I walked past her desk and into my office.

I debated turning my own computer on and checking emails, or playing chess, but my mind had been on the case all night, and I was still running possible scenarios through my mind. At this point, with no additional information to base actions on, it was just an academic exercise, but that's the way I roll. By the time Heather gave me her data dump and Buster got his info to me, I'd probably have two or three possible courses of action in mind, and would end up doing something entirely different. It was an old military habit, this constant planning. Even though no battle plan has ever survived the first shot, the military still plans constantly, under the theory that he who fails to plan plans to fail. It's not the content of the plan that matters, but the process of planning that's important.

When I'm doing this kind of mental planning, to an outside observer, I might look like I'm drifting off to sleep, but believe me, it takes as much energy to do that level of thinking as it does to run a marathon—you're just not breathing as hard at the end.

I sat in my scuffed old executive chair, swiveled around and leaned back against the edge of my desk, and focused on the sky beyond the window. In early May, the foliage on the trees between my building and the channel and river is so thick, it's almost impossible to see anything. The sky was a bright blue, with just a smattering of wispy clouds, and the occasional quick glimpse of an airplane taking off from National Airport across the river just down from Crystal City.

With hands clasped behind my head, I began reviewing what I knew—and, what I didn't.

The victim: Sydney 'Slick' Simpson, con man running a real estate pyramid scheme. Killed by person or persons unknown.

Suspects: Other than Loretta Palmer, our client, the other victims of Simpson's scam had to be considered suspects, but I was waiting for Heather to come up with names.

Plan of investigation. My initial focus would be on Simpson's victims. While Heather thought our client was innocent, and I trusted her judgment, she would have to remain on the list of suspects until I could come up with something to conclusively rule her out. That was my Plan A. Given what Quincy had told me about criminals using real estate deals to launder money, Plan B meant we would also have to look at Simpson's other possible contacts. If he was laundering money for a drug cartel, and somehow crossed them, he'd be toast. I'd yet to come up with a Plan C, but the two I had would take up a good chunk of my time.

The phone on my desk rang just as I was beginning to see some coherence in the shapes of the clouds that were floating lazily across my view. I stabbed the button with the picture of a megaphone, which Heather had finally explained to me caused the damn thing to act like an intercom.

"Yeah, what is it?"

"Buster on the line, Al," Heather said, her cheery tone in contrast to my surly sound.

"Thanks, Honeybunch," I said, using a nickname that she grudgingly allowed me to use, provided I only did it when no one else was around. I pushed the lit-up button. "Hey, Buster, what's up?"

"Got some skinny on that dude you asked me about yesterday," he said in that booming voice of his, and loud enough, that if I'd had the phone to my ear, I would've held it away. Buster only has two voice volumes, loud and off.

"Do I need to take notes?" A few years ago, I would've just told him to give me whatever he had, but with birthday number fifty-six just two months away, I was finally accepting that my ability to retain large volumes of information wasn't what it once was.

"Yeah, maybe you better," he said. "I got a shitload of names and dates."

Hell, even Buster's starting to treat me like an old man. I opened the top drawer of my desk and pulled out a new steno pad and a ballpoint pen. I opened the pad. "Okay, shoot."

He'd been busy, and as usual, amazed me with the amount information the government at all levels has on citizens. Here's what I jotted down in my pad:

Sydney Aaron Simpson, born October 12, 1968 in Bayonne, New Jersey. Known on the street as Slick, because of his flashy clothes and his ability to part people from their money. Killed May 2, 2003, at his residence in Rockville, Maryland, when someone stuck a nine-inch letter opener into his chest, piercing his heart. A single stab wound, Buster said, indicating that it probably wasn't a crime of passion, which seemed to rule my client out—but, not completely. Simpson had been in trouble with the law since his teens, with, according to Buster, a juvie record as long as his arm, but since it was sealed, he couldn't tell me what our dead friend had done. He was known to work with an accomplice, a grifter named David Devlin.

David Gerard Devlin, born June 1, 1972 in Lexington, Kentucky. In and out of the juvenile system since the age of 12, Devlin served 18 months in state prison in his home state for fraud. Moved to the DC area in 2000, where he met Simpson. Reported to be shy and socially awkward, not much known about him.

Loretta Lynne Palmer, born March 15, 1973 in Bournemouth, UK to Godfrey Palmer, a member of the British aristocracy, and lord of Palmer Manor near Bournemouth, and Elizabeth Saunders, a stage actress from New York City. Saunders and Palmer divorced when Loretta was five, and Saunders returned to the U.S., living first in New York until her stage career foundered, and then moving to DC, where she used the generous divorce settlement from her husband to establish an acting school in Georgetown, just north of Georgetown University, near Thirty-Sixth and R Street. Palmer grew up hobnobbing with the elite of Washington society, attending private schools and enrolling in Georgetown, where she dropped out after three years and took over her mother's acting school when the elder woman's health began to fail.

Buster had even gotten the names of the other members of the real estate investment club—like I said, the government knows who and where you are like you wouldn't believe.

There wasn't much on them beyond names and addresses, but that didn't bother me. With those bits of information, Heather could do a deep dive into the World Wide Web and come up with even more information than Buster could. I've always been reluctant to ask her how she manages to do it, and while I'm pretty sure she doesn't break any national security laws—she's never tried to get information from NSA, the CIA, or the Pentagon, for example—I ascribe to the view that what I don't know, I can't be made to testify to.

The club members were a really diverse group:

Tamara Braxton, 48, owner of Braxton's Boutique, a high-end beauty salon that catered to Washington's rich.

Isabel Frontis, 69, widow and heir of William Frontis, owner of one of the largest construction companies in the DC region.

Harrison Hillsworth, 60, a retired engineer who made a fortune from inventing some gizmo that sped up manufacturing processes in auto factories.

Dudley Wiggins, 52, a semi-retired plastic surgeon.

Liana Kolchek, 61, owner of a chain of bakeries.

Walter Reid, 64, a retired army colonel.

Jessica Travis, 50, a best-selling romance author.

Roberta Davis, 40, a well-known fashion model who

now has her own fashion line.

Harriet Gold, 62, an artist, whose work sells well in Europe and Asia.

Except for the army colonel, who I couldn't figure out, everyone on the list sounded like money, lots of money. I imagined he must have inherited from a rich relative. Other than that, though, nothing stood out. Buster didn't provide addresses, but that wasn't a problem. With just their names, Heather could coax more information out of the ether about them.

When Buster hung up, I tore off the pages of notes, and took my list out to Heather, and asked her to start doing work ups on them. I went back to my office and started refining my plan of attack—no, I wasn't planning on attacking anyone, but the use of army jargon is something that's hard to avoid when you were in uniform as long as I was. What I was doing was mapping out how I planned to conduct the investigation.

I started with the basic assumption that my client had not lied to me, and was innocent. If, in the course of the investigation I uncovered information that contradicted that assumption, I would make the appropriate adjustment. In other words, if my client was guilty, I would turn whatever I found over to the authorities. It would probably mean we wouldn't get paid—beyond the deposit we always insist on—but, that's the way the ball bounces.

Back, though, to the steps in my investigation. Assuming my client was innocent, I had to narrow down the list of people with motive, means, and opportunity. It would start of course with the names I currently possessed, with the other scam victims at the head of the list. My instinct was to eliminate the four older women, but I realized that, not only would that be somewhat sexist, it also ignored two things; it doesn't take a lot of strength to stab someone one time with a sharp object, and anyone with enough money could always hire a professional to do their dirty work. In fact, the more I thought about it, the more this killing bore the stamps of a professional job. One well-placed thrust to the chest, and, bingo, the victim's toast. No muss, no fuss, and no sign of any emotion in the act. Okay, that left all the con victims on the list.

Simpson's partner, Devlin, was also an interesting character. Not that I considered him high on the suspect list, but he might be able to give me more background on Simpson, his habits, other associates, and the like. Often, the key to catching a killer is to focus on the victim, and try to determine what it was about the victim that attracted the killer.

That, I decided, would be my primary effort—learn as much as I could about Sydney 'Slick' Simpson. It would involve visits to his home and place of business, neither of which would be easy. I had no easily-explainable reason for visiting his office—once Heather learned the address—and, his house would be a crime scene, which the cops might or might not be finished with. If they were still investigating, they'd be pretty miffed if I came snooping around, and even if they were finished, they might not be too happy to have a private gum shoe sticking his nose in their investigation.

I've not had much contact with the Montgomery County police; not that there's no crime in the county. On the contrary, despite being one of the wealthiest counties in the state of Maryland, places like east Rockville, Gaithersburg, and Silver Spring experience robberies, assaults, drug use, and even murder—not quite as much as DC or parts of northern Virginia, but significant. It's just that I hadn't been approached by anyone in the county for help on a case. That meant I would have to tread lightly. In addition to DC, I have a PI license in both neighbors, and didn't plan on doing anything to jeopardize my ability to practice my profession.

So, that meant coming up with a cover story for visiting Simpson's office—maybe I would find his partner, Devlin, there, and planning a nighttime reconnaissance of his residence.

After that, I would split the list up with Heather, and we'd interview each of the other members of the real estate investment club.

I made a few more notes in my steno pad, and was just about to go out front to brief Heather, when she breezed in with a smile on her face.

Chapter Eight

I've mentioned that Heather is something of a Svengali when it comes to coaxing information from online files, right? Well, in the time it had taken me to decide to visit Simpson's office and plan a midnight run at his house; a grand total of maybe thirty minutes; she'd come up with contact information for everyone on the list Buster had given me.

"Wow, that was quick," I said, when she put a paper with neatly typed entries on my desk in front of me.

"Huh, it's just basic information," she said. "I still have to get more background on them."

"Yeah, about that; I was thinking we could split the list up and pay them a visit."

She looked at me, her eyes wide with . . . surprise, or suspicion, I wasn't sure which. "I could get just about anything we need by doing research."

"It's time you earned your spurs kid," I said. "What

you get off those Internet files of yours is statistical crap . . . well, not crap, but just data. If you want to *know* a person, you have to look 'em in the eye. We need to determine if one of these people could be a killer. You don't get that from files."

Understanding dawned in her bright blue eyes. "Uh, yeah, I see what you mean."

She didn't look too comfortable, though. Good at pulling data from the ether, and not too bad schmoozing with her former secretarial colleagues over the phone, Heather hadn't done a lot of face-to-face stuff, and like a lot of computer people, she wasn't comfortable with strange people in their corporeal form. But, if she was going to be a full-fledged PI, she'd have to get over it.

"Hey, it's not that hard," I said. "Just remember that you're in charge. You know what you want to learn from them, and you don't let them side track you."

"How on earth do you do that if someone doesn't want to talk to you?"

"It just takes practice, kid. Tell you what, why don't you take the easy ones from the list; Isabel Frontis, Liana Kolchek, and Harriet Gold. I'll do the others."

"What am I supposed to ask them?"

"Well, it'd be nice to establish if any of them feel as strongly toward the dead guy as our client, and see if you can get a sense of whether or not they're capable of violence, or of having violence done. And, before you ask, it's a sense you get of someone. If they're hinky, you'll feel it."

"Oh, I get it. It's like when you're in a strange neighborhood and you get that itchy feeling at the base of your skull that tells you you're in the wrong place."

Exactly like that. It's that feeling you get when you meet someone, and regardless of how they're dressed, or what their title is, your gut tells you they're off. That's your lizard brain at work. It's gone dormant in most people, but with a little training it'll come back.

So, you ready to hit the bricks?" I asked.

"Wait a minute, what if someone calls while we're both out?"

"That's what we've got an answering machine for, isn't it?"

"Yeah, I guess so. Okay, let's do this."

With Frontis north of Georgetown, near Montrose Park, Gold near the DC Convention Center, and Kolchek on Georgia Avenue in Wheaton, Maryland, I figured she'd be most of the day. My plan was to combine checking out Simpson's office, in one of the strip malls on Rockville Pike, just north of the Beltway where Bethesda ends and Rockville begins, and none of the remaining names on the list were conveniently located nearby, so I decided I'd hit the retired army colonel, Walter Reid, who lived on Decatur Place near Dupont Circle, on my way out.

We debated calling ahead, but only Braxton had an active job, so we took a chance that we'd find the others at home. If it turned out we were wrong, at the least, we'd get a sense of them from where they lived. If it sounds like an inefficient way to do an investigation, it probably is, but my gut was telling me, coming at them without warning was preferable to giving them a chance to prepare stories, something that would happen after the first few interviews anyway, but even that would tell us something about them.

Decatur Place, an east-west street that runs from Massachusetts Avenue to Twenty-First Street, is a tree-lined, restricted-parking street northwest of Dupont Circle. Stately brick town homes line both sides, and the sidewalks are perpetually shaded by the overhanging branches that protrude over the brick walls.

Walter Reid's place was a three-story, gray brick structure, without a surrounding wall, but with knee-high, neatly trimmed hedges on either side, marking his property line. I had to drive four houses past to find a vacant spot to park, making a note that only residents with a sticker could park longer than two hours. I locked the Volkswagen and walked back.

It took nearly a minute for Reid to respond to his doorbell. Not that he was frail. He looked remarkably fit for a sixty-four-year-old. About an inch shorter than me, he stood ramrod straight, with his shoulders squared, and only the slightest sign of softness around his midsection. His tan slacks had sharp creases, the collar of his beige shirt lay perfectly flat, and the sleeveless, dark brown sweater he wore highlighted, a chest, shoulders, and arms that had benefited at some point in the past from a weight-lifting regimen. His iron-gray hair was cropped close on the sides and short on top, and icy-blue eyes regarded me from beneath neatly trimmed gray brows. He had the square-jawed look of someone accustomed to command.

"Something I can do for you?" he asked.

I took my wallet from my pocket, removed my PI ID, and held it up so he could see it. "I'm Al Pennyback, a private investigator," I said. I decided to use his military rank as a way to establish some rapport. "Colonel Reid, I was wondering if I might have a few moments of your time."

His brows came together as he squinted at my ID.

"Why does a private investigator want to talk to me?"

"You're part of a real estate investment club organized by Sydney Simpson, correct?"

His eyes narrowed as his gaze shifted from my ID to my face.

"Why do you want to know?"

"As you probably know, Mr. Simpson was murdered six day ago. I've been hired to look into his business dealings."

That was close enough to the truth without

revealing more than I wanted him to know.

"Who hired you?"

This guy was sharp. I'd have to be on my toes with him.

"I'm sorry, colonel, but I'm not at liberty to disclose that information at the moment. My client wishes to remain anonymous. May I come in? I promise, I'll only take a few minutes of your time."

He seemed hesitant, but I could also see curiosity in his expression. Curiosity won out. He stepped aside and motioned me inside.

The entrance foyer was small, with a door, probably a closet, to the right, and a narrow stairwell to the left, leading up to the next floor. Beyond was a small living room, with a large black leather couch, a matching chair, and a low, kidney-shaped coffee table made from dark mahogany. The walls were decorated with plaques, photos, and shadow boxes with medals and military insignia. A bottle of Johnny Walker Black and a glass with an inch of amber liquor in it sat in the middle of the coffee table, and it wasn't even mid-morning yet. Despite the lowered level in the bottle, he looked sober.

He motioned me to the chair, and sat on the sofa, precisely in the center, straddling two of the cushions.

"Now, Mr. Pennyback, how may I help you?"

"How long have you been involved with Mr. Simpson?"

He hesitated, giving me the once-over. Then, he shrugged and frowned.

"About a year, maybe ten months."

"How did you become involved?"

"I was introduced to Mr. Simpson by Harrison Hillsworth," he said. "I know Harrison from before he retired. He did a few DOD contracts when I worked procurement at the Pentagon, and we've kept in touch."

"Could you tell me how this investment club

works?"

"Uh, well, I'm not comfortable discussing my personal finances with a total stranger."

"No, colonel, I don't want personal information. Just the basics; how does one go about making money in a venture like this?"

"Well, it's actually quite simple. A group of people pool their money, and buy property. That property is either sold or developed and the investors share the profits in proportion to their investment."

"And, was your club making money?"

His brows came together again. "We were . . . at first," he said.

I sensed a 'but,' followed by bad news, but he clamped his lips shut.

"What happened?" I asked.

He glared at me, and when he spoke, I could hear the anger in his voice. "Everything was fine at first. For the first four months, we received regular monthly payments. It was a long way from recouping our investments, but it looked to be on track to do that within eighteen months, or so. Then, two months ago, the payments stopped." He was making no attempt to hide the anger now. "Some of us approached Simpson, but he kept putting us off, something about a couple of potential buyers that he had to deal with first. Then, about three weeks ago, in a meeting with him, Loretta . . . that's Loretta Palmer, a bit of a firebrand, came into the meeting and accused him of cheating us. Said he was running a pyramid scheme, and she wanted her money back. Of course, he denied it. He said he had almost made a deal with one of the two mystery buyers he'd previously mentioned, and that we'd all make a handsome profit as soon as the deal went through. Loretta wasn't having any of it, though, and said it he didn't give her back every penny she'd invested she'd, and these are her words, not mine, cut his fucking heart out."

"And, now," I said. "He's dead."

"Yeah, I heard it on the news. I've been trying to get through to his associate, Mr. Devlin, but the woman who answers their phone says she doesn't know where he is."

"Devlin's an active part of the deal?"

"Hell, I don't know. Simpson always introduced him as his associate, but I thought he was just a flunky. Of course, with Simpson dead, he's the only lead we have to trying to find out what happened to our money."

"If Simpson was really running a con, there's probably no land, which means your money's probably in some offshore bank where you can't touch it."

"Oh no, there's land." He shook his head. "I saw the papers. Several hundred acres north of Germantown, east of I-270. The papers looked real as far as I could tell."

That, of course, didn't say that Simpson actually had title to the land, but it was worth checking out.

"What exactly did Simpson say the land would be used for?"

"You been up 270 lately? They're building office buildings from Rockville to Germantown. Lots of medical research and tech firms. Won't be long before they'll be expanding past Germantown, which will shoot land prices up there through the stratosphere."

"So, the plan was to sell it to a developer? Did he give you any idea who?"

"No. He just said he had two potential buyers, and he was playing them off against each other to get the price up. Now that he's dead, though, I imagine the deal's off."

I wondered. That would be an interesting question to ask Devlin when we found him.

Charles Ray

Chapter Nine

I thanked Reid for his time and headed over to Wisconsin Avenue for the drive north. Once past the National Naval Medical Center in Bethesda, Wisconsin Avenue becomes Rockville Pike, and keeps going as Maryland Route 355, with a number of name changes through Rockville and on up past Germantown.

I didn't get a good sense of the colonel, other than not taking him off our list of suspects. Despite his age, he looked fit enough to tackle someone my size, and being ex-military, he probably knew a number of ways to kill someone. In fact, the clinical way Simpson's death was described by Buster, tended to point toward someone who'd been trained in the deadly arts. I would have to have Heather pay special attention to Reid's background.

The office Simpson had been using was just north of the White Flint Metro Station, on the west side of the pike, in one of the smaller strip malls. A green, two-story building, with stores on the ground floor, and offices on the second, accessed through a central opening that was sandwiched between a jewelry store and an ice cream shop.

At the top of the stairs, a narrow hallway stretched in both directions with eight offices, four in each direction. According to the directory sign at the bottom of the stairway, Simpson Land Holdings was the last office on the right.

The hallway was dimly lit and looked like it hadn't been swept in a week. The inside of Simpson Land Holdings was nothing to write home about, either—except for the receptionist.

A platinum blonde, nearly my six-one height, she looked like she'd been poured into the gold pants and blouse, and was in danger of spilling over at the top. To her credit, she wasn't wearing any more makeup than clothing, just a pink blush on her lips, and a slight turquoise shading over her noon-day-sky blue eyes.

She looked up and smiled when I entered. "Sorry, but we're closed for business today," she said.

I flashed my ID at her, which she didn't even bother to do more than glance at. "I'm not here to invest or buy real estate," I said. "I'm here to get information."

"Well, Mr. Simpson and Mr. Develin are both out," she said. "Actually, Mr. Simpson is . . . dead. I'm not sure about Mr. Devlin. He hasn't come in for the past two days."

She delivered that news in the same tone of voice she might've used to tell me that Simpson was at the local deli. I didn't know what to make of her—was she really that uncaring, or was she just, well, dumb?

"How long have you worked here?" I asked.

"Since they opened the office two years ago."

"And, your duties?"

"I answer the phone, schedule appointments, and keep their calendars."

And, sit around making the office look inviting.

More expensive than a pinup calendar, but a lot more interesting from where I was standing.

"Then, it stands to reason that you know pretty much everything that's gone on here."

That got a smile from her. She was actually quite pretty when she smiled.

"Yeah, I suppose I do." She pointed at the chair beside her desk, and sat in the one behind it. "What do you want to know?"

"How about, is there really land in this deal?"

She gave me a funny look. "Of course, there's land, silly. Mr. Simpson and Mr. Devlin bought several hundred acres from farmers north of Germantown."

"You've seen this land?"

"Well, no, but I got the title transfer papers notarized."

I sort of assumed that meant there *was* actual land, which meant the scam Simpson was pulling was selling shares in that land to different groups, probably using the investment from newcomers to pay off the old timers. But, that was just a guess.

"Was he making a lot of money?"

She held her hands up in mock surrender. "Now, *that* is one thing they never let me do. Other than the fact that they pay me on time, I have no idea how much they made. I did get a look at a couple of the checks they got from the latest club they started, and there were a lot of zeroes—"

"Whoa," I said. "The latest club? How many of these investment clubs did they have?"

"Well, let me see." She began counting on her well-manicured fingers. "I think there were four of them."

"How many people in each?"

"Each club has ten members," she said.

"And, the buy-in's what, a hundred thousand?"

She shook her head, causing her blonde tresses to bounce and sway across her face. "Uh-uh. Try five."

I did some quick mental calculations. Five million

taken in from each club, times four clubs—holy crap! These two guys had pulled in twenty million bucks from just the four scams she'd mentioned. I figured they tossed a few crumbs to the members of the clubs, especially the earlier ones, but they still had a lot of money stashed somewhere, either in an offshore account—I was hoping Heather would be able to determine whether one existed—or in cash. If the latter, that was another motive for murder, and that meant a killer running around with a shit load of cash.

"That's a lot of money," I said. "Where did these two guys do their banking?"

"I have no idea. I've never gotten any mail from a bank here."

That didn't surprise me.

"Do you happen to have their home addresses?" I had both, thanks to Buster and Heather, but wanted to double check.

"Sure, but I don't know if I should give you personal information like that."

Shit, she must've gone to a secretarial school, or else she'd been watching too damn much TV.

"Aw, come on," I said. "Simpson's dead, so it doesn't matter, now does it. He has no privacy to protect. As for Devlin, I could always go to the cops and ask them to help me find him, but I don't think he'd like that very much, do you?"

She screwed up her face, as if thinking of an answer was a strenuous exercise.

"I suppose you have a point," she said finally. "Just don't tell Mr. Devlin I gave you the information, okay?"

"Scout's honor. It's just between you and me."

She picked up a pencil, licked the lead, and wrote two addresses on a Post-it™ note, which she pulled off the pad and handed to me. They matched what I already had. That still didn't mean they didn't have hidey-holes somewhere that the authorities didn't know about, but it was a starting point. I folded the little yellow square and put it in my shirt pocket.

"So, other than the investment clubs, did they have any other deals going?"

Again, she did the scrunched-up face thing. Thinking wasn't her forte, apparently.

"I'm not absolutely sure, but the two of them were discussing something last week, a few days before . . . you know, Mr. Simpson was . . . anyway, it was something to do with these two potential buyers for the land. Mr. Devlin wanted to sell to one guy, but I got the feeling that Mr. Simpson was leaning toward the other one."

"Did you get the names of these two buyers?"

"No, sorry, and I only overheard part of the conversation." She tilted her head back, and regarded me down the length of her nose. "I'm not a snoop, or anything. I just happen to be passing the office door when they were talking, and they were talking pretty loud."

"Of course. I would never think such a thing of you. Anything else you can think of that might help me locate Devlin?"

"Not off the top of my head. Sorry."

I gave her one of my name cards. "Well, if you do think of anything, or if Devlin comes in or contacts you, would you have him call me? If I'm not there, my partner will answer."

I left her sitting there staring at my card.

Chapter Ten

I made a stop at a Popeye's Louisiana Kitchen for fried chicken, home fries, and a biscuit, and then drove back to the office, arriving about the same time Heather pulled her little blue Honda Civic into the adjacent slot.

We went upstairs and compared notes; not really much to show for our efforts. She'd only been able to contact Frontis, who she described as ancient, but not too frail, and Gold, a manic painter who specialized in an abstract form that Heather called 'disturbing.' She said she didn't see either as the killer, but wouldn't rule out the possibility that they'd hired someone. I gave her roughly the same assessment of Reid, with the additional information that he was retired military and *could* have done it himself.

Temperamentally, none of the three impressed us as having the *will* to kill, especially the clinical way Simpson seems to have been done. It's one thing to kill in the heat of the moment, but to coldly shove a sharp object into someone's chest; well, that takes a certain personality. Reid was still a possibility, but a distant one.

I was leaving all options open until we'd talked to everyone.

I briefed Heather on my plan to visit Simpson's house, and decided to go home to get some rest. Nighttime operations take a lot out of a body, and when they have to be done on the quiet, even more so.

Sandra arrived at the farmhouse two hours after I did, and we had an early light supper, cream of mushroom soup and tossed salad with toast, washed down with unsweetened ice tea. After allowing an hour for our food to partially digest, we spent another hour in the bedroom, showered, and by 9:00, I'd decided to get a couple hours of sleep before my evening foray, while Sandra decided to read a bit before going to bed—to sleep, that is.

My internal clock woke me at 11:00. Sandra was lying next to me, her hands tucked under her chin. I hadn't even felt her get in bed.

I eased out of bed, careful to keep the sheet up to her neck without waking her, and took my night gear, that I'd put in a pile on the floor of the closet, into the bathroom, where I got dressed.

My night recon outfit is always pretty much the same: black cargo pants with extra pockets in the legs; long-sleeved black shirt, nylon for breathing; black commando boots with soft soles; a K-Bar knife in an ankle sheath; and, thanks to my retired CIA buddy, Carlton 'Blood' Raine, a pair of portable night vision goggles, that fit in one of the thigh pockets of my cargo pants. If I'm going to do any climbing, up or down, I have a 25-foot coil of nylon rope. The 300-pound test of the thin rope easily carries the weight of me and most equipment, but, it's still thin and light enough that I can clip it to my belt and it's not much of a burden.

This mission, though, was a simple 'slip in and look

around,' so the goggles were the most essential. The knife was just in case. Unlike the detectives you see on TV, I do not carry a weapon, don't even own one, and have only fired one in anger once since leaving the army—in self-defense when a rogue FBI agent tried to take me out. Heather and I, in order to keep our PI licenses current, especially in Virginia, a state that seems to be in love with guns, go to a shooting range in Fairfax City twice a year, but that's it. If I need a weapon in my cases, I call the cops. If I can't talk my way out of a situation, or handle it with fists and feet— using the skills I picked up earning black belts in judo, karate, and taekwondo—I can run like hell in the opposite direction. Thankfully, not many of our cases involve gunplay.

After getting dressed, I eased out of the bedroom. Sandra shifted a bit in the bed, making little burbling sounds, but didn't wake up.

I was outside and in my Volkswagen by 11:30. Could have made it faster if I hadn't had to dress in the dark.

Thanks to a little upgrade, the engine started on the first try, with a soft purring sound.

East on River Road, I didn't encounter another car until I arrived at Falls Road in Potomac Village, where I saw late-night delivery trucks pulling into the shopping mall on the right. I turned north on Falls Road, which runs through quiet housing estates until it crosses I-270, where I saw a lot of northbound traffic—probably late-working commuters on the way home—and enters the city of Rockville. Again, a couple of county police cars and a few delivery vans was about the only traffic until I crossed Rockville Pike, which, like I-270, had a pretty steady flow of northbound traffic, and a few cars and trucks heading south. On the east side of the pike, the street changed to Viers Mill Road, which is primarily small, single-family, working class homes and a few shopping malls, gas stations, and churches. The gas stations were open all-night, and a few had cars gassing up, with the attendants ensconced behind plate glass windows watching, and one or two of the eateries still had a few cars parked in front, late workers grabbing a bite before going on or after just coming off shift. Few of the houses had lights on, except for the occasional light over a front door. In working class neighborhoods like this, when people weren't night workers, at this time of night, they were probably asleep. I saw no pedestrians.

Simpson's address was on a cross street to the left, a two-lane street lined with modest looking houses and long lines of beat-up sedans, vans, and pickups lining both sides. His house, number 7707, was on the left. I found a spot to park about six houses beyond his, did a U-turn and pulled in.

I waited a few minutes, to make sure there was no traffic, and then got out, locked the doors, and made my way back to Simpson's house. The light over the front door was on, probably left on by the cops after they did their investigation. A strip of yellow crime scene tape hung loosely across the door. I turned and walked up the grass strip between his house and the house next door, moving quickly, but not so fast that, if someone saw me, I'd be mistaken for a stalker or burglar.

A graveled service road ran behind the houses, and a few old junkers were parked, partially blocking it. Garbage cans and recycling containers sat in back yards, along with mounds of other odds and ends. The area behind 7707 was bare earth, with nothing but an overturned garbage can, the lid lying a few feet away. Simpson apparently didn't recycle; his was the only house within sight without a blue recycling container.

Wooden steps led up to a screen door. I pulled on it, slowly. It made soft squeaking sounds as it swung out. I held it open and waited, but there were no other sounds, other than the muffled sound of passing cars on Viers Mill. I tried the wooden door. It was locked. I took out my K-Bar and slid it between the door and the frame, jiggling it until I encountered the latch bolt. A few twists, and the bold slid back just enough to allow me to put my shoulder against the door and pop it open without too much noise. I went inside and closed the door.

With my back against the door, I removed the night vision goggles from my pocket and put them on. After I pressed the button on the right side, the room, a small kitchen, sprang into sharp relief, all green and black. Pizza boxes, some still containing crumbs and pieces of crust, were scattered across the kitchen counter and a small table near the center of the room, along with several glasses and an empty Jim Beam bottle. A trash can near the sink was filled to overflowing with more empty pizza boxes and beer cans. The place reeked of grease and something else I wasn't sure I wanted to identify. It was for sure this place would never be featured in *Good Housekeeping.*

I checked the refrigerator. Empty except for a milk cartoon that gave off a sour odor and a block of moldy cheese. The cabinets over the sink had a few plastic plates and cups, and the drawers were empty except for plastic cutlery, some with bits of food still sticking to them.

From the kitchen, it looked like Simpson was just using the place as a hangout. It looked like the living room of a frat house after a rush party or a kegger, and smelled like a locker room that was also used to cook greasy food. I took shallow breaths to try and minimize the rank odor that crawled up my nostrils like caterpillars.

I moved through the kitchen and into the front room. There wasn't much in the way of furnishings; just a sofa, a coffee table, and a couple of mismatched wooden chairs, and even through the goggles, it all looked tatty, like someone had picked up castoffs at a garage sale and just dumped them haphazardly around the room. More empty pizza boxes and empty beer cans littered the coffee table. The smell, thankfully, wasn't as oppressive as the kitchen. A closet near the front door was empty except for a pair of frayed running shoes. A dark circle at the side of the sofa caught my eye. I knelt for a closer look. It was dry, but the metallic smell of blood still lingered in the air. This, no doubt, was where Simpson fell after being skewered. I checked the front door. There was no sign that it had been forced open—the same thing at the back, too. So, unless his assailant came in through a window, he . . . or she had been allowed in, meaning it had likely been someone Simpson knew, and trusted enough to open the door for. That didn't reduce the number of suspects at all, but it also did nothing to tell me who it might have been.

The place had two bedrooms. The first one was empty, closets included, but in the second was a queen-sized bed with rumpled bedclothes, and a pair of pants crumpled on the floor near the closet. A couple of suits, some jeans, and three or four dress shirts hung in the closet. Four pairs of dress shoes were in the back of the closet. The dresser, off to the left, had underwear and socks, and nothing else.

The one bathroom, located between the two bedrooms, had the usual; shaving gear, toothbrush, a half-used tube of toothpaste, and a hairbrush. Nothing in the medicine cabinet, or in the toilet's water tank, and no sign of cubby holes in which a few million bucks could be stashed in the bathroom. Back in the master bedroom, I even checked under the bed and dresser—nothing.

It was beginning to look more and more that Simpson had the money in a hidden bank account, and there were no clues indicating who had killed him.

I took a glance at my watch. The luminous dial read

1:25. I'd spent a good hour already in the house, and had come up empty.

I decided to call it a night, and go home.

As I entered the living room, a movement in the air currents to my left, caught my attention. I began turning, and, as I made it about a quarter way around, I saw a dark, greenish black shadow moving toward me. I raised my left arm, but was a fraction of a second too late.

There was a bright flash of green before my eyes, and a dull thud, followed by complete darkness.

Charles Ray

Chapter Eleven

The first sensation I felt was a throbbing pain at the back of my head, followed by a tickling sensation in my nose. I sneezed, and the throbbing pain turned to a jackhammer, causing me to squeeze my eyes shut and cry out.

In my peripheral vision I could see what looked like a light brown tree trunk against a dark background, but after a few seconds of squinting, that turned into the back leg of a chair about four feet from my nose. The tickling in my nose was from the dusty carpet that the right side of my face was mashed into.

I was lying face down on a floor, in a room, that I could now see from the ambient light coming through some really ratty looking curtains over a window to the right of the chair, was a living room, with a sofa that looked even rattier than the wooden chair, and a scarred wooden coffee table with a bunch of what appeared from my low vantage point to be pizza boxes and Miller beer cans. Oh, and the place stank of stale beer and grease.

Slowly, I lifted my head, which caused the stabbing

pain to increase. I lifted my shoulders, and bracing on my left elbow, reached my right hand around behind my head. I felt warm, wetness, and it hurt when I touched my skull. Pulling my hand away, I saw red stains on my fingertips.

Realization came slowly, and as it did, my anger and embarrassment grew. Someone had cold-cocked me in the dark. I pushed myself up into a sitting position and leaned against the wall. Looked at my watch. It read 4:40. I remembered looking at it before and it had read 1:25. I'd been face down on that dirty floor for three hours and fifteen minutes. Whoever hit me, really put some oomph into it. I felt my skull again. The blood didn't seem to be flowing, but it hurt like hell; I mean, really, really hurt. I could feel a bump the size of an egg, and when I moved my head, I felt a little woozy. A part of my brain, the part that wasn't cursing my clumsiness in allowing myself to be ambushed, and the part that wasn't confused as hell from the bonk on the noggin, was cataloguing my injury. I was pretty sure I'd suffered a minor concussion, thus the wooziness, and initial confusion. But, I remembered where I was, so I reasoned it wasn't *too* bad.

Using the wall for leverage, I stood, and took a few tentative steps. I could walk without reeling, so I figured I could drive. But, head injuries can be dangerous. I wanted a medic to take a look and give me a clean bill of health. Of course, I wasn't about to go to the nearest civilian hospital. A black dude, dressed in black, reporting to an emergency room at 4:00 or 5:00 in the morning with a head injury was likely to generate a call to the cops, and I wasn't up to explaining anything to Montgomery County's finest at that moment. Then, I remembered. I was only about ten miles from the Navy Hospital in Bethesda. All I had to do was drive up to Rockville Pike and hang a left. As a retired army officer, I had access to the finest medical care in the world; the Navy Hospital is on standby to treat the president in an emergency, as well as other senior government officials, and I, as a retired army colonel, wouldn't be likely to have any story I told questioned.

I made my way through the living room and into the kitchen. The door was wide open. Whoever had bopped me hadn't bothered to close it when he—and, I assumed it was most probably a man—made his getaway.

There were a few early walkers, early shift workers, on the sidewalk on Viers Mill, but no one paid me much attention.

Traffic on Viers Mill going southeast toward Wheaton was starting to pick up, and the southbound traffic when I got to Rockville Pike was almost at rush-hour levels. By the time I crossed the I-495 Beltway and reached the gate into the hospital, across the street from the National Institutes of Health and the Medical Center Metro station, traffic in both directions was full bore, with buses, trucks, vans, and commuters all vying for the three lanes in each direction, backing up in the inner lanes because of cars making the left turns into the two respective medical facilities.

The Naval Medical Center is an unusual building, a tall tower in the center, with wings flaring out from both sides, the site was selected and the facility was designed by Franklin D. Roosevelt in 1938. He laid the cornerstone for the central tower on Armistice Day, November 11, 1940, and it was completed and opened for operations as the Naval Medical Hospital, Bethesda, in 1942, soon after the U.S. entry into World War II. The original center was a 1,200-bed hospital, Naval Medical and Dental Schools, and the Naval Medical Research Institute. By 1945, it had been expanded to accommodate 2,464 wounded sailors and marines. Though it was originally designed for treatment of military personnel only, because he'd dedicated it, and because of the paralysis of his lower limbs from polio, the hospital offered to provide him treatment to enable him to function as president, starting the tradition of presidents and other senior officials receiving treatment—at their own expense— either there or at Walter Reed Army Hospital on Georgia Avenue, in DC, just south of Silver Spring. Home to the National Military Medical Institution, and with extensive renovations and additions over the years, it was now one of the largest medical facilities in the United States, and is on the National Register of Historic Buildings. In addition to treating all active duty servicemembers and their families, it provides medical services to retirees and their spouses, yours truly included. I preferred it to Walter Reed, because it was several miles closer to my house, and the parking was better.

The hospital's emergency room is the first wing of the south annex off the central tower, just in from the gate. Despite the increasing traffic, I pulled up to the gate, and showed my military retiree ID to the uniformed naval policeman at 5:15, and five minutes later had parked in the ER parking lot and was entering the waiting room.

A naval corpsman, a youngster with close-cropped hair and a face full of freckles, dressed in the blue dungarees that are the navy's work uniform, sat behind a high desk with a glass window. He spoke to me through a soft-ball-sized hole in the glass. After looking at my ID and making a note of my complaint and condition, and considering that I was neither bleeding or fainting, had me take a seat to wait for the next doctor. I joined six other patients on the plastic chairs facing the desk; two were elderly men with wispy strands of white hair, one of whom was clutching his wrist, while the other held a hand over his stomach; a youngster who had his army held tightly against his chest as he huddled against a man I took for his father; and a young couple, the woman pregnant and splayed back in the chair moaning in pain. By comparison, my injuries appeared minor, so I sat apart from them, and killed time by thumbing through a *Reader's Digest* that was on the low table near my chair.

Ten minutes later, I was jerked away from an article on 'How to Travel with Colicky Kids,' by a childish sounding voice calling, "Colonel Pennyback, would you please go to cubicle two." I looked up to see the corpsman pointing at me, and then pointing to a curtained opening to the right. I stood and headed in the direction he'd pointed. "Second one to your left," he said.

A young woman, clad in dusty green scrubs, with her brown hair pulled back in a severe bun, and no-nonsense looking brown eyes peering at me through horn-rimmed glasses, waited for me as I pushed through the privacy curtains. She pointed to the examination table, a mid-thigh-high aluminum tray covered in thin white paper.

"Have a seat, please. I'm Lieutenant, j.g., Karen Murphy," she said. "I'll be examining you. So, had a bump on the head, did we?"

Except for her eyes, she hardly looked a day over twenty-five. The eyes, though, belonged to someone who'd seen a lot, and who was probably near the end of a long night shift.

"Yeah, clumsy me," I said.

She consulted a sheet of paper on a metal clipboard.

"Colonel Alfred E. Pennyback, retired," she said. "What service were you in, colonel?"

"Army."

She grasped my chin and shone a light into each eye. "Does the light bother you?"

"No," I said. I resisted shaking my head. It still hurt

a little.

She examined the back of my head.

"A small abrasion on the back of your head. It didn't bleed much. How'd this happen?"

I thought carefully about what I'd say. Sure, she was military, and I was military, but I couldn't be sure what she might do if I made her suspicious. In other words, as much as I hate to lie, in this case, it was for the greater good.

"I can't sleep, so I was working on my heavy bag in the barn behind my house. A roundhouse kick went wrong, I slipped, and banged my head on the post of my *makiwa* board, describing the padded upright board used for kicking and punching practice in taekwondo.

She lifted my hands, and examined the knuckles. I have the prominent knobs of calcium deposits on the knuckles of the second fingers from many years of pounding the board, bricks, or slates; and occasionally an opponent's head.

"Karate or taekwondo?" she asked.

"Both."

Her mouth made a little 'O'. "What degree?"

"Fifth degree in karate, fourth in taekwondo," I said.

She whistled. "Wow, that's awesome. I'm studying taekwondo, but I'm only up to green belt."

All the while she was talking she was moving my head from side to side and up and down, and examining the injured area.

"Will I live?" I asked.

"You don't seem to have any lingering side effects. I imagine there's still a little pain. Any dizziness?" I shook my head slowly. "Good. You're lucky. Barely broke the skin, and only mild concussion. I would advise you to take the rest of the day off, and you might want to move your *makiwa* board so it's not so close to your kicking bag."

"Yeah, you're right. It's not as if I don't have enough

space in my barn to do that."

"I'll give you some ibuprofen tablets, about 500 mg, for the pain," she said. "Take them as needed, and be careful. You're pretty fit for a man your age, but at the same time, you have to remember falls are the number-one cause of injury for people in your age group."

Ow; that hurt worse than the blow to the head. No one likes to be reminded that they're getting old. I winced, and she laughed. She left me for a few minutes, and then returned with a small plastic container with twenty white tablets, 'to save me having to wait for the pharmacy to open,' she said. And, that was it. Less than an hour after arriving, I was on my way home, and thankfully, most of the rush-hour traffic was moving in the opposite direction.

The first sensation I felt was a throbbing pain at the back of my head, followed by a tickling sensation in my nose. I sneezed, and the throbbing pain turned to a jackhammer, causing me to squeeze my eyes shut and cry out.

In my peripheral vision I could see what looked like a light brown tree trunk against a dark background, but after a few seconds of squinting, that turned into the back leg of a chair about four feet from my nose. The tickling in my nose was from the dusty carpet that the right side of my face was mashed into.

I was lying face down on a floor, in a room, that I could now see from the ambient light coming through some really ratty looking curtains over a window to the right of the chair, was a living room, with a sofa that looked even rattier than the wooden chair, and a scarred wooden coffee table with a bunch of what appeared from my low vantage point to be pizza boxes and Miller beer cans. Oh, and the place stank of stale beer and grease.

Slowly, I lifted my head, which caused the stabbing pain to increase. I lifted my shoulders, and bracing on my left elbow, reached my right hand around behind my head. I felt warm, wetness, and it hurt when I touched my skull. Pulling my hand away, I saw red stains on my fingertips.

Realization came slowly, and as it did, my anger and embarrassment grew. Someone had cold-cocked me in the dark. I pushed myself up into a sitting position and leaned against the wall. Looked at my watch. It read 4:40. I remembered looking at it before and it had read 1:25. I'd been face down on that dirty floor for three hours and fifteen minutes. Whoever hit me, really put some oomph into it. I felt my skull again. The blood didn't seem to be flowing, but it hurt like hell; I mean, really, really hurt. I could feel a bump the size of an egg, and when I moved my head, I felt a little woozy. A part of my brain, the part that wasn't cursing my clumsiness in allowing myself to be ambushed, and the part that wasn't confused as hell from the bonk on the noggin, was cataloguing my injury. I was pretty sure I'd suffered a minor concussion, thus the wooziness, and initial confusion. But, I remembered where I was, so I reasoned it wasn't *too* bad.

Using the wall for leverage, I stood, and took a few tentative steps. I could walk without reeling, so I figured I could drive. But, head injuries can be dangerous. I wanted a medic to take a look and give me a clean bill of health. Of course, I wasn't about to go to the nearest civilian hospital. A black dude, dressed in black, reporting to an emergency room at 4:00 or 5:00 in the morning with a head injury was likely to generate a call to the cops, and I wasn't up to explaining anything to Montgomery County's finest at that moment. Then, I remembered. I was only about ten miles from the Navy Hospital in Bethesda. All I had to do was drive up to Rockville Pike and hang a left. As a retired army officer, I had access to the finest medical care in the world; the Navy Hospital is on standby to treat the president in an emergency, as well as other senior government officials, and I, as a retired army colonel, wouldn't be likely to have any story I told questioned.

I made my way through the living room and into the kitchen. The door was wide open. Whoever had bopped me hadn't bothered to close it when he—and, I assumed it was most probably a man—made his getaway.

There were a few early walkers, early shift workers, on the sidewalk on Viers Mill, but no one paid me much attention.

Traffic on Viers Mill going southeast toward Wheaton was starting to pick up, and the southbound traffic when I got to Rockville Pike was almost at rush-hour levels. By the time I crossed the I-495 Beltway and reached the gate into the hospital, across the street from the National Institutes of Health and the Medical Center Metro station, traffic in both directions was full bore, with buses, trucks, vans, and commuters all vying for the three lanes in each direction, backing up in the inner lanes because of cars making the left turns into the two respective medical facilities.

The Naval Medical Center is an unusual building, a tall tower in the center, with wings flaring out from both sides, the site was selected and the facility was designed by Franklin D. Roosevelt in 1938. He laid the cornerstone for the central tower on Armistice Day, November 11, 1940, and it was completed and opened for operations as the Naval Medical Hospital, Bethesda, in 1942, soon after the U.S. entry into World War II. The original center was a 1,200-bed hospital, Naval Medical and Dental Schools, and the Naval Medical Research Institute. By 1945, it had been expanded to accommodate 2,464 wounded sailors and marines. Though it was originally designed for treatment of military personnel only, because he'd dedicated it, and because of the paralysis of his lower limbs from polio, the hospital offered to provide him treatment to enable him to function as president, starting the tradition of presidents and other senior officials receiving treatment—at their own expense— either there or at Walter Reed Army Hospital on Georgia Avenue, in DC, just south of Silver Spring. Home to the National Military Medical Institution, and with extensive renovations and additions over the years, it was now one of the largest medical facilities in the United States, and is on the National Register of Historic Buildings. In addition to treating all active duty servicemembers and their families, it provides medical services to retirees and their spouses, yours truly included. I preferred it to Walter Reed, because it was several miles closer to my house, and the parking was better.

The hospital's emergency room is the first wing of the south annex off the central tower, just in from the gate. Despite the increasing traffic, I pulled up to the gate, and showed my military retiree ID to the uniformed naval policeman at 5:15, and five minutes later had parked in the ER parking lot and was entering the waiting room.

A naval corpsman, a youngster with close-cropped hair and a face full of freckles, dressed in the blue dungarees that are the navy's work uniform, sat behind a high desk with a glass window. He spoke to me through a soft-ball-sized hole in the glass. After looking at my ID and making a note of my complaint and condition, and considering that I was neither bleeding or fainting, had me take a seat to wait for the next doctor. I joined six other patients on the plastic chairs facing the desk; two were elderly men with wispy strands of white hair, one of whom was clutching his wrist, while the other held a hand over his stomach; a youngster who had his army held tightly against his chest as he huddled against a man I took for his father; and a young couple, the woman pregnant and splayed back in the chair moaning in pain. By comparison, my injuries appeared minor, so I sat apart from them, and killed time by thumbing through a *Reader's Digest* that was on the low table near my chair.

Ten minutes later, I was jerked away from an article on 'How to Travel with Colicky Kids,' by a childish sounding voice calling, "Colonel Pennyback, would you please go to cubicle two." I looked up to see the corpsman pointing at me, and then pointing to a curtained opening to the right. I stood and headed in the direction he'd pointed. "Second one to your left," he said.

A young woman, clad in dusty green scrubs, with her brown hair pulled back in a severe bun, and no-nonsense looking brown eyes peering at me through horn-rimmed glasses, waited for me as I pushed through the privacy curtains. She pointed to the examination table, a mid-thigh-high aluminum tray covered in thin white paper.

"Have a seat, please. I'm Lieutenant, j.g., Karen Murphy," she said. "I'll be examining you. So, had a bump on the head, did we?"

Except for her eyes, she hardly looked a day over twenty-five. The eyes, though, belonged to someone who'd seen a lot, and who was probably near the end of a long night shift.

"Yeah, clumsy me," I said.

She consulted a sheet of paper on a metal clipboard.

"Colonel Alfred E. Pennyback, retired," she said. "What service were you in, colonel?"

"Army."

She grasped my chin and shone a light into each eye. "Does the light bother you?"

"No," I said. I resisted shaking my head. It still hurt a little.

She examined the back of my head.

"A small abrasion on the back of your head. It didn't bleed much. How'd this happen?"

I thought carefully about what I'd say. Sure, she was military, and I was military, but I couldn't be sure what she might do if I made her suspicious. In other words, as much as I hate to lie, in this case, it was for the greater good.

"I can't sleep, so I was working on my heavy bag in the barn behind my house. A roundhouse kick went wrong, I slipped, and banged my head on the post of my *makiwa* board, describing the padded upright board used for kicking and punching practice in taekwondo.

She lifted my hands, and examined the knuckles. I have the prominent knobs of calcium deposits on the knuckles of the second fingers from many years of pounding the board, bricks, or slates; and occasionally an opponent's head.

"Karate or taekwondo?" she asked.

"Both."

Her mouth made a little 'O'. "What degree?"

"Fifth degree in karate, fourth in taekwondo," I said.

She whistled. "Wow, that's awesome. I'm studying taekwondo, but I'm only up to green belt."

All the while she was talking she was moving my head from side to side and up and down, and examining the injured area.

"Will I live?" I asked.

"You don't seem to have any lingering side effects. I imagine there's still a little pain. Any dizziness?" I shook my head slowly. "Good. You're lucky. Barely broke the skin, and only mild concussion. I would advise you to take the rest of the day off, and you might want to move your *makiwa* board so it's not so close to your kicking bag."

"Yeah, you're right. It's not as if I don't have enough space in my barn to do that."

"I'll give you some ibuprofen tablets, about 500 mg, for the pain," she said. "Take them as needed, and be careful. You're pretty fit for a man your age, but at the same time, you have to remember falls are the number-one cause of injury for people in your age group."

Ow; that hurt worse than the blow to the head. No one likes to be reminded that they're getting old. I winced, and she laughed. She left me for a few minutes, and then returned with a small plastic container with twenty white tablets, 'to save me having to wait for the pharmacy to open,' she said. And, that was it. Less than an hour after arriving, I was on my way home, and thankfully, most of the rush-hour traffic was moving in the opposite direction.

Charles Ray

Chapter Twelve

Sandra was in the shower when I got back home. I stripped and joined her. She noticed the lump on the back of my head as she was soaping my back.

"What the hell happened?" she asked.

I told her.

She leaned in and put her forehead against mine.

"You know, Al, I worry sometimes about stuff like this happening."

"Hey, I've got a hard head. I had the doc at Bethesda check it out, and I'm okay."

"Yeah, but you could've been killed."

True, but I wasn't, was I? I hadn't thought about it, but her comment kicked my brain into gear. Who the hell was it in Simpson's house, why were they there, and why did they just knock me out and skip? All good questions that I was determined to get answers to.

"I'm fine, babe," I said.

"But, you're going to take it easy today, right?"

"Of course. I'll probably only do one or two interviews. The rest of the time, I'll just chill out at the office."

She made a face. "Chilling out at the office is not quite what I had in mind. I was thinking more along the lines of you not *going* to the office."

She had that determined look on her face, but I was just as determined. Sitting around at home would really make me sick. Besides, I'd only taken two of the ibuprofen.

"Tell you what," I said. "Let me cook you a big breakfast and get you off to school, and I'll think about hanging out here this morning, and go in at noon."

She looked skeptical, but I'd offered the olive branch of compromise, so I had the advantage. Besides, I make a killer breakfast when I want to; scrambled eggs with onion, garlic, and jalapeno peppers; hashed browns with cheese, and buttermilk biscuits that melt in your mouth. To top that off, I'd recently bought a new bag of Colombian beans; best coffee going. That won her over, that and a little tongue tickling at the base of her neck.

I almost kept my word. It *was* nearly noon when I got to the office; like 11:15. I'd called Heather to let her know I'd be late, which was okay with her, because she wanted to do some more computer research.

She had a 'I found something' smile on her face when I walked in. I stopped at her desk.

"You have something," I said. "Tell me you have something."

"I have something, but first, tell me what happened to you."

So, I told her. She made faces. "It could've been a lot worse," I said. "Whoever hit me could've stayed and finished the job."

"I wonder why they didn't," she said.

"Don't sound so disappointed."

She made another face.

"That's not what I meant, and you know it." She stood. "It's just . . . what were they doing there? Looking for something? What? And, why not just hide and wait for you to leave?"

"Well, there aren't a lot of hiding places. I'm thinking whoever it was heard me in the back room, and just waited against the living room wall for me to come out. I was out for a while, so if they were looking for something, there was plenty time."

"Curious. Anyway, I do have some additional data, so grab your coffee and let's go into your office." She picked up her note pad, while I poured a mug of coffee.

In my office, I leaned back in my chair, and she perched on the edge of one of my visitor chairs, her notebook opened on her knee. I took my own steno pad out and positioned it at the center of my desk, just to the left of my laptop, then held my pen poised over a blank page.

"Okay, partner, I'm ready, so shoot."

"You don't need to take notes," she said, a peevish note in her voice. "I'll remind you of anything you need to remember."

I put the pen down, and leaned back with my hands crossed over my chest. "Fine, if that's the way you want it."

"For starters," she said, flipping open her notebook. "After lunch I'm going to visit Liana Kolchek out in Wheaton, and I was thinking on the way back, maybe I could drop in on Tamara Braxton, and then go and talk to Roberta Davis."

"Any particular reason you want to do that, interview Braxton, I mean?"

"Well, yesterday, when I was talking to old lady Frontis, she casually let it drop that Braxton has a bit of a hot temper. I thought it might be useful for me to feel her out, you know, see if maybe she has it in her to kill someone."

I wasn't so sure we needed to be looking for someone with a temper. Anger, yes, or at least, a grudge against Simpson, but I still kept going back to that single, precise stab wound. Not a 'heat of the moment' action. No, I had a feeling we were looking for someone cold and calculating.

"Sure, go ahead. I might drive out to McLean and talk to Hillsworth, the retired engineer."

"Didn't the doctor tell you to take it easy?"

"Hey, I rested all morning. Besides, it's an easy drive down Chain Bridge Road, and a few minutes conversation. No strain."

She shrugged. "Okay. One more thing. I followed up on the information you got from the receptionist yesterday, about the two mystery buyers. On a hunch, I called the mall management office, and spoke to the security guy. Turns out he does periodic walk-arounds, and he saw at least one person talking to Simpson in the parking lot that might just be one of them."

"Oh yeah, what did he say about him?

"He said the guy was a swarthy looking foreigner, Mexican or maybe Indian, he said. I asked him how he knew the guy was foreign, and all he could tell me was he just *looked* foreign. What was interesting, though, was that the guy and Simpson were having a heated discussion, lots of finger pointing and arm waving."

"Interesting. I don't suppose the mall has security cameras?"

"A few of the stores, but they're all inside. They don't have anything covering the parking lot. I know, it's not much help, but it does support the other buyers' theory. And, if Simpson and this guy were having a dispute, it means at least he is also a suspect."

"I'll bet Devlin knows," I said. "We need to find him."

"I agree. All the more reason for me to interview Braxton, Travis, and Davis. You talk to Hillsworth, and if you get time, Wiggins, and then we can focus on finding Devlin."

I couldn't argue with her logic. If we could knock

out the rest of the interviews with members of the investment club before going home, we could move on to what I was beginning to think were more lucrative hunting grounds. I was convinced that Devlin was the key person to get to the bottom of what was going on, and that, somehow, these two mysterious buyers were also involved.

"All right, let's go for it. But, if you run into any problems give me a buzz."

She smiled. "Same for you, boss, same for you."

She was up and out of the office before I realized that she'd taken a shot at me for getting hit in the head. I'm not usually that slow. Maybe I *was* still suffering the after effects of the blow to the noggin.

Chapter Thirteen

We left together, up Fourth Street to Maine Avenue. I peeled off at the Southwest Freeway, and got on Fourteenth Street Bridge, exiting onto George Washington Memorial Parkway northbound, while Heather stayed on Maine to Fourteenth Street.

Traffic on the parkway was heavy near the Pentagon and Rosslyn exits, but eased off just past Theodore Roosevelt Island. I exited the parkway onto Chain Bridge Road south, toward the headquarters of the CIA. There was a lot of noontime traffic once I passed the CIA, with cars exiting the tree-covered campus and heading south to the eateries between there and McLean, or even as far south as Tyson's Corner.

My destination was two blocks south on Old Dominion Drive, a stately, two-story colonial on a heavily-wooded lot. The driveway rose up a slight grade, curved past the colonnaded entrance, and then on to the detached garage, with a loop that reconnected with the exit to the street. Except for the silver BMW parked in front of the three-car garage, it looked like a scene from 'Gone with the Wind.' I wouldn't have been surprised to see field hands working out back, or liveried servants hovering near the entrance. I parked behind the BMW, walked back to the entrance and rang the doorbell.

It wasn't a liveried servant who answered the door, but a tiny, brown-skinned woman in a black maid's uniform with white collar.

"Yes," she said in a Caribbean accent. "May I help you?"

"I wish to speak to Mr. Harrison Hillsworth," I said, flashing my ID.

She looked wide-eyed at it, and then at me, like maybe I was some alien from another universe. Then again, I suppose in this neighborhood, a private investigator at the door is an alien.

"Just a moment, I will see if Mr. Hillsworth is in."

She closed the door, and left me standing there staring at the wood panels. A few seconds later, the door opened, and she was back, smiling up at me.

"Please, come in," she said. "Mr. Hillsworth will see you in the parlor."

She actually said parlor. I hadn't heard anyone use that word for years. I didn't think anyone called a living room a parlor any more.

I followed her into the house, through a modestly long entrance foyer, and into a large room with a vaulted ceiling, filled with early American furniture and what appeared to be original oil paintings from the colonial period on the walls. The place reeked of money.

Harrison Hillsworth, standing in front of one of those futuristic looking leather couches, his hand extended as I approached, was also not what I'd expected. I figured a retired engineer would be tousled, wearing rumpled chinos, a plaid shirt, and a vest, with lots of pens in his shirt or vest pockets, and slightly ruffled hair. Instead, I saw a portly man, with thinning black hair slicked back on his round head, his blue eyes looking at me through a pair of half glasses. He wore dark brown pants, sharply creased; a beige silk shirt, with open collar; and a deep red smoking jacket with black cuffs. He looked like a man who was comfortable with his money.

"Mr. Pennyback," he said, as I grasped his hand. "I've been expecting you." When my eyebrows twitched upwards, he said, "Walter called right after you visited him yesterday, so I figured you'd be making your way to me soon enough. Have a seat."

I looked around. The couch was one of those abstract things, with lots of curves, that looked like it'd been designed for a science fiction movie—not at all comfortable for an earth-human's body shape, and the chairs opposite it looked just as rough on the back. I opted for the one directly opposite the couch, and perched on the edge of the cushion. As I'd expected, it had no give. It felt like sitting on a concrete bench. He sat opposite me on the couch, looking a lot more at ease on the weird looking seat than I felt.

"Now, Mr. Pennyback, what can I do for you?"

He hadn't asked to see any ID, and his expression was open, making direct eye contact with me. He was either prepared to be completely open and honest, or was one of those rare people who can completely mask emotions. It was too early in our relationship for me to determine which, so I decided to just go with the flow and see what developed.

"I'm looking into this real estate investment club you belong to," I said.

"On behalf of Loretta Palmer, no doubt," he said.

I kept my expression neutral. "Why would you think that?"

He regarded me with an expression of equal neutrality. "Just a matter of putting two and two together. You're asking about the investment club, I heard on the news that the guy running it has been killed, I was present when Loretta threatened to cut his heart out if he didn't give her her money back, ipso facto, you must've been hired by her to prove that she didn't do it. How's that?" He sat back and folded his hands in his lap.

I'm not sure which was most impressive; that he had pieced things together so effectively, or that he could sit back so comfortable looking in that torture chamber of a couch. Then, I decided that it was the latter. After all, the guy was an engineer, and engineers, like PIs, solve problems. He'd very effectively put the pieces together and come to the most logical conclusion.

"Because of client confidentiality, I can neither confirm nor deny that," I said. "But, who else do you thing might've had a reason to do Sydney Simpson in?"

"Well, if Loretta's accusations are correct," he said. "And, I'm beginning to believe that they are, then anyone of us in the club would have an excellent motive . . . on the surface. However, if you think about it, that really doesn't make sense. Killing him means it's just that much less likely we'll get out money back."

Yup, this guy had an engineer's mind. I was beginning to develop a fondness for him.

"What about David Devlin, Simpson's accomplice; what was his role in all this?"

He rubbed at his fleshy chin, his eyes narrowed in concentration.

"An interesting question," he said finally. "I didn't see much of Devlin. Simpson was clearly the boss of the operation, sort of the alpha male. Devlin was kind of a nonentity. Mostly, when he was around, he was running errands for Simpson."

That didn't tell me much, so I decided to move to

who might've killed Simpson.

"You said that Loretta, Ms. Palmer, accused Simpson of fraud, and threatened to cut his heart out if he didn't give her money back. Do you think she's actually capable of killing him?"

"Nah," he answered without hesitation. "Loretta's a drama queen. Sure, she has a fiery temper, but she's actually just a spoiled, self-absorbed rich girl, accustomed to having her own way. Her kind kills with words and cutting looks. You have to get your hands dirty to actually kill someone, and she's definitely *not* the type to get those well-manicured hands of hers dirty." He leaned forward and slapped his hands on his knees. "Say, I'm not being a good host. It's a bit early in the day for a true libation, but would you like a coffee or tea?"

I hadn't finished my coffee at the office, and my day hasn't officially started until I've finished my second cup.

"I wouldn't mind a cup of coffee," I said.

"Black, of course." The guy was pretty perceptive, or just a good guesser. "Celeste," he called in a loud voice. "Two cups of coffee, black, please."

As if she'd been waiting in the wings for her cue, the maid appeared with two china cups on a silver tray, which she put on the coffee table. After a curtsy, right out of a vintage movie, she backed out of the room. Hillsworth sat back and smiled. He was truly living the dream. He picked up his cup, and waited for me to retrieve mine. The aroma wafting up from the cup was . . . intoxicating. A rich smell of southern hemisphere hillside; the distinctive bouquet of Colombia. I blew on it, and took a sip. Yes! Fresh-brewed from freshly-ground beans, with nothing added.

"Good coffee," I said.

He took a sip without blowing, and then nodded. "I get beans shipped from Bogota every month," he said.

"Got hooked on it when I worked an engineering project in Santa Marta ten years ago."

"I like Jamaican sometimes, but no one grows coffee beans quite like the Colombians."

"Yes, too bad they get so much competition from the Vietnamese. Did you know that most of the big coffee companies mix Vietnamese beans with the Colombian? The taste is not too bad, I mean, Vietnam grows some good beans, but I like pure Colombian."

We could've gotten sidetracked by a discussion of how, when bad weather disrupted the Colombian coffee crop one year, buyers had shifted a lot of their purchases to Vietnam, but I was more interested in solving my current puzzle. The world coffee market would have to wait for another day.

"So, if you think Loretta Palmer's not good for Simpson's murder, who do you think might've done it?"

"I'm assuming, here, you're talking about the other members of the club," he said. "We *all* were cheated by the man—and, there's no doubt he was running a scam, but I don't see how killing him helps us get our money back. Beyond motive, who in our group has the capability of murder? I'd have to include myself, of course. As an engineer, I've worked in some hard places, and seen some terrible stuff, so death doesn't really phase me much. Of course, I didn't do it. Why would I? Sure, I'm pissed about losing half a million, but it hasn't impoverished me, so I'll survive, and I'm not the vengeful type. There's Walter, of course. He's army, and I suppose he would know *how* to kill someone, but I don't think he'd do it for the same reason I wouldn't. What would he get out of it? As for the rest of the group, except for Tamara Braxton, who's a real tough broad, I doubt if any of them have the balls to commit a murder."

"What about Dudley Wiggins," I said. "He's a doctor. He would certainly know how to end someone's life."

"Yeah, he does have the knowledge." He smiled wryly. "But, Dudley's got this thing about blood. I know, a doctor, right, but he can't stand the sight of blood. His specialty is podiatry, so the only blood he has to deal with is a poorly extracted hangnail. And, to top it off, the man is about fifty pounds overweight."

I hadn't met any of the women other than Palmer, but what he was saying about them, except for Braxton, Davis, and Travis, whom we had yet to contact, fit with what Heather had told me. As for Reid; yeah, he was army, and would've been trained to take a life, but I hadn't gotten that kind of vibe off him, and his description of Wiggins didn't fit the profile of a man capable of sticking a blade into someone's chest. If you have a blood phobia, stabbing someone is not something you're likely to do. As for him, my gut was telling me he wasn't the killer. I know you can't take a gut to court, but my gut's seldom wrong about these things.

So, where did that leave me? I couldn't shake the nagging feeling, more a subliminal nudge, really, that the two mysterious buyers somehow figured into the case.

"We've picked up information that Simpson was courting two potential buyers for the property your club bought," I said. "What do you know about that?"

"Nothing." He shook his head. "When Loretta accosted him, he said he had two possible buyers for the property, and when he got the deal finalized, we'd all have a windfall payday. My instinct at the time was that he was making up the story on the fly to wriggle out of her clutches. When I asked him about them, he got real cagey; wouldn't identify them, other than to say they were well-heeled and might get into a bidding war over the property."

"So, you don't think they exist?"

"I don't know enough to say with assurance," he said. "But, you have to remember; we're dealing with a con man. I have no proof of their existence."

Maybe, maybe not. We had evidence that at least one of them *did* exist, and if Simpson was maneuvering them into a bidding war over this property, I wondered about the possibility of that changing into a real war, and him becoming collateral damage. At any rate, I felt that I'd gotten all I was going to get from Hillsworth. I finished my coffee, thanked him for his time, and left.

As I pulled out of his driveway, and headed back toward the main road, I decided to keep going to Rockville Pike and have a face to face with the security guy at the mall. Heather had gotten some information from him about Simpson's encounter with an individual who might be one of the mysterious buyers, but that was by phone. Nothing beats talking to someone face to face.

I took Chain Bridge Road, back to the George Washington Memorial Parkway, and the over to the Beltway. For getting to Rockville Pike, it was a tossup between going back through the District to Wisconsin Avenue or getting on the Beltway. Wisconsin Avenue, from Georgetown until you pass American University near the dividing line between the District and Montgomery County, is a maze of mixed traffic, trucks parked partly in the traffic lanes while the drivers unload their wares, and people not sure what lane they want to be in until they're at their turn and realize they need to cross two lanes to make it, while the Beltway between the GW Parkway on-ramp and the Rockville Pike off-ramp is filled with Indy 500 wannabes who insist on driving twenty miles per hour over the fifty-five mile per hour limit, and court disaster by staying in the outer lanes until they're almost on top of the I-270 split and then darting across three lanes of high-speed traffic to be in the lane they should've been in five miles back. If none of this dare devil driving results in an accident, which can back traffic up for ten miles, the Beltway's half the time, so I took a deep breath and headed up GW for the Beltway.

Luck was with me. I made it to the Rockville Pike off-ramp in twenty minutes, and only had three close calls in the process. Northbound Rockville Pike traffic was light, giving me time to get my heart rate back to something approaching normal by the time I pulled into the mall's parking lot.

The mall's admin office was on the second floor, at the opposite end of the hallway from Simpson's office. The reception area was staffed by a clone of Simpson's secretary, wearing faded jeans and a Redskin's sweatshirt that bulged out in all the right places. The mall security manager, Hiram Watkins, was in his office, so there was no waiting. She smiled as he waved me in.

I held out my ID, which he took and scrutinized carefully as he sat himself behind a gray, battered desk, piled high with stacks of folders. I sat in a folding, gray metal chair to the right side of the desk. He smiled as he handed me back my ID.

"So, Pennyback," he said. "What can I do for you?"

He got right down to business. No looking confused or worried by my being there, and the way he'd eyed my ID I pegged him for a former cop. He was about half an inch shorter than me, but a lot broader in girth, especially around the midsection. His hair, thinning on top, was beginning to show a lot of gray in with the brown, and he had deeply-etched crows feet at the corners of his eyes. Some people call them laugh lines, but he didn't look like he laughed a lot, and his eyes didn't look like they missed much.

"You spoke to my colleague, Heather Bunche," I said. "About a visitor to one of the mall's clients?"

"Ah, yeah. The lady with the sexy voice. Wanted to know about a visitor that the late Sydney Simpson had. What more do you want to know about that?"

"You told her this person you saw was swarthy, maybe Hispanic or East Asian?"

He laughed. "Actually, I said he looked like he might be either Mexican or Indian, but the more I think about it, I'm not sure."

"Why is that?"

"I dunno. There was something about him that I can't quite put my finger on. I only saw him talking to Simpson from a distance, and I guess, the brown skin and dark hair made me think that. But, there was something else. I just can't remember what it was."

"Let's talk about something else, and maybe it'll come to you."

"You an ex-cop, or military?" he asked.

"Military, what makes you ask."

"Just the way you do things. That interrogation technique, for example. That's kinda a cop thing. But, the way you carry yourself, says GI. Know what I mean?"

I nodded. I did know. Certain behaviors you pick up after years in a profession stay with you.

"Yeah, I noticed the same thing about you. Former cop?"

"Yup. Twenty-five years with the Montgomery County police. Took this job six months after hanging up my badge. Pay's not all that good, but along with my pension, it keeps me in beer. My third wife divorced me five years before I retired—one of the drawbacks of being a cop, you know—so, my needs are few. I get by. What about you, you do a full career?"

I nodded again. "Okay, back to business. Did you ever see anyone else visiting Simpson?"

"Well, there were these people in his investment clubs. He approached me about that once, but the buy-in was a bit too rich for my blood. Who do you think iced him? One of his customers?"

"Anything's possible. I heard, though, that he had potential customers besides the clubs; this swarthy guy, for example, so I'm also looking at them."

"Why would they do that, though? I mean, the guy who was talkin' to him in the parking lot didn't seem too happy, but why would he want to kill him?"

Without knowing *why* the mystery man was unhappy, I couldn't even begin to answer that question.

"Why does anyone kill another person?" I asked. "Money's a good reason, and Simpson was handling a lot of money. Then, there's jealousy, but I don't see that at work here. And, of course, there's anger or revenge. You piss someone off enough, and they just might kill you."

Yeah, suppose you're right about that. Say, I just remembered the strange thing that happened. When Simpson was arguing with that guy, one of his club members, the hot black chick, Baxter or something like that, came up to them. Well, they stopped talking right away, and Simpson shook her hand. But, when she offered her hand to the other guy, he pulled back like she was offering him a snake or something."

"What was that all about?" I asked.

"I wasn't close enough to hear what went down," he said. "At first, I thought maybe the dude was being racist, or something; which is pretty funny when you consider he's actually darker than she is. But, then, he smiled and bowed, so I guess he just has a thing about touching a woman. Now that I think about it, that pretty much rules out him being Mexican, don't it? Could he be one of them Indian Hindus or Buddhists, or something?"

Could be, I was thinking, but I wasn't aware of any Hindu prohibition of physical contact between different genders, nor of any Buddhists who would be as dark as he'd described this man. There was, though, one other possibility, and one that set warning bells clanging in my head.

I needed to get out of there and call Heather, so I

thanked Watkins for his time, assured him that he'd in fact been quite helpful, and beat feet for the parking lot and my car.

Chapter Fourteen

I caught Heather just as she was about to get into her car and head for Tamara Braxton's interior design shop.

"When you get there," I said. "Wait outside for me. I'd like for us to both interview her together."

"Why? So far, my interviews have been routine. In fact, they've been downright boring."

"I can promise you this one won't be boring. Braxton just might be able to identify one of our mysterious buyers."

That got her attention. "How?" she asked.

"I'll brief you when I see you."

She protested, but I held firm. Finally, she agreed to wait. I fired up the Bug and headed south on Rockville Pike, which becomes Wisconsin Avenue in Bethesda, and played tag with the traffic lights until I got to Dumbarton Street in Georgetown. Heather was parked a couple of buildings north of the four-story, gray brick structure that housed Braxton's company. I found an empty slot half a block past her and walked back. She was out of her car and waiting for me.

"Okay, tell me what's going on," she said.

I told her. She snapped her mouth shut and nodded her head. This was going to be an interesting interview.

Braxton's shop was on the first and second floor of the building. The first floor was mostly a display floor, showing the different furnishings and accoutrements, as well as various designs she'd done, while the second floor was her office and workshop. She had a wood workshop, a clay modeling room, and a large room with six ladies bent over sewing machines.

Her receptionist, a tall, willowy Asian woman, welcomed us, offered us herbal tea, and said Ms. Braxton would be with us shortly.

She was; about five minutes after we arrived, and Watkins' description of her as a 'hot black chick' was an understatement. Even Heather gaped when she walked through the door from her office into the reception area.

Tamara Braxton was just a shade under six feet tall. An oval head sat on a long, regal neck, and she looked at us through amber eyes with flecks of gold in the pupils. Her hair, close-cropped curls, was glossy black, and her skin was a rich caramel, absolutely flawless. Broad shoulders encased in a pearl jacket with a white silk blouse underneath. Breasts, prominent without being grossly large. Nipped in waist and hips that flared out provocatively under a knee-length pearl skirt, showing shapely calves that flowed down to narrow ankles and small feet encased in two-inch black heels. She flowed rather than walked across the room to greet us, and when she spoke, her voice had the slightly raspy sound of the old-time blues singers.

"You must be Mr. Pennyback and Ms. Bunche," she said. "I didn't expect both of you. Come on into my office, and we'll talk."

No hesitation, no confusion; a real take-charge kind

of person.

"How did you know who we were?" Heather asked as we followed Braxton into her office.

"Grapevine, honey. Isabel called me as soon as you left her place." She waved at two not too uncomfortable looking chairs in the left corner of a large, modernistic office. "Make yourself comfortable. Would you like coffee or tea, or maybe water? I have Evian."

"Water's fine," I said. "Me, too," said Heather.

She walked past a desk that looked to be made almost entirely of glass, a large slab on uprights with no drawers, more a work table, actually, to a black cabinet which, when she opened the door, revealed a small fridge, from which she took three bottles of water. From the shelf over the cabinet, she got three crystal tumblers. All this she brought back to the corner and placed them in the center of the glass coffee table. She took a seat across from us, picked up one of the water bottles, opened it, and took a long, unladylike swig.

"So, you want to talk about the little real estate investment scheme we got ourselves hooked into," she said. "Fire away. What do you want to know?"

Heather shot me a glance. The question in her eyes; which one of us leads this interview? I answered by turning to Braxton and asking, "When did you realize it was a scam?"

She laid an index finger alongside her aquiline nose and cocked her head to the left. "I think I had some misgivings early on. Nothing I could put my finger on, just an itch. But, when Loretta went off on Simpson that day, I knew it."

"Must've made you mad."

"Being taken for five hundred grand isn't exactly something you want for Christmas," she said. "But, if you mean mad enough to kill Simpson, not really. Sure, it put a crimp in my bank account, but with the fees I charge, I'll make it back before the year's out."

"What about Loretta Palmer?" Heather asked. "She threatened to cut Simpson's heart out."

She laughed, a deep, throaty sound. "Oh, that girl's all mouth. I mean, she was pissed, no doubt about that, but she wouldn't actually *kill* anyone. Too much danger of getting her designer clothes soiled."

That was the second reference to the lack of substance in our client, which, frankly, squared with my own view of her. She still wasn't on my list of people to like, but it's always nice to know you're working for an innocent person. Tamara Braxton, on the other hand, struck me as someone who *could* kill if sufficiently provoked. I decided to play devil's advocate.

"What about you?" I asked. "Were you upset enough with Simpson to kill him?"

She didn't blink. She didn't flinch. She just regarded me coolly with those amber eyes, and with a half-smile on her ruby red lips. "I was upset with the little weasel, no doubt about that. But, not enough to kill him. How in the hell could I get my money back from him if I did that?"

Logic, pure sweet logic, delivered in a deep, raspy, cool voice. And, she never broke eye contact once during the delivery. I believed her.

"What about the other members of your club? Any of them capable of it?"

She responded as if she'd been with me during my interviews; Reid, the retired soldier, would know how to kill, but he would, like her, be more interested in getting his money back; Hillsworth, the engineer, would want his money back, and was, if anything, more analytically logical than she was; the doctor, Dudley Wiggins, was too fat to get around well enough to go out and kill anyone, and had once almost fainted when the writer, Harriet Gold, had shown up with a bloody bandage on her finger from a paper cut; and the other women just didn't have it in them to kill.

"That doesn't give us much to work with," Heather said, when Braxton finished her account.

"Well," Braxton said. "There is this dude Sydney was arguing with one day. He's one of the buyers Sydney claimed was interesting in our land, and he was pissed because Sydney was playing him off against someone else."

"How do you know this?" I asked. She'd moved on to identifying the mysterious buyer, and I hadn't even had to bring it up.

"I ran into the dude quite by accident." She brushed at her tight curls. "I was out in Rockville, meeting with one of my commercial clients, and thought I'd just drop by and ask Sydney how things were going . . . it'd been a while since we'd gotten a royalty check. Anyway, when I arrived in the parking lot, he was out front, arguing with this guy, and when I approached, they both got real quiet, and tried to act like nothing was happening."

"Can you describe this person?" Heather asked. I gave her points for not mentioning anything about him, a common rookie mistake. If she'd mentioned what he looked like, it could've thrown Braxton's memory off. By asking it open-ended like that, we were more likely to get a more accurate recollection.

"Yeah, he was dark, I think they call it swarthy, but this dude was darker than me," she said. "And, he had this thick, jet black hair, and a kind of hooked nose."

"Was he Hispanic?" I asked, already knowing the answer.

"Hell, no," she shot back. "This guy looked like a desert Arab, straight out of central casting. Muslim, too."

Heather looked puzzled. "How do you know that, that he was Muslim, I mean?"

"Because when I offered to shake his hand, he took a step backward, smiled shyly, and did that little hand to the heart thing they do. And, I happened to overhear Sydney call him Mr. Sayeed, as I was approaching them."

I didn't tell her that the name she heard wasn't necessarily Arab; could be from south Asia, like Pakistan, for example, but I thought she'd nailed it on the guy's religion. Now, I don't like to stereotype, but even I'd fallen ill to a bit of the post-9/11 hysteria. Mysterious men of that religious persuasion, keeping in the background, kind of made me nervous. As a person of color, I always felt guilty whenever I did it, but there you go.

Braxton looked at me, a querying look in her eyes. "Is that significant?"

"Probably not," I said, hoping that was the case. The country had experienced far too much religious hysteria without me adding to it. "I'd heard, though, that Simpson had two buyers for the land."

"Yes, that's what he told us, and from the fragmentary bit of conversation I overheard, that's what they were arguing about."

Oh, is that so, I thought. Maybe we were closing in on a motive for the murder.

"What did you hear?"

"Sayeed had said something like, 'you can't play games with me, I already promised you two million for that land,' and Sydney responded, 'Hey, it's just business, Sayeed, Hodges has topped your bid."

"You have any idea who this Hodges is?" I asked.

"Not a clue."

I shot Heather a look. "Let's assume it's a surname, and run it," I said.

"Are you thinking Sayeed might've killed him?" Braxton asked.

"If he felt he was being stiffed on a deal, anything's possible. First, though, we need to try and identify both these guys."

Just then, the door to her office banged open, causing Heather and I to turn and look. A red-haired, whirling dervish of a woman, came bouncing through the door, arms waving, and mouth moving. "Tamara, darling," she said. "I came as soon as I could." She looked at the two of us. "This is them, the detectives, I mean. What have you told them? What do they want to know?"

Braxton came from behind her desk, and the red head grabbed her and pulled her into a bear hug. They kissed; not the air kiss, or kiss on the cheek of two old friends, but the lip-on-lip, tongue-action of a GI home from the war kind of kiss, their bodies glued together from hip to thigh. Heather's cheeks turned pink, and I looked at the floor. After a few moments, they released each other and turned to face us.

"Ms. Bunche, Mr. Pennyback, may I introduce Roberta Davis," Braxton said. "She's a member of the real estate investment club . . . and, my significant other."

Davis, according to Heather's research, an actress whose career was on the downslide, but who was still quite attractive, in an over-the-top kind of way, beamed at us around Braxton's shoulder. Six inches shorter than her partner, but about the same weight, she had one of those ivory complexions that keep from looking sickly because of little circles of pastel color in the cheeks that make her look like a life-sized porcelain doll, the kind that little girls collect and hold until they're old women, when they keep them on shelves where they collect dust.

"Please to meet you," she said.

I nodded. Heather said, "Likewise."

"What do you want to know?" she asked.

"They were asking questions about the real estate deal," Braxton said. "But, I think they're really trying to figure out who killed Sydney."

She looked at me with wide blue eyes, looking even more like a doll on display. "Oh, and how are you coming on that? Have you discovered who did it?"

I shrugged, and Heather looked like she wasn't sure whether to laugh or vomit. The question was so innocently asked, I couldn't help but jump straight to the conclusion that, in no way could this woman be guilty of murder. I kept a straight face. "No," I said. "So far, we've run into nothing but dead ends. The people who would, on the surface, have a reason for wanting him dead, and that, by the way, is the entire investment club, also have every reason to want him alive—to get your money back."

"Unless one or more of you got your money back when he was killed," Heather said.

I looked at her with appreciation and pride. She was learning the business well. Statements like that can throw a guilty, but unsuspecting, suspect off balance. With the two women standing there, arms around each other and staring at us, it didn't upset their balance an inch.

"I doubt that anyone in our group would be able to conceal getting their hands on that much money, or even a fraction of it," Braxton said. "I know that neither of us did it."

I agreed with her, I didn't think any of them did it. I didn't tell her that, though. Keep options open, just in case I was being overly optimistic.

"Well," I said. "We'll just have to keep digging. By the way, can either of you tell us how to get in touch with David Devlin, Simpson's accomplice?"

They looked at each other, shaking their heads.

"Devlin? I don't recall seeing him around much," Davis said.

"And, when he was, he never said much," Braxton added. "He seemed more an errand boy than a real accomplice, though. Sydney was always bossing him around."

A little more chit chat, little useful information gained therefrom, and we thanked them both and left.

I walked Heather to her car, not out of any sense of

chivalry, but to talk to her about the things we needed to focus on.

"We have *got* to find Devlin," I said. "I've got a feeling that these two mystery buyers are deeply involved in this, and Devlin is probably the only person who can identify them."

"If you're right, and one of them was Simpson's killer, Devlin's life could also be in danger . . . provided he hasn't already been killed."

That thought had crossed my mind as well. "All the more reason to find him as soon as possible."

She gave me one of her pixie smiles. "So, it's off the streets and back to the computer for me, right?"

"We each serve where we serve best, kiddo. You know I'm no good trying to use one of those infernal machines, while you work magic with it. Pull out all the stops. Find Devlin."

She put a hand over her heart and stood with her shoulders squared. "Yes, oh fearless leader. I'll get right on it."

Charles Ray

Chapter Fifteen

We went south on Wisconsin, with me following behind Heather, took a right on M, and while she took a left, across Francis Scott Key Bridge into Rosslyn, to get to her little brick house in North Arlington, I kept on going on M to Canal Road, toward Clara Barton Parkway and River Road. It was 5:25 when I made the left onto Canal Road, which was now one-way traffic westbound, but not quite up to full rush hour volume.

The traffic started to pick up by the time I got to the Chain Bridge turnoff, and was at normal rush hour levels by the time I'd reached the weird left turn, right merge onto Clara Barton Parkway. That was also when I noticed the blue Ford Taurus that had been four cars behind me since I passed Key Bridge.

People, when they're behind the wheel of a car, do the strangest and most self-indulgent things in their little cocoons of anonymity, but they're the strangest in the DC area for some reason, probably having to do with the ego-centric nature of the region's main industry, politics. Washington drivers hate to drive behind anyone, and if they see an empty space ahead of you that's even a foot more than a car-length, they will try to fill it. People execute dangerous passing maneuvers just to get one or two car lengths farther in their journey, or to get in front of the driver who had the temerity to be in front of them. So, for a car to maintain the same position relative to mine for more than three miles, especially given the number of times I'd let a bit of space open up between my car and the one in front in order to maintain my usual two-second distance between cars to allow for reaction time in case the idiot in front of me makes a sudden stop, something is off. I think my mind registered it at a subconscious level shortly after entering Canal Road, but by the time we reached Clara Barton, the conscious mind was beginning to sit up and take notice.

I was being followed.

I sped up, and pulled a Washington maneuver, by darting out into an empty space, pulling past three cars, and then cutting in front of the third one, putting on the brakes to keep from rear-ending the car ahead. Sure enough, a few seconds later, the Taurus pulled out and then cut back in, forced to do it five cars back because of a lack of empty space to pull into.

As far as I knew, they, whoever the hell they were, had been on my tail since I left the shopping mall in Rockville, or even earlier. In the heavy downtown and suburban traffic, I'd not noticed. It was only out here, with all the traffic heading in one direction, that I noticed a vehicle that wasn't following the usual traffic patterns.

The question was, who was following me, and why; and what was I to do about it?

One thing for sure; I didn't want to lead them to my house. So, instead of taking the I-495/River Road exit, I stayed on the parkway, heading toward the C&O Canal National Historical Park and Falls Road. The blue Taurus kept its position.

I was becoming more pissed than worried. I don't like being followed. I was pretty sure it wasn't the police. What police department would use a powder blue car, and a Ford at that, for vehicle surveillance? Was it connected to our present case, and was another car following Heather? Was she in danger?

Using a mobile phone while driving is not only dangerous, it's illegal in Maryland, but I did it anyway. With one hand gripping the steering wheel, I took my phone from my shirt pocket and hit number two on the speed dial. Heather answered after two rings.

"Are you okay?" I asked.

"Sure, just got home, and was about to take a shower, why?"

I didn't want to worry her. "I just remembered," I said. "In addition to working on finding Devlin, I have a couple of leads on the two mystery buyers. One is named Sayeed. I'm pretty sure that's his last name, and he's Middle Eastern or South Asian, maybe Pakistani. The other is Hughes, also probably a last name. I know that's not a lot to go on, but see if you can tie either of those names to Simpson or real estate."

If she was suspicious of such a vague request, she didn't let on. "It's not a lot to go on, but I'll give it a shot. Right now, though, all I want is a hot shower, a salad and a glass of wine. Street work takes a lot out of a person."

"Don't I know it. I'm almost home now. See you tomorrow."

I broke the connection before she got suspicious, and put my mind to work on how to ditch my tail.

Once Clara Barton reaches I-270, it becomes Cabin John Parkway, and then Falls Road at the C&O Canal Park. Falls Road runs north and intersects with River Road in Potomac Village. From the park to the intersection, even during rush hour, is about three or four minutes. When I reached River Road, instead of turning, I stayed on Falls Road, heading northeast toward downtown Rockville. I could see the Ford in the rearview mirror, it had dropped back to about six cars now, but was still keeping pace with me.

There was no doubt about it. I was being followed.

A major thoroughfare, Falls Road didn't offer me a lot of options for ditching my tail, until it crossed I-270 and entered the historic neighborhoods of west Rockville. Home at the turn of the century to people like F. Scott Fitzgerald, who is buried in the Catholic cemetery near the Rockville Metro station, the neighborhood has the old homes of some of the city's past elites. This is also where Falls Roads not only narrows, but where it curves a lot, and where small feeder roads and side streets are in abundance. As I barely managed to get in front of a large utility van coming off the expressway, I saw my opportunity.

I pushed the gas pedal to the floor. The Bug farted out a white puff of smoke from the exhaust pipe, and my reconditioned engine belched thanks for finally being used. I felt the force against my chest, pressing me against the seat as my Volkswagen surged forward. I whipped into the outer lane to go around the car in front of me, cutting back in immediately, causing the driver to hit his brakes, and creating an accordion effect of brake lights and deceleration, I was pretty sure all the way back to the Ford on my tail. Falls Road curved around to the right, momentarily shielding me from the Ford. I made a quick left onto a narrow side street bordering a large parking lot that, thankfully, even at that time of evening was still mostly filled. I made a screeching turn into the parking lot, drove halfway across, turned and slipped into the first empty space I saw. I turned off the engine and lights and sat back, looking over my shoulder at the entrance to the parking lot.

I sat there for twenty minutes. No other cars went past the parking lot entrance, and the movement of headlights to my right, on Falls Road, was at a normal pace. I could just imagine my pursuers, craning to see through their windows, wondering where the green Volkswagen had gotten to.

Finally, convinced that I'd ditched them, I left the parking lot, turned right and drove to Montgomery Avenue, hung a left across I-270, and drove home.

All the way west on Route 28 to Travillah Road, I kept watch in the rearview mirror, but the Taurus didn't reappear. Travillah Road winds through mostly residential neighborhoods—some new developments along with a lot of the original frame dwellings of the working-class people who live north of Potomac—until it comes to River Road, where, after waiting for a few minutes for a break in the evening rush hour traffic, I turned right, and drove the rest of the way home without incident.

I said nothing to Sandra about the incident, but couldn't get it out of my mind.

I was convinced that it was related to the case I was working, but couldn't for the life of me figure out why.

Charles Ray

Chapter Sixteen

I was up early Saturday morning, well before the sun made its first appearance at the horizon. By 5:45, just as the eastern horizon was turning pink, I was on my back porch, in gray sweats and tattered sneakers, stretching in preparation for a morning run through the forest that makes up a good portion of my backyard. Sandra looked so peaceful, curled in a fetal position, with her fists tucked under her chin, I decided to let her sleep and run solo.

A herd of five deer was startled when I dashed into the woods, starting off my run at a fast clip for the first two miles, mostly downhill. After that, I settled into an easy loping pace, down toward the river, along a muddy trail that ran parallel to the river, and then back upslope toward the house, doing a total of about four miles. There's nothing magic about four miles, but it was what they'd had us do in the army back when the jogging craze caught on—four miles, five days a week—and, it had been my standard run for so long, I just did it without thinking much about it.

I finished the last hundred yards, from the trees to

my barn, a level stretch, at a flat out run, and then spent a few minutes walking around to cool down, before doing twenty minutes on the heavy bag suspended from the rafters of the barn. I followed that up with ten minutes of meditation, sitting cross-legged on the back porch.

Sandra was just coming out of the shower when I went inside to wash up.

"Why didn't you wake me to run with you?" she asked, toweling her still damp hair.

"You looked too peaceful," I said. "You know, a guy hates to disturb a woman's sleep."

She gave me a funny look. I knew that she was waiting for me to say, 'unlike women, who want everyone awake when they get out of bed,' but I decided not to. She waited a few heartbeats, and then visibly relaxed.

"I'm skipping exercise this morning. I'll go fix us some breakfast," she said.

"But, Saturday's my day to do breakfast."

She gave me another funny look. "You forget, we're having lunch with Carlton and Elizabeth today, so we need to eat a light breakfast."

"I can do us a light breakfast." I *never* skip breakfast if I can avoid it, and with us planning to leave home around noon for the trip to Blood Raine's cabin, there was no way I was skipping today.

She made a sniffing noise. "Babe, your idea of a light breakfast is having only bacon instead of bacon *and* sausage. You can do tomorrow and Monday. *I'll* do a truly light breakfast this morning." She said it in a tone that was as hard as tempered steel.

Her idea of light breakfast, while wise under the circumstances, often left my stomach wondering when the real meal would be served. I have, though, learned never to argue with her when she uses her school-marm tone of voice.

"Okay, milady," I said. "I'll wash the stink off while

you cook.

Mollified by my surrender, she closed the gap between us and gave me a sisterly peck on the cheek. When I reached for her, she scooted back. "After you shower. Now, scoot."

She grabbed for her clothing, which was hanging over the back of a chair near the door to the bathroom, and started pulling it on. Chastened, I began stripping as I entered the bathroom. It was comfortably warm from her recent use, and I didn't have to wait for the shower to reach a nice temperature.

Twenty minutes later, showered, shaved, and clad in jeans and a Dallas Cowboys polo shirt, I joined her in the kitchen. She hadn't been kidding about preparing a *light* breakfast. Two slices of whole wheat toast, a hard-boiled egg, a small glass of grapefruit juice, and a cup of black coffee. That's usually what I snack on while I'm preparing breakfast, but at least it meant that I'd have a healthy appetite for whatever fine viands Blood was preparing for us.

I tried to look like I was enjoying it as I chewed the dry toast—Sandra opted against jam or jelly, because sugar is too filling, she says—and washed it down with grapefruit juice. The boiled egg wasn't too bad, because she let me put salt on it, and the coffee, freshly ground Colombian, was delicious.

We cleaned up after finishing, and then went out to the back porch where we sat and watched the deer herd I'd spooked earlier return to graze.

Twenty minutes before twelve, we got in my Volkswagen and started for Blood's place. It's about eight miles west on River Road from my farmhouse, and then another mile down an unmarked dirt road, lined on each side by a pine forest. Somewhere in that forest, Blood has a network of cameras and sensors, which I've been unable to spot, and I'm pretty good at that. Even though he's been long retired from the agency, he still does consulting work for them, and tests new gadgets, so his cabin, which is almost as fortified as the Pentagon, has all the latest monitoring technology. No one can get within a mile of the place without him knowing it.

And, as usual, he was waiting on the porch for us when we pulled up.

We got out and approached him.

"Well, well, my two most favorite people," he said. "Come on up here and sit down. Elizabeth, Al and Sandra are here."

Elizabeth Sung, half an inch shorter and thirty years younger than Blood, came out of the cabin. She stepped up beside him and slipped an arm around his waist. They were wearing matching outfits, plaid shirts and faded jeans, his rather loosely on his slender frame, hers hugging curves that rivaled Sandra's.

"Hi, guys," she said. "Glad you could make it."

I'd introduced Elizabeth to Blood several years earlier, when I needed a safe place to stash her to keep a Chinese gangster from killing her. What started as a favor to me, developed first into a close friendship, and finally with her selling her Chinatown condo and moving in with him permanently. Despite the age difference, the two acted like an old married couple.

We stepped up onto the porch. Sandra and Elizabeth embraced, and I shook hands with Blood. Then, we switched places, and Elizabeth kissed me on the cheek, while Sandra did the same to Blood.

"It's always nice to visit you two," Sandra said. She patted Blood's shoulder. "You're looking sexy as always."

He slipped his arm around her waist, lifted her left hand and kissed it. "You'd better watch yourself, young lady," he said. "Al's a friend of mine, but if Elizabeth ever decides to leave me, I'm giving him a run for his money."

Elizabeth poked him gently in the ribs. "That's not going to happen, you old flirt. Guys, would you like some refreshment while we wait for Carlton's ham to finish roasting?"

"I'd love something," I said.

"We made a fresh batch of eggnog this morning. Sandra, would you help me get it?"

The two women went into the cabin. Blood and I sat on the big carved wooden bench that sat beneath the double-glass window next to the reinforced wooden door.

"You look like you got a bee under your bonnet, youngster," he said, as I slumped back against the polished wood.

He might be in his eighties, but he's still no slouch when it comes to reading people.

"Yeah, I've got this case that's perplexing." I filled him in quickly.

"Your client didn't do it, but there's evidence linking her, and you have no other suspect, is that about the gist of it?" Like I said, he's sharp.

"That's it." I was just about to tell him about the car following me, when Sandra and Elizabeth came back to the porch. Sandra carried a large glass pitcher containing a beige liquid, and Elizabeth had a large silver tray with four large glass tumblers on it.

"Who wants eggnog?" Sandra asked.

"Why is it that color?" I asked.

Elizabeth smiled and winked at Blood. "Carlton went a little wild with the rum. There's nearly half a bottle in here."

Whoa! That explained the color. Eggnog that's nearly fifty percent alcohol by volume, and me with nothing more than one boiled egg and two pieces of dry toast in my stomach.

"I'll have half a glass," I said. Sandra poured, stopping just a bit above the half-way mark. She then filled glasses for Elizabeth and Blood, and poured about four fingers in her own glass, from which she took tiny sips.

"You were telling Carlton about your latest case I see," Sandra said. "It's a real puzzler, guys. I think the great detective has finally met his match."

Blood rubbed at his chin, the stubble making a rasping sound. I'd not noticed until then that he wasn't as clean-shaven as usual.

"Well, he's had tough cases before," he said. "Just need to take a close look at the elements to start forming a clear picture, is all." He looked at me, and winked. "Let's show these ladies how it's done, youngster. Tell me what you have so far."

In the past, I'd often found him to be a good sounding board when I was dealing with a particularly perplexing problem. His years in the CIA, although mostly involved in field operations, had given him the ability to pierce the murkiness of a situation and find that one gleaming ray of light that was the key to pulling aside the veil of uncertainty. So, beginning with Loretta Palmer's arrival in my office, I laid the case out for him, bit by bit, watching Sandra's eyes widen when I reached the coda of the blue Taurus tailing me.

When I finished, and awaited his revelation, Sandra preempted him by grasping my forearm, her nails denting the flesh. "Al, you didn't tell me about someone following you." There was an accusatory tone in her voice.

"I didn't want to worry you last night," I said. "Besides, I ditched them in Rockville."

Her expression showed that she was only partly mollified. While I often shared cases with her, trusting her insights almost as much as Blood's, I tried to keep her insulated from as much of the danger as possible. When she'd been kidnapped, along with Buster's wife, Alma, by a gang of militia men, I'd determined that I wouldn't involve her in anything that might physically harm her. The psychic harm, though, when she discovered that I was treating her like a fragile little toy, something she definitely was not, was another matter. Fortunately, she's not one to create a scene in front of others, friend or stranger, so she sat there and looked at me, her lips compressed and her cheek muscles tight.

Blood looked from me to her, sensing, I think, the tension between us.

"I imagine he just didn't want to have to tell the story twice," he said. "This way, he gets both our perspectives on it."

Nice recovery on his part. Sandra's expression relaxed . . . a little.

"I suppose that makes sense."

Even though it hadn't been my reason for keeping it from her, it *did* make sense. She was second only to Blood in her ability to see through the fog of confusion and discern what was really going on. Something to do with having worked with inner city kids for so long.

"Okay," Blood said. "Here's what I see. You have this con artist, bilking money from wealthy, but naïve suckers. He has land, but it's probably not worth anywhere near the amount he's taken them for, and he's using the *investments* from new victims to keep the older ones happy. A classic pyramid scheme, and like most pyramid schemes, it eventually collapses, with everyone but the con artist losing their shirts."

"Yeah," I said. "That's the way I see it. But, someone shoved a letter opener into the guy's heart, and I can't come up with a viable suspect. The victims of the con might seem like the most likely suspects, but I'm having trouble seeing any of them doing it."

He nodded his agreement. "Right. Getting their money back would make sense, but it doesn't look like that happened. The only other motive that works is anger and just making the guy suffer, but a single stab wound doesn't sound like anger. That sounds like a cold, calculating killing. Any of the club members strike you as the type?"

I thought about it for a few seconds. "The army guy and the engineer are possible, but I don't get that vibe from either of them. And then, there's the interior designer, Tamara Braxton. She's an 'in-control' type, but she didn't strike me as the type who'd do it just out of anger. As for the rest, no, I don't see them as suspects."

"And, you're convinced that your client is innocent?"

"Yeah, I am. She's a spoiled, rich kid with a big mouth, but I don't think she's a murderer."

"So, that brings us back to the two mystery buyers," he said. "You said Simpson had an argument with one, and he was upset about the presence of the other?"

"Yeah; at least, that's what Braxton said. She seemed to be telling the truth, and I'm assuming she remembered correctly."

"Well, it's simple then. You have to identify those buyers."

"Easier said than done," I said. "I only have a single name for each, and I'm assuming they're surnames, along with a description of one that could match thousands of people in the greater DC metro area alone. It's not like finding a needle in a haystack, it's like finding a needle in a barrel full of needles."

He waggled a finger at me. "Not necessarily, son. I have some friends who can take what little we know about these two, such as their involvement in real estate, for example, and build profiles that can narrow it down a little."

I'd never heard of such a capability, but Blood has some unusual friends, so I had no choice but to believe him. After all, I had nothing else. So, I told him what I knew about the two mystery men—took all of two minutes.

He nodded at me as I gave him the information. Out of the corner of my eye, I noticed Elizabeth, her body slanted away from him, rapidly writing on a piece of paper. When she saw me looking, she frowned, stopped writing and snatched the paper up, folded it and tucked it into the pocket of her shirt. She then stuck the pencil into her hair which was arranged handily into a bun at the back of her head.

"Now, I want to hear about the car that was following you," Sandra said. I thought she'd forgotten about that, which was pretty stupid of me. The woman forgets nothing.

"There's not much to tell, really," I said. "I'm not sure where they began following me, but I picked it up on Canal Road. A blue Taurus, probably last year's model, and it never got close enough for me to even get a glimpse at the driver."

"It's probably safe to assume, though, that it's connected to your current case," Blood said. "I'll have my friends factor the blue Ford into the profile of our mystery men."

There was that sharp mind again. I hadn't really considered it, but the person or persons following me could be related to the mysterious buyers. They'd probably seen me at Simpson's place of business, talking to the security chief, even visiting his office, and been curious enough to want to know more about me.

I was about to comment on that, when Elizabeth laid a hand on his arm, "Carlton, honey," she said. "When we were getting the eggnog, I was telling Sandra about your special ham recipe, and she'd like to see it, wouldn't you, Sandra?"

The two women shared a look. "Of course," Sandra said. "Elizabeth tells me that you're basting it with bourbon and coke. I'd love to see how that works."

With a broad smile on his face, Blood stood, and bowed at Sandra. "Of course, deal lady. Always happy to share my cooking secrets with someone who appreciates the finer things. Come with me, the grille is just around the corner."

She stood and linked her arm in his, and they walked to the end of the porch, which stretched the width of the front of the cabin, with steps on both ends as well as the center. When they were around the corner, Elizabeth looked at me, her brow wrinkled.

"You're probably wondering why I was taking notes," she said.

"Not so much that, as why my noticing seems to have upset you."

"It's his memory. Lately, he's been having these episodes of forgetfulness. They're not often, and are usually brief in duration, but when he snaps out of it, he's unaware of what has happened."

I felt a chill. "How long has this been happening?"

"For about a month or two," she said. "He's otherwise healthy, and because he doesn't remember having these episodes, when I mentioned that he should maybe talk to a doctor, he thought I was being too much of a worrier, and refused."

"Do you have any idea what's causing it?"

Her eyes glistened, and she wiped at them. "Yes, unfortunately, I do. I had an uncle who had the same thing happen to him. I hope I'm wrong, though."

"Well, don't keep me in suspense," I said. "What is it?"

"It looks like the onset of dementia. If it is, it could continue to develop slowly, or he could just wake up one day, and not know who I am, or where he is." A tear oozed slowly from the corner of her left eye and flowed down her cheek. She didn't bother wiping at it.

I felt like I'd been punched in the gut. Not Blood. The man was indestructible. This couldn't be happening.

"What will you do?"

She finally wiped at her cheek. "Whatever it takes," she said. "Eventually, I *will* get him to a doctor, even if I have to slip him a mickey and haul him in unconscious. Maybe I can find some medication that will delay or ease it. After that, well, I'll just take care of him."

She said it quietly, but with a fierce determination in her voice. I had no doubt that she meant exactly what she said.

I was up early Saturday morning, well before the sun made its first appearance at the horizon. By 5:45, just as the eastern horizon was turning pink, I was on my back porch, in gray sweats and tattered sneakers, stretching in preparation for a morning run through the forest that makes up a good portion of my backyard. Sandra looked so peaceful, curled in a fetal position, with her fists tucked under her chin, I decided to let her sleep and run solo.

A herd of five deer was startled when I dashed into the woods, starting off my run at a fast clip for the first two miles, mostly downhill. After that, I settled into an easy loping pace, down toward the river, along a muddy trail that ran parallel to the river, and then back upslope toward the house, doing a total of about four miles. There's nothing magic about four miles, but it was what they'd had us do in the army back when the jogging craze caught on—four miles, five days a week—and, it had been my standard run for so long, I just did it without thinking much about it.

I finished the last hundred yards, from the trees to my barn, a level stretch, at a flat out run, and then spent a few minutes walking around to cool down, before doing twenty minutes on the heavy bag suspended from the rafters of the barn. I followed that up with ten minutes of meditation, sitting cross-legged on the back porch.

Sandra was just coming out of the shower when I went inside to wash up.

"Why didn't you wake me to run with you?" she asked, toweling her still damp hair.

"You looked too peaceful," I said. "You know, a guy

hates to disturb a woman's sleep."

She gave me a funny look. I knew that she was waiting for me to say, 'unlike women, who want everyone awake when they get out of bed,' but I decided not to. She waited a few heartbeats, and then visibly relaxed.

"I'm skipping exercise this morning. I'll go fix us some breakfast," she said.

"But, Saturday's my day to do breakfast."

She gave me another funny look. "You forget, we're having lunch with Carlton and Elizabeth today, so we need to eat a light breakfast."

"I can do us a light breakfast." I *never* skip breakfast if I can avoid it, and with us planning to leave home around noon for the trip to Blood Raine's cabin, there was no way I was skipping today.

She made a sniffing noise. "Babe, your idea of a light breakfast is having only bacon instead of bacon *and* sausage. You can do tomorrow and Monday. *I'll* do a truly light breakfast this morning." She said it in a tone that was as hard as tempered steel.

Her idea of light breakfast, while wise under the circumstances, often left my stomach wondering when the real meal would be served. I have, though, learned never to argue with her when she uses her school-marm tone of voice.

"Okay, milady," I said. "I'll wash the stink off while you cook.

Mollified by my surrender, she closed the gap between us and gave me a sisterly peck on the cheek. When I reached for her, she scooted back. "After you shower. Now, scoot."

She grabbed for her clothing, which was hanging over the back of a chair near the door to the bathroom, and started pulling it on. Chastened, I began stripping as I entered the bathroom. It was comfortably warm from her recent use, and I didn't have to wait for the shower to reach a nice temperature.

Twenty minutes later, showered, shaved, and clad in jeans and a Dallas Cowboys polo shirt, I joined her in the kitchen. She hadn't been kidding about preparing a *light* breakfast. Two slices of whole wheat toast, a hard-boiled egg, a small glass of grapefruit juice, and a cup of black coffee. That's usually what I snack on while I'm preparing breakfast, but at least it meant that I'd have a healthy appetite for whatever fine viands Blood was preparing for us.

I tried to look like I was enjoying it as I chewed the dry toast—Sandra opted against jam or jelly, because sugar is too filling, she says—and washed it down with grapefruit juice. The boiled egg wasn't too bad, because she let me put salt on it, and the coffee, freshly ground Colombian, was delicious.

We cleaned up after finishing, and then went out to the back porch where we sat and watched the deer herd I'd spooked earlier return to graze.

Twenty minutes before twelve, we got in my Volkswagen and started for Blood's place. It's about eight miles west on River Road from my farmhouse, and then another mile down an unmarked dirt road, lined on each side by a pine forest. Somewhere in that forest, Blood has a network of cameras and sensors, which I've been unable to spot, and I'm pretty good at that. Even though he's been long retired from the agency, he still does consulting work for them, and tests new gadgets, so his cabin, which is almost as fortified as the Pentagon, has all the latest monitoring technology. No one can get within a mile of the place without him knowing it.

And, as usual, he was waiting on the porch for us when we pulled up.

We got out and approached him.

"Well, well, my two most favorite people," he said. "Come on up here and sit down. Elizabeth, Al and Sandra are here."

Elizabeth Sung, half an inch shorter and thirty

years younger than Blood, came out of the cabin. She stepped up beside him and slipped an arm around his waist. They were wearing matching outfits, plaid shirts and faded jeans, his rather loosely on his slender frame, hers hugging curves that rivaled Sandra's.

"Hi, guys," she said. "Glad you could make it."

I'd introduced Elizabeth to Blood several years earlier, when I needed a safe place to stash her to keep a Chinese gangster from killing her. What started as a favor to me, developed first into a close friendship, and finally with her selling her Chinatown condo and moving in with him permanently. Despite the age difference, the two acted like an old married couple.

We stepped up onto the porch. Sandra and Elizabeth embraced, and I shook hands with Blood. Then, we switched places, and Elizabeth kissed me on the cheek, while Sandra did the same to Blood.

"It's always nice to visit you two," Sandra said. She patted Blood's shoulder. "You're looking sexy as always."

He slipped his arm around her waist, lifted her left hand and kissed it. "You'd better watch yourself, young lady," he said. "Al's a friend of mine, but if Elizabeth ever decides to leave me, I'm giving him a run for his money."

Elizabeth poked him gently in the ribs. "That's not going to happen, you old flirt. Guys, would you like some refreshment while we wait for Carlton's ham to finish roasting?"

"I'd love something," I said.

"We made a fresh batch of eggnog this morning. Sandra, would you help me get it?"

The two women went into the cabin. Blood and I sat on the big carved wooden bench that sat beneath the double-glass window next to the reinforced wooden door.

"You look like you got a bee under your bonnet, youngster," he said, as I slumped back against the polished wood.

He might be in his eighties, but he's still no slouch when it comes to reading people.

"Yeah, I've got this case that's perplexing." I filled him in quickly.

"Your client didn't do it, but there's evidence linking her, and you have no other suspect, is that about the gist of it?" Like I said, he's sharp.

"That's it." I was just about to tell him about the car following me, when Sandra and Elizabeth came back to the porch. Sandra carried a large glass pitcher containing a beige liquid, and Elizabeth had a large silver tray with four large glass tumblers on it.

"Who wants eggnog?" Sandra asked.

"Why is it that color?" I asked.

Elizabeth smiled and winked at Blood. "Carlton went a little wild with the rum. There's nearly half a bottle in here."

Whoa! That explained the color. Eggnog that's nearly fifty percent alcohol by volume, and me with nothing more than one boiled egg and two pieces of dry toast in my stomach.

"I'll have half a glass," I said. Sandra poured, stopping just a bit above the half-way mark. She then filled glasses for Elizabeth and Blood, and poured about four fingers in her own glass, from which she took tiny sips.

"You were telling Carlton about your latest case I see," Sandra said. "It's a real puzzler, guys. I think the great detective has finally met his match."

Blood rubbed at his chin, the stubble making a rasping sound. I'd not noticed until then that he wasn't as clean-shaven as usual.

"Well, he's had tough cases before," he said. "Just need to take a close look at the elements to start forming a clear picture, is all." He looked at me, and winked. "Let's show these ladies how it's done, youngster. Tell me what you have so far."

In the past, I'd often found him to be a good sounding board when I was dealing with a particularly perplexing problem. His years in the CIA, although mostly involved in field operations, had given him the ability to pierce the murkiness of a situation and find that one gleaming ray of light that was the key to pulling aside the veil of uncertainty. So, beginning with Loretta Palmer's arrival in my office, I laid the case out for him, bit by bit, watching Sandra's eyes widen when I reached the coda of the blue Taurus tailing me.

When I finished, and awaited his revelation, Sandra preempted him by grasping my forearm, her nails denting the flesh. "Al, you didn't tell me about someone following you." There was an accusatory tone in her voice.

"I didn't want to worry you last night," I said. "Besides, I ditched them in Rockville."

Her expression showed that she was only partly mollified. While I often shared cases with her, trusting her insights almost as much as Blood's, I tried to keep her insulated from as much of the danger as possible. When she'd been kidnapped, along with Buster's wife, Alma, by a gang of militia men, I'd determined that I wouldn't involve her in anything that might physically harm her. The psychic harm, though, when she discovered that I was treating her like a fragile little toy, something she definitely was not, was another matter. Fortunately, she's not one to create a scene in front of others, friend or stranger, so she sat there and looked at me, her lips compressed and her cheek muscles tight.

Blood looked from me to her, sensing, I think, the tension between us.

"I imagine he just didn't want to have to tell the story twice," he said. "This way, he gets both our perspectives on it."

Nice recovery on his part. Sandra's expression

relaxed . . . a little.

"I suppose that makes sense."

Even though it hadn't been my reason for keeping it from her, it *did* make sense. She was second only to Blood in her ability to see through the fog of confusion and discern what was really going on. Something to do with having worked with inner city kids for so long.

"Okay," Blood said. "Here's what I see. You have this con artist, bilking money from wealthy, but naïve suckers. He has land, but it's probably not worth anywhere near the amount he's taken them for, and he's using the *investments* from new victims to keep the older ones happy. A classic pyramid scheme, and like most pyramid schemes, it eventually collapses, with everyone but the con artist losing their shirts."

"Yeah," I said. "That's the way I see it. But, someone shoved a letter opener into the guy's heart, and I can't come up with a viable suspect. The victims of the con might seem like the most likely suspects, but I'm having trouble seeing any of them doing it."

He nodded his agreement. "Right. Getting their money back would make sense, but it doesn't look like that happened. The only other motive that works is anger and just making the guy suffer, but a single stab wound doesn't sound like anger. That sounds like a cold, calculating killing. Any of the club members strike you as the type?"

I thought about it for a few seconds. "The army guy and the engineer are possible, but I don't get that vibe from either of them. And then, there's the interior designer, Tamara Braxton. She's an 'in-control' type, but she didn't strike me as the type who'd do it just out of anger. As for the rest, no, I don't see them as suspects."

"And, you're convinced that your client is innocent?"

"Yeah, I am. She's a spoiled, rich kid with a big mouth, but I don't think she's a murderer."

"So, that brings us back to the two mystery buyers," he said. "You said Simpson had an argument with one, and he was upset about the presence of the other?"

"Yeah; at least, that's what Braxton said. She seemed to be telling the truth, and I'm assuming she remembered correctly."

"Well, it's simple then. You have to identify those buyers."

"Easier said than done," I said. "I only have a single name for each, and I'm assuming they're surnames, along with a description of one that could match thousands of people in the greater DC metro area alone. It's not like finding a needle in a haystack, it's like finding a needle in a barrel full of needles."

He waggled a finger at me. "Not necessarily, son. I have some friends who can take what little we know about these two, such as their involvement in real estate, for example, and build profiles that can narrow it down a little."

I'd never heard of such a capability, but Blood has some unusual friends, so I had no choice but to believe him. After all, I had nothing else. So, I told him what I knew about the two mystery men—took all of two minutes.

He nodded at me as I gave him the information. Out of the corner of my eye, I noticed Elizabeth, her body slanted away from him, rapidly writing on a piece of paper. When she saw me looking, she frowned, stopped writing and snatched the paper up, folded it and tucked it into the pocket of her shirt. She then stuck the pencil into her hair which was arranged handily into a bun at the back of her head.

"Now, I want to hear about the car that was following you," Sandra said. I thought she'd forgotten about that, which was pretty stupid of me. The woman forgets nothing.

"There's not much to tell, really," I said. "I'm not

sure where they began following me, but I picked it up on Canal Road. A blue Taurus, probably last year's model, and it never got close enough for me to even get a glimpse at the driver."

"It's probably safe to assume, though, that it's connected to your current case," Blood said. "I'll have my friends factor the blue Ford into the profile of our mystery men."

There was that sharp mind again. I hadn't really considered it, but the person or persons following me could be related to the mysterious buyers. They'd probably seen me at Simpson's place of business, talking to the security chief, even visiting his office, and been curious enough to want to know more about me.

I was about to comment on that, when Elizabeth laid a hand on his arm, "Carlton, honey," she said. "When we were getting the eggnog, I was telling Sandra about your special ham recipe, and she'd like to see it, wouldn't you, Sandra?"

The two women shared a look. "Of course," Sandra said. "Elizabeth tells me that you're basting it with bourbon and coke. I'd love to see how that works."

With a broad smile on his face, Blood stood, and bowed at Sandra. "Of course, deal lady. Always happy to share my cooking secrets with someone who appreciates the finer things. Come with me, the grille is just around the corner."

She stood and linked her arm in his, and they walked to the end of the porch, which stretched the width of the front of the cabin, with steps on both ends as well as the center. When they were around the corner, Elizabeth looked at me, her brow wrinkled.

"You're probably wondering why I was taking notes," she said.

"Not so much that, as why my noticing seems to have upset you."

"It's his memory. Lately, he's been having these

episodes of forgetfulness. They're not often, and are usually brief in duration, but when he snaps out of it, he's unaware of what has happened."

I felt a chill. "How long has this been happening?"

"For about a month or two," she said. "He's otherwise healthy, and because he doesn't remember having these episodes, when I mentioned that he should maybe talk to a doctor, he thought I was being too much of a worrier, and refused."

"Do you have any idea what's causing it?"

Her eyes glistened, and she wiped at them. "Yes, unfortunately, I do. I had an uncle who had the same thing happen to him. I hope I'm wrong, though."

"Well, don't keep me in suspense," I said. "What is it?"

"It looks like the onset of dementia. If it is, it could continue to develop slowly, or he could just wake up one day, and not know who I am, or where he is." A tear oozed slowly from the corner of her left eye and flowed down her cheek. She didn't bother wiping at it.

I felt like I'd been punched in the gut. Not Blood. The man was indestructible. This couldn't be happening.

"What will you do?"

She finally wiped at her cheek. "Whatever it takes," she said. "Eventually, I *will* get him to a doctor, even if I have to slip him a mickey and haul him in unconscious. Maybe I can find some medication that will delay or ease it. After that, well, I'll just take care of him."

She said it quietly, but with a fierce determination in her voice. I had no doubt that she meant exactly what she said.

Chapter Seventeen

The rest of the afternoon went well. Blood's ham, roasted until it was almost black on the outside, but nicely pink and juicy underneath the crusty exterior, was the hit of the meal. The smoky flavor of Kentucky bourbon and the sweetness of Coca Cola combined to create an unforgettable taste. We had it with cornbread, mashed potatoes, roast corn, and sweet potato pie, all dishes from the south that Blood and I had grown up with, prepared lovingly and served in large portions. By the time the meal was done, the rum in the eggnog had been thoroughly absorbed. Sandra even let me drive home.

We had a quiet Sunday. Just lounging around in our pajamas, after a light breakfast of scrambled eggs, ham, and biscuits, and then hitting the hay early to prepare for the week ahead, with me working on my case, and her getting ready for end of school year tests.

She left before me Monday, and I called Heather to let her know I was swinging by Capitol Hill to talk to the last member of the investment club before coming into the office.

Dudley Wiggins lived in one of the older three-story townhouses on Third Street, near Maryland Avenue, northeast of the Capitol Building. A narrow street, with a few flowering trees planted in embedded iron pots to provide a modicum of shade, Third Street was, like most of the District's neighborhood byways, restricted parking, rigorously enforced. I ended up parking at a metered space on Maryland Avenue, nearly six blocks from Wiggins' place. It was warm for May, and my shirt and pants were sticking to my sweaty body by the time I climbed the stone steps and rang his bell.

Wiggins had been described as overweight. That was like describing the Grand Canyon as a big hole in the ground. The man was immensely obese; bad for anyone, but especially disturbing for a medical professional. One would think he would at least try to display a good example to potential patients. About five-eight, he looked almost as wide. His hips filled the doorway. His eyes were almost hidden in the folds of flesh that made up his face, and his lips were little pink blobs that looked like the tied-off end of an inflated balloon.

"Good morning," he said. "You must be Mr. Pennyback. Harrison called me Friday and said that you'd probably be paying me a visit. Come on in. Would you care for a cup of tea, or coffee, perhaps?"

I was still one cup short of my usual morning intake. "A cup of coffee, black, would be fine, thanks."

He turned and waddled into the living room. A white coffee urn sat in the middle of a kidney-shaped mahogany coffee table, in front of a wide leather sofa that sagged in the middle. Opposite the sofa was a matching black leather chair. Two cups, a sugar bowl and a creamer sat near the coffee urn.

"I was just about to pour myself a cup." He poured a cup and pushed it in the direction of the chair, and then sat in the depression in the sofa cushion, and poured another cup for himself. Into the cup, he dropped four teaspoons of sugar and then so much cream the dark brown liquid turned an ivory color. I saw the explanation of his size. He lifted the cup, blew, and slurped loudly. "Hm, nice. That first cup in the morning is good, but it's the second cup that I really enjoy," he said.

I took a sip of mine. Good coffee. Tasted like Jamaican. "I quite agree," I said. I'm not sure why I spoke in such a stilted manner, except that with this guy, it seemed appropriate.

He took one more drink, spilling a bit on his triple chin, and then put his now-empty cup on the coffee table. "I suppose you'll be wanting to ask me questions about the real estate investment club, how I got involved, and how I felt when I discovered that Sydney Simpson was cheating me . . . us."

"Yes, as a matter of fact, I do. Let's start with the last question; how did you feel when you learned that you'd been victim of a scam?"

"Well, disappointed, of course, and a bit angry. I would so love to get my money back, but I suppose, with Sydney dead that's impossible."

He didn't seem overly disappointed. "You don't really seem all that disappointed," I said.

"Oh, not now, of course. I was at first. I guess I'm kind of resigned to it now. Water under the bridge, you know. Say, would you care for a small snack." He looked at the gold Rolex almost hidden by rolls of fat on his wrist. "It's almost time for my after-breakfast snack. My metabolism's out of whack, so I have to eat every two hours to keep my blood sugar under control."

I held my hands up in a two-handed traffic stop. "No, thanks. Coffee's enough for me." I'm strictly a three-meals-a-day kind of guy. Occasionally, on weekends I'll do a mid-afternoon snack, but I try to avoid snacking during the week. I'd also come to the conclusion that, in addition to disrupting the good doctor's eating schedule, I was wasting my time. Not only did his size argue against him being the killer, he just didn't seem to have the energy or desire to move too far from his snack cabinet.

I thanked him for his time, and left.

Chapter Eighteen

I arrived at the office at 9:25. Heather was pecking away at her laptop's keyboard, a cup of chamomile tea at her left elbow. I waved, poured myself a mug of coffee, and retreated to my office, where I booted up my laptop, and opened the chess game when the screen finally quit flashing.

The computer was three moves from checkmate when the phone rang. Heather informed me that it was Buster calling.

I paused the game and picked up the phone. "Hey, amigo, what's happening?"

His booming voice echoed in my ear. "Got some more dope on that case you're workin', bro, but you ain't gon' like it."

"Well, it's not gonna get any better by being held back," I said. "So, what's the bad news?"

"A contact of mine at the Montgomery County cop house says they're close to makin' an arrest in the Simpson case. You know what that means. They finally got enough hard evidence to point the finger at your girl, and the county attorney's about to file charges."

Shit, I thought, and I was no closer to coming up with any hard evidence that she didn't do it. Like her or not, I couldn't let a client down.

"That sucks, but right now, there's not a lot I can do about it. I'm still a long way from identifying these two mysterious buyers."

"Oh, yeah, about that," he said. "I ran the two names you gave me through the local and national databases. Nothing on this Sayeed, but Hodges came up with a couple of interesting possibilities."

"Don't keep me in suspense. What did you find out?"

"One is Stanley Hodges, a con man himself, and he just happens to specialize in high-end real estate, so for my money, he's your man. He usually works up north, around Wilmington, Delaware and Philadelphia, but if there was a big-bucks deal going down in this area, my bet is he'd swoop down like flies zoomin' in on cow pies. I have to be careful, since we don't have any jurisdiction on this, and there's no case in the District, but I'm discretely tryin' to see if old Stanley's been in the area lately."

It sounded like a good lead, and I could only hope he came up with something I could use before the authorities pushed their case against my client too far. Getting the law to change course when it's invested a lot in moving a case in one direction is like trying to put toothpaste back into the tube. If they were close to filing charges against Palmer, I was going to have to come up with something that proved her innocence beyond doubt.

"Okay, pal," I said. "That sounds like a real possibility. You said you had a couple of possibilities?"

"Yeah, but I don't see the second one bein' interested in buyin' land. I only pulled the info 'cause of our past history with militias. Dude's name's Keith Hodges, 'n he's the head honcho of an outfit called the

True Sons of America. Can you believe it? Their initials are TSA, just like the turkeys who make your life miserable at the airport. Anyway, these shitheads are all about preparing for the country to be invaded and taken over by the 'darker' races. They're all into cuttin' off immigration, 'n crap like that. There've been reports that Brother Keith's been in DC lately, lobbyin' some of the right-wing Tea Party types in congress on immigration."

"I hope you guys are keeping him on your radar. Remember the last time we had militia in the city; they tried to blow up the metro and kill a senator."

"How the hell could I forget that," he said. "Problem is, the dude's done nothin' against the law. It ain't illegal to lobby your congressman, and these militia and white supremacist groups have become pretty sophisticated in the past few years. They're pretty quick to holler suppression of free speech or police harassment, if we get too close to 'em, and with the congressional finger on DC's government, especially the budget, the powers that be are reluctant to push the envelope."

"In other words, no one in metro police is watching this guy."

"You got it."

My gut was churning. People like Keith Hodges and his group pose a greater danger to the average American than all the radical Islamic groups in the world, but it's almost impossible to get the average American to understand that. I like nothing better than to run turkeys like him to ground, and truss them up nicely, and at any other time, I would've dropped what I was doing and made a run at him. But, I had an ethical responsibility to my client. I had to find the evidence to get John Law off her case. After that, though, Mr. Keith bloody Hodges, look out.

"Okay," I said. "Let me know if you learn anything else."

I hung up. The news of a new militia group operating in the area, even if only the innocuous activity of schmoozing with members of congress, had me too aggravated to go back to my chess game, so I shut my computer down, got up, and went out to the outer office to bug Heather.

It just wasn't my day. Rather than being bugged by my unannounced presence, Heather was waiting, notebook in hand, to fill me in on her latest findings. Unfortunately, she was running into as many brick walls as I was.

"I've tried finding someone with the last name Sayeed who might be connected to Simpson's real estate operations, but I keep coming up empty," she said. "So much of his dealings were undocumented. I did find proof that he'd bought several hundred acres of land north of Germantown, and had options on a few more, though, so that much we now know."

"But, nothing on potential buyers?"

She tapped her pen on the page of the notebook. "Nothing but chatter. Other than the fact that there *were* two potential buyers, no one I've been able to contact ever saw them."

"Any luck in tracking Devlin down?"

"No," she said. "It's like he just dropped off the map a week ago. No credit card activity that I can find, no mobile phone usage, nothing."

There were only a few reasons for that, either he had deliberately dropped off the net in order to hide, or someone had *taken* him off, which meant that he was no longer among the living. We couldn't rule out either possibility, nor could we stop looking for him until we knew one way or another.

"We need to find him, but I think trying to get IDs on these two mystery buyers should be our number-one priority."

"You still think one of them is responsible for Simpson's death?" She looked skeptical, sort of her default expression when we're stuck on a case.

"Right now, it's the only thing that makes sense, so until we get information pointing down another trail, let's follow this one."

Skeptical, she might be, but she didn't have a better answer, so she just nodded. Heather's like a bloodhound, though. She wouldn't give up on any of her searches until the case was closed. But, then, neither would I.

I stood, and was just about to go back to my office to mull over my next steps, when the outer door swung open.

Loretta Palmer, her hair a bit messy, with a stricken look on her face, stood there. "You've got to help me," she said. "Please."

Charles Ray

Chapter Nineteen

She didn't look anything like she did when I first saw her. Her polished, finely-turned-out look was gone. The clothing, though still expensive looking, was rumpled, making her look like someone who'd raided some rich person's closet and stolen a few items, and the look in her eyes was that of a hunted animal, chased into a blind canyon, with no way out.

She looked almost human as she tottered across the floor and grasped my upper arms, her nails digging into my biceps.

"What's the problem?" I asked, trying to pry her fingers loose before she did some real damage.

She looked down at my hands wrapped around hers, and seemed to understand that she'd invaded my personal space, and that I wasn't cool with it. Her cheeks darkened as she let my biceps go and retreated two steps.

"Uh, sorry," she said. "I'm just so, I mean—"

"Calm down." I patted her shoulders. "Take slow, deep breaths." When she looked a bit calmer, I said, "Now, tell us what's going on."

"Merriwether called. He said the police want me to come to their office to answer some questions." She started breathing faster. "I know it means they plan to arrest me, I just know it."

She was on the verge of hyperventilating, and, frankly, I thought she was overreacting. I'd never heard of the police inviting someone to come in to be arrested, but, I wasn't sure *how* the cops dealt with the rich. Maybe they did invite them to cooperate. I had to get her under control, though.

"You could be over-thinking this," I said. "Maybe they do just want to talk to you. If they wanted to arrest you, I think they'd come to you."

She stopped breathing for a few beats, and looked at me, her brow wrinkling. "You think so?"

Hell, I wasn't sure at all, but if it kept her calm it's the story I was going with. There was, however, one little problem; if she was invited to come to the Montgomery County police headquarters, and had come to DC instead, that might not go over so well, despite her wealth.

"Does your lawyer know where you are right now?"

"Yeah, I told him I was coming to see you, to get this mess straightened out. He's meeting me here."

I turned, eyebrows raised, to Heather.

"In that case, maybe you should have a cup of coffee, or tea, or something, and just relax until he gets here."

Heather took my cue. She got up, came around her desk, and took her by the elbow, steering her to the chair beside her desk.

"Let me get you a nice cup of chamomile," she said.

"That would be nice," Palmer said. "Tea does relax me."

Since the two of them seemed to be bonding nicely, I decided the prudent course of action for me was to exit stage left, so I went back to my office to wait for Baldridge's arrival. I was planning to let him explain to his client that this was one mess I couldn't clean up for her.

I'd barely settled myself into my chair, and was just about to boot up my computer, when Heather stuck her head around the edge of the door. "Mr. Baldridge is here," she said. She then stepped aside to allow Palmer, followed by her expensive lawyer to enter my office.

Without waiting for my invitation, the two of them took seats. Heather brought in a chair and sat by the door with a notepad on her knee.

"Sorry to barge in like this, Mr. Pennyback," Baldridge said. "I'm sure Ms. Palmer has told you, the police want her to come in for a few questions. She insists that you can prevent it, despite me telling her that you don't have that ability."

I pointed a finger at her. "He's right, Ms. Palmer. I'm must a private investigator. I can't keep the police from talking to you." I looked at Baldridge. "I'm pretty sure they just want to talk to you." He nodded. "And, I think it would be to your advantage to cooperate with them. You will have your lawyer present, and maybe he'll get some idea of what evidence they have that makes them even want to talk to you."

"My thoughts exactly," he said, nodding vigorously. "Now, my dear, why don't we go and let these two do their jobs."

The way she pouted, it was clear to me that Loretta Palmer wasn't completely satisfied. Accustomed to get whatever she wanted, no matter how inconvenient to others, or illogical, she was having a hard time processing the situation. Someone was telling her what to do, and she didn't like it. But, rich she was, dumb she wasn't. She could see the sense in what her lawyer and I were saying, and as much as her whole upbringing rebelled against it, she went along. Not, though, without one last attempt to get me to do the impossible.

"Are you sure you can't get me out of this?" she asked me.

"If you mean prove you didn't kill anyone, we're not stopping until we do that. If, on the other hand, you mean get you out of your appointment with the cops, sorry, but no can do."

"Oh well, you can't blame a girl for trying." She tried to act nonchalant, as if this was an every day occurrence, but I could see the fear in her eyes. So, she was human after all.

At that moment, I didn't dislike her quite as much.

Chapter Twenty

A few minutes after they left, Buster called.

"I got a line on your boy, Devlin," he said when I got on the line. "He's holed up in a rowhouse on Patterson Street, north of the bus station."

He was referring to the bus terminal at L Street and First Street, about four blocks north of Union Station, a rundown area of vacant lots, warehouses, and ratty old rowhouses that is yet to be affected by the gentrification taking place in much of the rest of the District. With streets that are often more pothole than pavement, crooked sidewalks that would challenge a triathlete, and parks with more empty liquor bottles and used condoms than grass, it's a perfect place for someone to hide out. Only the gangbangers who control the neighborhoods, addicts looking for a fix, or stupid men willing to play Russian roulette with STDs, go into the area after dark, and only residents who can't afford to move to safer neighborhoods or to the suburbs, walk the streets during the day. The bus terminal is at the edge of an urban combat zone, but even there, it's not exactly a place you want to park your car.

"Is he alone?" I asked.

"He's staying with an ex-con he met in stir, according to my CI, but the friend's workin' at a garage up in Hyattsville, so he'll probably be alone for the rest of the day. You plannin' on tryin' to bring him out?"

"For now, I just want to talk to him. Depends on what he has to say. Give me the address."

I wrote the address down, told Heather to keep looking for more information on our mystery men, and walked to the Waterfront metro station, a few blocks north of us. I took the Green Line to Gallery Place, and transferred to the Red Line for Union Station, three stops away. The train hadn't been crowded from Waterfront, but there were so many people in the car when I got on at Gallery Place, I was forced to stand, grasping one of the upright poles near the door, until a bunch of us were finally spewed out onto the platform at the train station. I took the escalator up to the street level, and crossed the street at the corner near the Postal Museum. Walking north along First Street, I watched the area deteriorate, getting seedier the farther I went.

Just past the one-story, glass-front bus terminal, I passed an overgrown park, with knee-high weeds, empty bottles and cans, and two young hookers in flimsy tops and super-short skirts, standing idly at the corner, trying not to look like they were soliciting the passing men, but somehow managing to show their thighs up to the junction each time a potential customer neared. At the far side of the park, a ratty looking kid, probably not much older than sixteen, with his pants hanging below the crack of his butt, lounged against a street light pole, hands in the pocket of his bright green jacket, a Baltimore Ravens cap sideways on his head. He might as well have had one of those sandwich board signs, saying, 'Drugs for Sale, Here!' There wasn't a cop in sight, except for one bored looking uniform walking through the waiting room at the bus station, which, regrettably, is par for the course in neighborhoods like this around the city. Neither the hookers nor the dealer paid me any attention as I passed the park.

The address Buster had given me was on a block that looked like a scene from one of those World War II movies of the London blitz. Abandoned and vacant buildings, window openings like monsters' eyes staring blankly at the empty street, outnumbered those that appeared to have human habitation. Two old men, sharing a bottle in a brown paper bag, sat on the steps, mumbling incoherently at each other. I had to step over them to get to the entrance. They didn't seem to notice.

I was looking for an apartment at the top, the third floor, end of the hallway, Buster had said. I made my way up the litter-covered stairs, trying to avoid stepping on the suspicious-looking stains on the floor. The apartment at the end of the corridor was near a large, grease-smeared window that opened onto a rusted fire escape. I knocked on the door, which rattled in the frame. No answer. I knocked again. Still no answer.

The door across the hall opened, and a wizened old man, his bullet-shaped head covered with gray peppercorn hair, peered out at me.

"You lookin' for that white boy what been livin' wit' Luther?" he asked in a shaky, cracked voice.

"Yes," I said. "Have you seen him today?"

"Yeah, seen him 'bout two hour ago. He's on his way out."

"I don't suppose you'd have any idea where he went?"

"Don't know, don't care. Ain't none of my business. What you want with him?"

"It's a business matter." I turned to go.

"Funny business, I bet," he said. I stopped and

turned back to face him.

"Why do you say that?"

"That white boy up to no good. I can smell it a mile away. Luther on probation, and he don't need the trouble that boy sure to bring."

"What kind of trouble?"

"Don't know, just know he trouble."

I wasn't going to get anything useful from him, so I turned again to leave. "Well, thank you for your time," I said.

"You see that boy, you tell him don't come back. We don't need his kind here."

As I made my way gingerly back down the stairs, I wondered what Devlin had done to get on the old guy's shit list.

I was stepping over the two drunks just outside the entrance, when I spotted him.

Chapter Twenty-One

If he'd been better at conducting foot surveillance, or if he hadn't been white, I might not have spotted him.

His quick move to turn away and not look at me as I exited the building caught my eye, and a six-two, two-hundred-pound-plus white dude in dark brown pants and light brown windbreaker, standing across the street in a neighborhood that was, except for David Devlin, as far as I knew, all black, stands out like a pimple on the tip of your nose on prom night.

I didn't break stride. When I stepped off the bottom step onto the sidewalk, I turned smoothly left, and headed back in the direction of Union Station. At the bus terminal I turned right on L and walked to North Capitol Street, where I turned left. This gave me the chance to get a glimpse via peripheral vision of the big guy, who was tagging along about a block behind, looking at everything but me—a dead giveaway. There was a danger that he'd be suspicious of me returning to the subway by a slightly different route, but he wasn't acting as there was anything out of the ordinary. I took another quick peek when I went left on F Street in front of the Postal Museum, and, sure enough, he was still a block behind me, but picking up his pace. My guess was he wanted to get closer to avoid losing me in the subway, causing him to make a real amateur move by speeding up. I slowed down as I came to the crosswalk just before the metro entrance. Taking my time, I crossed the street and got on the escalator leading down to the train platform.

Bracing my hip against the railing, I stood facing the wall opposite the down escalator. Out of the corner of my eye, I saw the big guy step on the escalator, his head down. At the bottom, I moved to the side of the platform for the Shady Grove-bound train, standing next to a couple with rollaway suitcases. I surveyed the platform idly, staring for a long time at the tunnel from which the train would emerge, which also gave me a view of my tail, who'd positioned himself on the platform where he'd be able to get into the car behind me.

The way he fidgeted, and strained to keep from looking my way, he hadn't done this before. When he reached up to scratch his ear, I saw the dark mark of ink on his wrist, and as his arm dropped I saw a dark horizontal line with a tail peeking up from the collar of his windbreaker. This guy had spent a lot of time under a tattoo artist's needle. The needle on my curiosity meter was pegged all the way to the right. Who the hell did he work with, and why was he following me? I wondered if he was the idiot in the blue Taurus from the previous week.

The arrival of the train was signaled by blinking lights at the edge of the platform, and a rumbling sound from the tunnel. I stepped back from the edge. Unlike most subway riders who push forward, dangerously close to the platform edge, just for a chance to be first through the door—sometimes before the passengers in the car get a chance to get out. Sort of like the way people in the area drive, thinking of themselves first.

When the train slid to a stop, and the doors whooshed open, a crowd of people, most carrying or pulling luggage, poured out of the car. When the last one exited, I used my bulk to push my way in, and stopped just inside the door, against the plastic panel beside the inward-facing seat that's supposed to be reserved for the handicapped and the elderly, but which was immediately taken by a young man with his blond hair pulled back in a pony tail. To add insult to his infraction, he had a greasy, smelly cardboard container, which opened, putting his large burger and fries on display for all to see and smell.

Looking through the window, toward the car behind, I saw the big guy wait until most of the people around him had entered the car, and then, with a last glance at the car I was in, he got in.

The 'library-lady' voice of Metro's recorded train message announced, 'The doors are closing, please stand clear of the door,' a 'ding-ding' sounded, and the doors swooshed close. With a jerking motion, the train began moving, and was soon in the tunnel.

At the Judiciary Square station, I endured the glares and an occasional jab from passengers getting off and on, for not relinquishing my position flattened against the partition near the door, and the same again at Gallery Place, but at Metro Center, as soon as the door opened, I stepped out onto the platform, and began walking at a brisk pace toward the escalator to the lower level to the Blue and Orange Line trains. As I turned and stepped onto the escalator, I saw the big guy's head bobbing in a crowd of tourists as he legged it toward the escalator.

So far, my plan was working. He didn't seem agitated, so maybe the fact that I'd gone one station past what should have been my stop hadn't aroused his suspicions. I got off the escalator at the bottom and moved to a position on the platform that would put me at about the center car of an eight-car train. A sidewise glance showed my pursuer at a spot that would put him in the car behind me.

I'd come up with a Hail Mary of a plan as the train departed Union Station. It wasn't the best of ideas, requiring precise timing and predictable behavior, but was the best I could think of under the circumstances.

The Blue Line train for Largo Town Center pulled into the station and, after a minor adjustment of a few feet, stopped. The doors opened and passengers, mostly laborers from Prince Georges County, Maryland, began spilling onto the platform, while impatient soon-to-be riders strained forward, anxious to board.

When the way was clear, I pushed forward to claim the spot just inside the door. There was no partition or inward facing seat, just a space, normally reserved for passengers in wheelchairs. Since there was no one fitting that description, I stood with my back against the wall, just inside the door. When the final passenger boarded, I turned to face the open doors, and as soon as the bell and announcement of 'doors closing' sounded, I tensed. Just as the doors began to slid close, I jumped out onto the platform. I heard a few gasps behind me as the doors clicked shut, and the train started moving.

I turned just in time to see an angry red face staring at me through the window of the car following the one I'd just exited.

It worked. My tail had probably stood near the door, but to keep from annoying fellow passengers, moved inside the car to be able to watch the platform through the window. It had probably never occurred to him that I would get back off the train—I mean, who does that, right? Even if he'd happened to spot me leaving my car, which was doubtful, given the angle of view, he wouldn't have had time himself to get to the doors of his car before they closed.

As the train disappeared into the tunnel, on its way to the next stop at Federal Triangle, with three stops before it reached L'Enfant Plaza, the transfer station to the Yellow and Green Lines, whereas I only had to go back upstairs, get on a Red Line train to Gallery Place, and then go downstairs to catch the Green Line to Waterfront. With luck, I'd be halfway down Fourth Street before he even got to L'Enfant.

Now, I just had to figure out who he was, who he worked for, and why the hell he was following me.

Charles Ray

Chapter Twenty-Two

I'm pretty sure I had an ugly scowl on my face when I walked into our outer office, because Heather's teacup paused halfway to her mouth, and she looked at me with an expression of wide-eyed curiosity.

"I take it you didn't find Devlin," she said from behind her cup.

"No, but I did pick up a tail."

"And, by that, you don't mean a prehensile appendage, do you?"

"No, I mean the two-legged variety," I said, and gave her a description of the guy who was following me, with as detailed account of the tats I saw as possible. "See what you can find."

"You know, I'm not going to be able to identify this person from what you've given me."

"Of course, I do. But, I'm hoping you might be able to get a line on who he might be associated with. The guy looked like a foot soldier, not a boss. I'd be interested in knowing who's above him in his chain of command."

Okay, I *know* I had a scowl on my face—and,

there's no such thing as a pretty scowl. I was justified, though. I'm the private detective. It's my job to follow people, not to be followed, and twice in less than a week was . . . irritating, especially the part about not knowing why. It might sound like I'd given Heather an impossible task. It wasn't easy, and probably would be impossible for the average person. But, Heather Bunche is *not* your average person. In addition to being a total magician when it comes to coaxing information out of that ethereal realm called cyberspace, she's as much of a puzzle fanatic as I am. She can take seemingly unrelated pieces of data, and assemble them into a coherent picture better even than I can, and now, in the relative quiet of the office, I was already beginning to make some assumptions about the guy following me based upon a few fragments I'd observed.

The first was that his hair was cut high and tight; that is, close on top, and even closer on the sides; common among military and ex-military. Since I hadn't done anything lately to piss the Pentagon off, I ruled out active duty military. So, my guy was probably a former soldier, who was now working as a mercenary, or was associated with one of the hundreds of militias that have sprung up around the country. The guy's body art, that I'd gotten quick glimpses of, could've been prison tats, but some of the military guys get tattoos as well. Then, I remembered the two names Buster had given me, Stanley Hodges and Keith Hodges, and that brother Keith was associated with a militia outfit. But, that then raised the question, why the hell would a militia be involved in a real estate scam?

I decided to call Buster and see what he thought.

He sounded a bit busy and put upon when he answered his phone.

"Sorry to bother you, compadre," I said. "But, I'd like to ask a few more questions about one of the guys you told me about."

"I told you everything I know when I gave you the names," he said. "And, I ain't picked up anything new since."

"No, not new information, just your take on things." I told him about the goon who'd been following me.

"Whoa, bro, that don't sound like anybody who'd be hangin' with Stanley Hodges. Far's I know, that dude works alone. Danged if the dude you described don't sound like one of them militia bad asses."

"Kinda what I was thinking," I said. "But, what's the militia doing getting mixed up in a real estate scam?"

"You said this Simpson actually had some land, right? What if it ain't a scam, like, what if they really tryin' to buy land? You know how them dudes in West Virginia had all that land they used as a trainin' camp and storage depot."

How well I remembered that bunch. Buster and his wife, Alma, on vacation in West Virginia, had had the misfortune to witness their murder of an undercover agent, and Alma, along with Sandra, had been kidnapped by them in an effort to persuade Buster not to testify against them. That bunch of kooks had owned a large spread in the mountains, where they did their training, stored their equipment, and from where they conducted their weapon and drug smuggling business. Having isolated acreage made sense, but we were talking about land in a development corridor, adjacent to a major transportation route. Would a militia organization, as obsessed with secrecy and security as they tend to be, want to acquire land in such a setting? It didn't make sense, but it was something we'd have to investigate.

"Okay," I said. "Heather and I will check it out. Thanks for the info, buddy."

"Fine, bro. In the meantime, I'll check and see if any of Hodges' buddies are in the area with him."

Chapter Twenty-Three

After hanging up the phone, I sat there for a while, trying to decide what to do next. I was, by now, firmly convinced that the mystery buyers were critical to solving the case. I just needed to find that one crucial piece of evidence that would be the key to unlock the puzzle.

Simpson's house was a bust in my opinion. The place looked like he only used it as a hangout, and besides that, whoever had conked me over the head had probably thoroughly searched it—I was beginning to warm up to the idea of militia involvement—and, since I was being followed, my guess was that whatever it was they were looking for, they hadn't found. That left his office. I'd been there, but hadn't really searched it. While his receptionist was probably not in on the scam, that didn't rule out the possibility that he'd kept things, like money, for instance, secreted somewhere in the office.

I let Heather know my plan, went outside and fired up the Volkswagen. I was on Wisconsin Avenue, just passing over the Beltway, when I saw the blue Ford

Taurus in my rearview mirror. I decided that I'd just about had it with whoever it was dogging my tracks. I'd take care of this turkey, and then go over Simpson's office.

Whoever it was, he or she was markedly better than the turkey who'd tried to follow me on foot, but I had a few tricks up my sleeve. Even though I'd been an infantryman in the army, I'd also trained in intelligence and counterintelligence operations, including the six-month counterintelligence officer course at Fort Holabird, in Baltimore, when the army's intelligence command and school were located there— before someone got the bright idea to move to Fort Huachuca, on the fringe of the Sonora Desert in Arizona in the early 1970s. Among the many skills I'd picked up during my training in Baltimore, vehicle surveillance and counter-surveillance were included. I'd been at Fort Huachuca once when I was still in uniform, and after my intelligence training, and I'd wondered how the army was going to teach vehicle and foot surveillance, servicing of dead drops, and meeting with clandestine agents in the desert surrounding the fort, or even in the cowboy boots and string tie city of Tucson, about two hours to the northwest. Wisely, I'd not asked any of the officers I met during my visit. Senior officers can get very prickly when the wisdom of their stupid decisions is questioned.

I watched in my mirror as the Ford kept pace with me, this time only two car lengths back. As we passed Tuckerman Lane, with shopping centers on both sides of Rockville Pike, and large open parking lots, a plan began formulating in my mind. We were soon coming up on Strathmore Avenue, a relatively wide, winding thoroughfare that crossed Rock Creek and the railroad, but off of which ran a number of narrow residential streets, many curving back to Strathmore, but also a lot of them ending in cul de sacs or dead ends, especially when they came to the railroad tracks and a small MARC station, that serviced the regional rail service. I'd once done a job for Quincy's law firm that involved serving papers to an elderly lady who lived in the area, and had spent nearly half an hour trying to find her address, becoming disoriented by the maze of streets. I was banking on the person following me being as unfamiliar with the area as I was the first time I visited.

I moved to the right lane about a block away, and made the turn onto Strathmore, slowing down as I entered to make sure the Ford had taken the bait. Sure enough, I was less than a hundred yards from the turn when he popped into view.

I slowed, looking for just the right spot, and soon found it in an elevated, gravel-surfaced parking lot just past the little train station. With only one entrance, it was perfect. I pulled in and drove toward the back, slowly, as if looking for a parking slot. When the Ford pulled in behind me, I hung a sharp left, drove to the end of the row, did a double left and headed back to the entrance. At the entrance, rather than leave the parking lot, I pulled across the opening, effectively blocking it in both directions, and after stopping the engine, got out and stood at the front.

A scant ten seconds later, the Ford pulled out of the end of a row of cars, and turned right. I got a good look at the driver, eyes wide in his dark brown face as he saw me standing there glaring at him. He slammed on the brakes.

I walked to the driver's side of the vehicle, and stood there with my hands folded across my chest and a stern look on my face.

After a few seconds, he lowered the window.

"Okay, you want to tell me why you're following me, Mr. Sayeed?"

He shrank down in the seat, like a large balloon with a slow leak.

"I . . . I was afraid after you lost me last week, that

you'd spotted me. I apologize, but I had to know if you knew where Mr. Simpson put the paperwork."

"What paperwork is that?"

"The papers transferring title of the property north of Germantown to me," he said.

After hanging up the phone, I sat there for a while, trying to decide what to do next. I was, by now, firmly convinced that the mystery buyers were critical to solving the case. I just needed to find that one crucial piece of evidence that would be the key to unlock the puzzle.

Simpson's house was a bust in my opinion. The place looked like he only used it as a hangout, and besides that, whoever had conked me over the head had probably thoroughly searched it—I was beginning to warm up to the idea of militia involvement—and, since I was being followed, my guess was that whatever it was they were looking for, they hadn't found. That left his office. I'd been there, but hadn't really searched it. While his receptionist was probably not in on the scam, that didn't rule out the possibility that he'd kept things, like money, for instance, secreted somewhere in the office.

I let Heather know my plan, went outside and fired up the Volkswagen. I was on Wisconsin Avenue, just passing over the Beltway, when I saw the blue Ford Taurus in my rearview mirror. I decided that I'd just about had it with whoever it was dogging my tracks. I'd take care of this turkey, and then go over Simpson's office.

Whoever it was, he or she was markedly better than the turkey who'd tried to follow me on foot, but I had a few tricks up my sleeve. Even though I'd been an infantryman in the army, I'd also trained in intelligence and counterintelligence operations, including the six-month counterintelligence officer course at Fort Holabird, in Baltimore, when the army's intelligence command and school were located there—

before someone got the bright idea to move to Fort Huachuca, on the fringe of the Sonora Desert in Arizona in the early 1970s. Among the many skills I'd picked up during my training in Baltimore, vehicle surveillance and counter-surveillance were included. I'd been at Fort Huachuca once when I was still in uniform, and after my intelligence training, and I'd wondered how the army was going to teach vehicle and foot surveillance, servicing of dead drops, and meeting with clandestine agents in the desert surrounding the fort, or even in the cowboy boots and string tie city of Tucson, about two hours to the northwest. Wisely, I'd not asked any of the officers I met during my visit. Senior officers can get very prickly when the wisdom of their stupid decisions is questioned.

I watched in my mirror as the Ford kept pace with me, this time only two car lengths back. As we passed Tuckerman Lane, with shopping centers on both sides of Rockville Pike, and large open parking lots, a plan began formulating in my mind. We were soon coming up on Strathmore Avenue, a relatively wide, winding thoroughfare that crossed Rock Creek and the railroad, but off of which ran a number of narrow residential streets, many curving back to Strathmore, but also a lot of them ending in cul de sacs or dead ends, especially when they came to the railroad tracks and a small MARC station, that serviced the regional rail service. I'd once done a job for Quincy's law firm that involved serving papers to an elderly lady who lived in the area, and had spent nearly half an hour trying to find her address, becoming disoriented by the maze of streets. I was banking on the person following me being as unfamiliar with the area as I was the first time I visited.

I moved to the right lane about a block away, and made the turn onto Strathmore, slowing down as I entered to make sure the Ford had taken the bait. Sure enough, I was less than a hundred yards from the turn when he popped into view.

I slowed, looking for just the right spot, and soon found it in an elevated, gravel-surfaced parking lot just past the little train station. With only one entrance, it was perfect. I pulled in and drove toward the back, slowly, as if looking for a parking slot. When the Ford pulled in behind me, I hung a sharp left, drove to the end of the row, did a double left and headed back to the entrance. At the entrance, rather than leave the parking lot, I pulled across the opening, effectively blocking it in both directions, and after stopping the engine, got out and stood at the front.

A scant ten seconds later, the Ford pulled out of the end of a row of cars, and turned right. I got a good look at the driver, eyes wide in his dark brown face as he saw me standing there glaring at him. He slammed on the brakes.

I walked to the driver's side of the vehicle, and stood there with my hands folded across my chest and a stern look on my face.

After a few seconds, he lowered the window.

"Okay, you want to tell me why you're following me, Mr. Sayeed?"

He shrank down in the seat, like a large balloon with a slow leak.

"I . . . I was afraid after you lost me last week, that you'd spotted me. I apologize, but I had to know if you knew where Mr. Simpson put the paperwork."

"What paperwork is that?"

"The papers transferring title of the property north of Germantown to me," he said.

Chapter Twenty-Four

Omar Sayid, he corrected my spelling of his surname after getting out of his car and formally introducing himself, was a bookish looking Pakistani, who had immigrated from Pakistan with his parents when he was six, and had spent the last 24 years of his life in, of all places, Bowie, Maryland. His father, a structural engineer, worked for NASA in Greenbelt, but he'd decided not to follow in the family tradition, so, instead of studying engineering, he'd received a degree in teaching from the University of Maryland's College Park campus, and for nine years had been running a boarding school for young American Muslims near Bowie. His motivation for establishing such a school was the increasing efforts, he said, by radical groups to entice young American Muslims onto the path of extremism, an effort that was, unfortunately, aided by the ignorant reaction to Islam by many Americans after the events of September 11, 2001. His hope was to be able to teach young Muslims how to be true to their religion, while at the same time, be good citizens. He also hoped that such a school would help change some of the biased attitudes of many Americans regarding Islam.

With the numbers of students increasing, his school had outgrown its current facilities, and he'd been looking for a place to build a larger school and Islamic study center.

Sitting in my car, moved from the entrance to the parking lot, he and I had a fascinating conversation; one that caused a few pieces of what had become an extremely complicated puzzle to fall into place.

"I imagine you had images of me as some wild-eyed terrorist," he said, after I'd explained how I got his name.

"Uh, let's just say that, under the circumstances as they were described to me, I was unsure about you," I said, feeling a bit chastened and embarrassed at having jumped to just that conclusion about him. "So, tell me, why were you and Simpson arguing?"

"I had already given Mr. Simpson a quite substantial security deposit on the land. But, then, he said there was another bidder who was offering more, so he might not be able to sell to me. I'm afraid I became quite angry, and perhaps said a few things I should not have."

"Did he tell you who this other person was?"

"No, he only referred to him as Mr. Hodges." He ran a hand through his hair. "But, the day after our argument, he called me to apologize. He'd decided not to accept Mr. Hodges money after all."

"But, you said he told you this Hodges was offering more money. Why would he turn an offer like that down?"

"He told me that he had learned some things about Mr. Hodges that made him reluctant to do business with him, and that he would prepare the title transfer paperwork that day, and deliver it to me."

"And, did he?"

"No, he did not." He shook his head. "Then, I heard

on the news two days later that he'd been killed. I called the receptionist about the paperwork, but she knew nothing. That sounded strange to me, so I've been watching the office to see if I could discover what is happening. That's when I saw you, and decided to follow you. Have you learned anything?"

I don't usually share information about a case with outsiders, but I felt I kind of owed the poor guy because of my uninformed reaction to him merely on the basis of his name and heritage.

"Nothing yet," I said. "I can't seem to determine what the motive was for his murder."

"Do you think, perhaps, that this Hodges person might have reacted poorly to having his offer refused?"

That was, of course, always a possibility, but I couldn't see the logic. Killing Simpson because he refused to accept money didn't make a lot of sense. Not, mind you, that I had a better theory. I still didn't know which of the Hodges was involved.

"I'm still looking into that," I said. "Unfortunately, I haven't been able to identify Hodges."

"I would be most grateful if you could determine if, before his demise, Mr. Simpson completed the transfer papers. The people who have donated funds to build the school are quite anxious to see some progress, and if I cannot acquire this land, I will have to look elsewhere."

I got his phone number, which I wrote on the back of one of my name cards. If I happened to run across title transfer papers—as unlikely as that seemed—it wouldn't hurt to let him know. After cautioning him not to follow me anymore, not just because it was aggravating, but because it could put him in danger from whoever else was on my tail, I watched him get in his car and drive away.

One suspect eliminated, one unknown suspect remaining. But, first, I had to pay a visit to Simpson's office.

Chapter Twenty-Five

Business in the little strip mall wasn't exactly booming. The parking lot was practically empty, except for a couple of pickup trucks, a delivery van, and four cars.

The hallway on the second floor was also vacant. Simpson's office, however, was not.

The receptionist's platinum blonde hair was askew, and her beautiful face was contorted in a mixture of fear and pain as she cowered, her back to the wall behind her desk. Facing her across the desk, deep scowls on their faces, two gonzos stood in aggressive poses. One was short, with muscles straining his plaid shirt and jeans, the other, dressed in khaki pants and a faded army field jacket, was the goon I'd ditched in the subway.

"One last chance, bitch," khaki pants said. "Tell us where your boss hid his papers and dough."

"I t-told you I don't know." Tears flowed down her cheeks, and her lightly tinted lips quivered. "I just answered the phone and made coffee for the few guests who came."

"You're lying," the other goon said, taking a threatening step forward.

No one had noticed when I came in.

I made my presence known. "Is there a problem here?" I asked.

The two goons spun on their heels, glaring daggers at me. The receptionist looked almost glad to see me.

"Who the fuck are you?" the short one asked.

"Hey, this is the dude I was followin'," khaki pants said.

"You mean the one that ditched your ass in the subway?"

For a moment, they glared at each other.

"I'd like to see you try to follow somebody in a crowded subway," khaki pants said.

The little guy snorted. "Don't make no mind," he said. "He probably don't know nothin' anyway. Send him on his way."

Looked like the little guy was in charge, but, khaki pants didn't like it much. Still, he made a move toward me, raising his fists.

"I'd think twice before doing something stupid," I said.

Khaki pants was close to my height, and probably had ten pounds on me. He had the bulk of someone who spent a lot of time hefting free weights, which meant he was strong, but probably not too flexible. He was also, as I'd surmised when he was trying to follow me, not too bright.

"I don't have to think about poundin' your ass," he said. "Now, either you walk out, or I drag your ass out. Which is it gonna be?"

"Oh, neither, I think. Actually, I was going to suggest that you two gentlemen leave, and stop bothering the young lady."

The little guy laughed. "He's a real wise ass, Rollo," he said. "Whyn't you pound on him a little, maybe teach him some manners?"

That got a laugh from the big guy, and he slammed his right fist into his left palm. He began moving toward me, bent slightly at the waist, and going into a boxer's crouch.

That was his second mistake. His first, of course, was assuming that, just because he outweighed me, and had a lot more muscle, that I'd be an easy target. The second was coming at me like a boxer, left fist forward and protecting his face, right fist slightly lower. He was totally ignoring the part of the body that's essential in a fight, the legs. Take out a fighter's legs, and he's worse than useless.

And, that's what I went for. As he shuffled forward, sliding his left foot forward, I brought my right foot up and snapped it at his kneecap, making solid contact with the patella, and causing his face to contort in pain. He pulled his left leg back, lifting it, and that's when I pivoted slightly left and snap-kicked his right knee.

He went down, his knees hitting the floor first, causing him to howl in agony and flip to his right side to take the pressure off his knees. As he started swaying, I stepped forward and hit the left side of his head, just in front of his ear, with a backhand left fist. His eyes rolled back in their sockets, and his head bounced off the floor. He was not unconscious, but stunned, and all the fight had been knocked out of him.

But, I was still moving. The little guy was slow to realize what was happening. By the time he did begin to react, his friend was already stretched out on the floor and beginning to moan, and I was within striking distance.

He went for his pocket. My right hand, fingers together and stiff in a spear point, went for his larynx, and the side of my left foot, encased in a hard-soled shoe, went for his right shin. My fingertips hit his square on the little protrusion midway down his neck, causing him to make a 'gwok' sound, and his eyes to cross, followed immediately by the sharp edge of my shoe striking just below his knee, and sliding down his shin, which caused him to purse his lips, and the 'gwok' changed to an 'e-e-eep,' and he scrunched his eyes shut. His right hand had been going for his pocket, but when my fingers poked his throat, it changed direction and went toward the site of the stabbing pain in his neck. At the same time, he bent forward and grabbed his shin with his left hand.

His face turned red, and then purple as he tried sucking air down his throat, and he was making sounds somewhere between gurgling and sobbing. He sank to his knees, then lay on his side, curled up, holding his throat and his leg, and sobbing.

The big guy began to come to his senses. He sat up, swaying from side to side and blinking his eyes. Finally, he looked up at me, and his lips curled down in a scowl, until I stepped toward him. He scooted back, his butt making whishing sounds on the floor. Then, he managed to get up by bracing his back against the door, keeping his eyes on me.

The little guy, tears streaming down his face, pushed himself up to his knees, and then stood, a little unsteady, and still breathing raggedly. He, too, watched me carefully as he backed up to his buddy at the door.

The big guy opened the door. His pal squeezed past him, and was soon out of sight.

"This ain't over," the big guy said, as he limped backwards through the opening.

I stepped toward him. He whirled and followed his friend.

I walked over and closed the door.

"Wow, that was really something," blondie said.

I turned to face her.

"Wasn't all that much. You okay?"

"Yeah, I am now."

"What did they want?"

"They kept asking me about some papers," she said. "I don't know nothing about no papers. I just answer the phone and make coffee."

"Yeah, I heard you say that. Did they say who they worked for?"

"The short guy said some dude named Keith would be pissed if they didn't come back with the papers. That mean anything?"

Yes, it did. I now knew the name of the other mystery buyer, and Buster and I had pegged it wrong. The militia *was*, for reasons unknown, involved in the real estate business. I now also had a motive for Simpson's murder. He had something, some papers, that they wanted. Now, all I had to do was find those papers first, and maybe find the evidence I needed to pin these bozos to the wall.

"Say, do you mind if I look around? I'd especially like to check out Simpson's office."

She smiled and batted her lashes at me. "Honey, you can do anything you want."

Chapter Twenty-Six

"Oh, one other thing they were asking just before you came," she said. "They wanted to know where Dave Devlin was. I told them I hadn't seen him in several days, and I had no idea where he was. They didn't believe me about that any more than they believed I didn't know anything about the papers they were looking for."

She was following me as I examined Simpson's office, not that there was much to examine. It was pretty bare bones. A gray office desk, a bookcase, with a few copies of *Architectural Digest*, the Montgomery County *White Pages*, and several real estate flyers, a couple of chairs, and a coffee table. No pictures on the wall, not even a calendar. I tapped on the walls, looking for openings or dead spaces that could be used to hide things, and came up empty.

I sat in the chair behind the desk, and she sat in the other chair, at the left side. I leaned back and tried to visualize Simpson sitting there, wondering where he would put things, like documents, that he didn't want anyone else to find.

The office was a bust. Definitely low rent, with

fiberboard wall covering, painted a hospital green, and fake tile on the floor, scuffed from much foot traffic. No safe, no filing cabinet, no secret recess in wall or floor, and nothing in the desk drawers but dust bunnies.

"Tell me how things worked around here," I said. "What did they do? Where do they keep files? There had to be some paperwork."

She studied her fingernails. "You'd think so, wouldn't you? I remember when my parents bought their last house. They were drowning in paperwork, what with the inspections, loan applications, and stuff, but Mr. Simpson said he dealt with people who preferred paying cash, and it was mostly undeveloped land, so there was less paperwork. He had some, but he always took it with him when he left the office."

That brought up another question, one that I knew it was a waste of time to ask her—where did he store the papers he took out of the office?

"What about Devlin? What'd he do around here?" I asked.

"Good question." She shrugged. "He was hardly ever around, and when he was, Mr. Simpson was always bossing him around, and criticizing him. I think his job was to find customers, or *fish*, which is what Mr. Simpson called them."

Of course, he would.

"So, you don't have a home address for him?"

She shook her head, and studied her nails again. Then, she raised her hand, index finger wiggling at me. "I just remembered something," she said. "It's kind of strange, really. It's something Mr. Simpson said once when I asked him why he didn't file the paperwork here. He said, 'Babe, I'm a traveling man, so I keep everything I need in my shoes.' Do you have any idea what that means?"

At first, I didn't. Then, a mental image of Simpson's bedroom formed in my mind, and it came to me.

I had to get back into Simpson's house, and soon.

Chapter Twenty-Seven

"You can't go back there alone." Heather's tone was adamant. In fact, she quite literally put her foot down, stamping it on the floor.

"Look, kiddo," I said. "It'll be an easy in and out. I just need to check this guy's closet."

She stamped her foot again.

"Are you forgetting, the last time you were there, you got conked on the head? I could act as lookout."

"I'll be on the lookout this time. I'd really rather you sat this one out."

She gave me a squinty-eyed look. "If it's supposed to be so easy, why do you object to me going along?"

Did I really think it was going to be easy? I'd been asking myself that question all the way back to the office. It should be. The cops had gone over the place after Simpson's murder, and, except for the mystery visitor who had conked me over the head, I couldn't think of any reason anyone else should be interested. My guess was that whoever it was didn't know about the 'shoes,' so, whatever Simpson had secreted was still probably there. That was just a hunch, a gut feeling, but my gut was also telling me that going back in there was a calculated risk, and I wasn't sure I wanted to put Heather at risk. I know, it's chauvinistic, but Heather was like the kid sister I never had, and what else is a big brother to do, if not protect his little sister?

"Well, you know, this kind of operation can always go sideways. You have no experience at clandestine entry."

"Why don't you just call it what it is, Al; breaking and entering," she snapped. "And, how the heck am I supposed to get any experience if you never let me go with you?"

She had me there. I'd made her a full partner, so I guess it was time to make her a *full* partner.

"Okay, you win," I said. "We go in at midnight. Maybe we should rendezvous here at 11:00, and go in one car. Does that meet with your approval?"

She smiled. The phone rang. She answered it. "A.E. Pennyback, Confidential Enquiries, how may I help you? Sure, he's here, hang on." She handed me the phone. "It's Loretta Palmer's attorney, for you."

"Yeah," I said into the receiver.

"You can't go back there alone." Heather's tone was adamant. In fact, she quite literally put her foot down, stamping it on the floor.

"Look, kiddo," I said. "It'll be an easy in and out. I just need to check this guy's closet."

She stamped her foot again.

"Are you forgetting, the last time you were there, you got conked on the head? I could act as lookout."

"I'll be on the lookout this time. I'd really rather you sat this one out."

She gave me a squinty-eyed look. "If it's supposed to be so easy, why do you object to me going along?"

Did I really think it was going to be easy? I'd been asking myself that question all the way back to the office. It should be. The cops had gone over the place after Simpson's murder, and, except for the mystery visitor who had conked me over the head, I couldn't think of any reason anyone else should be interested. My guess was that whoever it was didn't know about the 'shoes,' so, whatever Simpson had secreted was still probably there. That was just a hunch, a gut feeling, but my gut was also telling me that going back in there was a calculated risk, and I wasn't sure I wanted to put Heather at risk. I know, it's chauvinistic, but Heather was like the kid sister I never had, and what else is a big brother to do, if not protect his little sister?

"Well, you know, this kind of operation can always go sideways. You have no experience at clandestine entry."

"Why don't you just call it what it is, Al; breaking and entering," she snapped. "And, how the heck am I supposed to get any experience if you never let me go with you?"

She had me there. I'd made her a full partner, so I guess it was time to make her a *full* partner.

"Okay, you win," I said. "We go in at midnight. Maybe we should rendezvous here at 11:00, and go in one car. Does that meet with your approval?"

She smiled. The phone rang. She answered it. "A.E. Pennyback, Confidential Enquiries, how may I help you? Sure, he's here, hang on." She handed me the phone. "It's Loretta Palmer's attorney, for you."

"Yeah," I said into the receiver.

Charles Ray

Chapter Twenty-Eight

"Mr. Pennyback, Merriwether Baldridge here. I have a bit of a problem." His voice was tense. "Loretta, Ms. Palmer, has been taken into custody by the police. They're charging her with first degree murder."

Well, so much for keeping my client out of jail.

"Did they tell you what evidence they have to support that charge?" I asked.

"No, the arresting officers referred me to the county attorney, and that worthy is stonewalling on meeting me, but I'm pretty sure they have something pretty damaging. They'd never risk a false arrest charge. Frankly, I'm worried."

At what she was probably paying him in billable hours, he should be worried, I thought. I, of course, didn't say that.

"Okay, I get it," I said. "I'm close to cracking this." Fingers crossed. "It'll just take a bit more time, so tell your client to hang in there. I assume you're pushing for bail?"

"Yeah, but I can't get a bail hearing before tomorrow, and she's going nuts now. Look, she's asking to see you, says she has some things you need to know."

"If she's in custody, that could be a problem."

"She's in the county detention center on Seven Locks Road," he said. "And, I was able to get you cleared to visit her today, but you'll have to hurry. Visiting hours will end in two hours. Please tell me you can do it."

I wasn't sure Palmer wasn't blowing smoke up her lawyer's skirt, but on the off chance that she did have useful information, it might be worth it.

"Okay, I'll go talk to her."

His sigh of relief was audible. "Thank you," he said. "Thank you very much."

Chapter Twenty-Nine

Montgomery's County's detention center is a multistory, cinderblock building on Seven Locks Road, about halfway between Falls Road and Wooton Parkway. The angular construction makes it look like something from a science fiction film, but there's no mistaking the barbed wire-topped chain link fence that surrounds it, or the signs on Seven Locks on both sides warning drivers to park ONLY in designated and approved parking places.

With less than two hours left in the authorized visitor period, I decided to forego using I-270 to get there, and went via Canal Road to River Road instead. The traffic on that route was, as I expected, very light, and I made good time to Falls Road in Potomac Village. A right turn onto Falls Road and a few minutes of driving northeast brought me to Wooton Parkway, where I turned right, and then left onto Seven Locks Road.

I pulled into the authorized parking lot on the left, locked the car and walked across to the main reception area. A burly sheriff's deputy found my name on the authorized visitors' list, had me dump the contents of my pockets into a plastic container, and put me through a body scanner. Satisfied that I had no contraband or anything that could be used as a weapon, he reminded me that it was a violation of the center's rules to pass anything to an inmate, and that, while they did not make audio or video recordings of the visits, the visiting area was open and under constant guard, so there would also be no prolonged physical contact between visitors and inmates, beyond brief hugs from family members.

A petite female deputy with a mean looking baton attached to her waist, and a no-nonsense look on her face, escorted me to the visitor's lounge. I'd only ever been inside the place once, and had forgotten the almost dormitory-like appearance of the room where most inmates met with their visitors. They did have more austere and secure meeting spaces for inmates considered dangerous or escape risks, but most met in what looked like the common area of a college dorm, or a dentist's office. Little conversation centers, two to four chairs, and in some cases a low coffee table, were scattered around a large, well-lit room. Only the desk with a plexiglass barrier between it and the room, behind which sat an armed deputy, let you know where you were. The rest of the room was empty. I was the only visitor coming in so late.

The deputy stopped at the door, repeated the rules and restrictions, and told me I could choose where to sit and wait for my inmate to be brought out. I chose a chair near the center of the room.

Loretta Palmer was escorted in three minutes later. She looked even worse than she had when she came to my office the last time. Her hair hung limply to her shoulders, and she had on no makeup. The dark smudges and puffiness under eyes indicated that she'd either been crying or not sleeping, or, knowing her, probably both. The orange jumpsuit that was a size too large for her didn't flatter her figure, and accented the pallor of her complexion.

When she saw me, she smiled weakly. The deputy escorting her, brought her to sit in the chair facing me, and then moved back to stand beside the door through which they'd come, a nonchalant expression on his face.

She sat, her hands clasped in her lap, looking at me like a puppy that's just been caught near a wet spot on your best carpet.

The silence hung in the air between us like wet gauze. I'm never comfortable meeting someone in surroundings like the detention center. What do you say; how's it going? Nothing that I could think of seemed appropriate, so I kept my mouth closed. She finally broke the silence.

"Thanks for coming." Her voice was just above a whisper, causing me to have to lean forward to hear her, and earning me a warning frown from the deputy at the door.

"No problem," I said. "What do you need?"

She twisted her fingers together, staring down at the floor. When she looked up at me, her eyes glistened. "I haven't been exactly straight with you, concerning my relationship with Sydney Simpson."

"You were sleeping with the guy." My words were a bit sharper than I intended. She flinched. "What could you have left out about that?"

"I . . . that is, we, Sydney and I, were planning to go away together," she said. "At least, that's what he'd led me to believe for the two weeks leading up to his death. At first, I bought into it completely, but it wasn't long before I saw that he was just using my feelings for him to try and keep me from discovering his scam."

I wasn't hearing anything that surprised me, but considering what she was going through, I felt sorry for her nonetheless.

"You wouldn't be the first person to be taken in by

someone like Simpson. Don't beat yourself up over it. I'm pretty close to figuring out who actually did kill him, so we can get you out of here."

That earned another weak smile. "That's good, but I hope you do it quickly. The officers who brought me in said they had a pretty strong case against me."

"What? Did they have a witness putting you at the scene of the crime?"

"Oh, no, not that. The fact is, I was never at his house. He always came to my place. I think it has to do with the letter opener he was killed with."

"They know it was yours, but you've already said you gave it to him. Unless they can put you at the scene, they're still working with circumstantial evidence. Your lawyer ought to be able to shoot holes in it."

"I hope you're right."

"Look, I'm not surprised that they have something solid. They wouldn't have arrested you otherwise," I said. "But, why else did you ask to see me?"

She made sniffling noises. "I don't know. I guess I just needed to see someone other than Merriwether. You have no idea how alone a person can feel in a place like this. I'm sorry. I know you'd probably rather be somewhere else."

"No need to apologize. I can understand how you feel. Don't worry. My partner and I won't rest until we get you out of here."

She lifted her hand and reached for me. The deputy at the door, seeing the movement, strode to her side and placed a hand on her shoulder.

"No touching allowed," he said. He looked at me. "Sorry, sir, but your hour is up."

I stood. "Thanks, deputy. Don't you worry, Loretta, we'll get you out of here."

There was a glimmer of hope in her eyes as the deputy led her away. As the door closed on them, I hoped her trust in me wasn't misplaced.

Chapter Thirty

I got home at 5:45. Sandra was waiting for me, dressed in a pants suit and carrying a large cloth shopping bag. I looked at her, wide-eyed.

"Oh no," she said. "You forgot, didn't you?"

"What?" I asked.

"You promised me you'd take me shopping this evening."

Damn, I had forgotten. I'd also promised her that when school was out, we'd take a few days off and drive to Myrtle Beach, one of the few places in what's known as the Deep South, that I'm comfortable visiting. She wanted to buy some beach attire.

"Oops, you're right, I forgot. Sorry," I said. "Okay, let's go. We can grab a quick bite at one of the fast food joints near there. By the way, where are we going?"

She gave me a sour look. "We talked about it this morning, babe. We're going to the Target store off Sam Eig Freeway."

It all came back to me. We'd argued over whether to go there, or to the J.C. Penny store at Lake Forest Mall. Since Target was closer, and the shops off Sam Eig tended to be less crowded than Lake Forest, I'd pushed for that, and she'd agreed.

We piled into my Volkswagen and headed out, thankfully, against the flow of rush hour traffic. There was a bit of a wait at Travillah Road, until a break in traffic allowed us to make the left turn giving us a fairly direct route, through a lot of new housing developments, to Dufief Mill Road, Muddy Branch Road, and Great Seneca Highway to make a light-controlled turn onto Sam Eig.

I spotted the pickup as we crossed Route 28, the Rockville-Darnestown Road route that was once the main east-west thoroughfare connecting Rockville to the western rural areas. The big, red Dodge Ram with roll bars stood out in this white-collar suburban area. As we approached the turn onto Great Seneca Highway, the truck began to close on us, pulling into the inner lane and speeding up. I punched the gas, and the Bug's tires squealed as the bit into the pavement. We shot forward.

The pickup pulled in behind us, about three car lengths back. A mini-van pulled in directly behind us as we pulled into the turn lane. The pickup didn't pull into the turn lane, but stayed in the outer lane, heading toward the intersection. The light was red, and cross traffic was beginning to move. I punched the gas again, curious as to what the pickup driver would do. The Bug swayed as we began the turn at high speed. The pickup approached the intersection, and instead of stopping, pulled onto Great Seneca, causing an oncoming sedan to come to a brake-screeching halt. The pickup did a sharp one-eighty right, its right wheels leaving the road for a brief moment, before slamming back down and smoking as they grabbed the surface of the street. We were almost out of the turn and onto Great Seneca, but even with the upgrade, the Bug's engine was no match for the Dodge. He was closing fast, and would be alongside us before I could merge into the traffic lanes.

I saw the barrel of what looked like a revolver,

sticking out of the passenger-side window as the Dodge grew closer.

As he came alongside, I slammed on the brakes. "Get down, Sandra," I yelled, and then was slammed forward as the car behind rear-ended us.

I heard the crash and crumple of metal on metal, the screeching of brakes, the boom, boom of the revolver, and the tinkling of broken glass, as I pushed back against my seat. Other than some soreness from the seat belt tightening across my chest, I felt okay, but I heard a moaning sound.

It took a second for my vision to clear, and I looked first to my left, where I saw two nickel-sized holes in the window, and then to my right, and my breath caught in my throat.

Sandra lay against the door, her left side covered in sticky, red blood, her eyes closed, and a moan coming from her half-open lips. Beyond her, I saw a single hole in the passenger-side door window.

The pickup driver didn't stop to check his handiwork. Up ahead, I could see the taillights as he roared east on Great Seneca. I'd gotten just a brief look at the shooter before everything went to hell, though. The big guy I'd roughed up in Sydney Simpson's office.

Chapter Thirty-One

Fortunately, the damage to the rear of my car had been minimal. The engine still worked, so, in the confusion that followed the crash and the shooting, I burned rubber up Great Seneca to Route 28, turned right and didn't slow down until I pulled into the driveway in front of the emergency room at Shady Grove Adventist Hospital. Two Montgomery County police cruisers, blue lights flashing and sirens wailing, pulled in behind me.

Four cops, weapons drawn, jumped out of the cop cars, but when they saw Sandra's blood-covered form, the put the weapons away and helped me get her to the door, just in time for a doctor and three nurses to arrive and put her on a gurney and wheel her away.

I made to follow, but the doctor barred my way, and his refusal to let me go with her was reinforced by one of the cops who insisted that I make a statement while the doctors did their thing.

I gave as complete a description of the vehicle as I could, but could only describe the shooter. A plainclothes detective arrived just as I was describing the shooter.

"Mr. Pennyback, I'm Detective William Harrison," he said, as he flashed his badge at me. "I see you've already given a description of the incident and the perpetrators to the uniformed officers, now, you mind telling me why these guys would be shooting at you?"

I was a little put off at the preemptory way he fired the question at me—the uniformed guys were a lot more sympathetic—but, I realized that he probably didn't get a lot of drive-by shootings in this upwardly-mobile middle-class area. So, I gave him the five-cent version of the case I was working, including my run-in with the shooter at Simpson's office.

"So, you're saying this guy shot at you because you kicked his ass? That's a bit extreme, don't you think?"

"Hey, we're talking about militia guys here," I said. "These guys are fifty percent testosterone. I reckon he and his buddy took a bit of ribbing when they got back to their buddies. A single old fart like me, besting both of them."

He scratched the tip of his nose. "Yeah, I guess you got a point there. You didn't happen to get the license plate number of the truck, did you?"

I laughed. "Nah, I was a little busy ducking bullets at the time, and the light wasn't too good."

The doctor, his green scrubs smeared with blood, came over to where we were sitting.

"Which one of you brought the patient in?" he asked.

I raised my hand. "That would be me, doc. How is she?"

"She lost a lot of blood. The bullet, a .45 caliber slug, hit just above the clavicle, and just missed her left lung by a couple of millimeters. No vital organs were hit, but she's still unconscious, from the shock. She'll be okay, but out of it for a while."

"When can I see her?"

"We'll need you to fill out the admission forms," he

said. "Are you her husband?"

"No, but we live together. She has no other relatives in the area."

"Okay, you'll do. We're moving her from to ICU tonight, and if her condition improves, to a regular room tomorrow."

"Can I stay with her?" Even though I was asking a question, the look I gave him was meant to make it clear that I was making a statement. Fortunately, he got my meaning.

"Yeah, that can be arranged." He looked at the cops. "Provided it's okay with these guys."

He'd been doing so well up to that point, then he had to go and ruin it by assuming that the black guy might be in custody. Harrison nodded. "Nah, if we have any more questions, Mr. Pennyback, I assume you'll be here?"

"Yeah," I said. "I'll be right here."

He stuck out his hand. "Don't you worry," he said. "We'll get these dirt bags."

"Thanks," I said. But, I had other things in mind. The militia had just made the whole thing personal.

Charles Ray

Chapter Thirty-Two

After having a forensic team examine my car, and tagging and bagging the slug the doctor took from Sandra, the cops left. I sat in the waiting room until they got her set up in a bed in a relatively quiet corner of the ICU, with a privacy curtain around it. One of the orderlies found a chair and blanket for me, and the doctor warned me that she would likely be unconscious for the rest of the night.

When the doctor closed the privacy curtain and left, I wrapped the thin green blanket around my chest and settled back in the chair.

Sandra looked so fragile and vulnerable, lying in the narrow hospital bed with tubes and wired attached to her body, and her left shoulder encased in white bandages. The machines she was hooked up to, recording her blood pressure, pulse rate, and who knew what else, sat silent and blinking. Her chest, under the blanket, rose and fell steadily. Her normally healthy complexion was pale, and her lush blonde hair had been pulled back and secured with a scrunchy.

Sitting there, looking at her, even though the doctor

had assured me she would pull through and there would be no problem with her arm or shoulder, I felt like crap. She was there because of me.

The physical pain would go away, but the mental baggage that comes with being shot would be with her forever. I couldn't shake the fear that she would subconsciously blame me as much as I was blaming myself.

I don't know how long I sat there, mentally beating myself up for what happened to Sandra, and feeling sorry for myself, but it seemed like forever. I was so lost in thought, Heather's voice seemed to be part of a dream.

"Hey, boss man, wake up." She snapped her fingers in front of my face. "Whoa! You were sitting there with your eyes open, staring off into space, like a zombie." She looked at Sandra. "The doctor says she'll be okay. She'll probably be awake by morning."

I yawned and stretched. "What time is it?"

"It's 10:00," she said. "We need to get ready to go if we're going to get in and out of Simpson's place before daylight."

I shook my head. "Sorry, kiddo, but we're gonna have to reschedule that. I'm not leaving her."

"Don't you worry, Albert, we will stay with her."

I looked over Heather's shoulder to see Elizabeth and Blood come through the curtain.

"W-what're you guys doing here?" I asked.

"Buster called," Heather said. "And, I called them."

"How did Buster know I was here?"

"Apparently, his contact in the police here called him," she said.

I turned back to look at Sandra. "Well, thanks for coming, but I'm staying with her."

"But, Al, what about our client?" Heather asked.

"To hell with it. Sandra comes first."

Elizabeth came to my side and put her arm across my shoulder.

"Al, I know how you are feeling right now. But, you do no good for Sandra by neglecting your duty. Carlton and I will stay here with her; I have already cleared it with the doctor. Now, you go do what you have to do."

My heart rebelled, but my mind agreed with her. I'd been assured that Sandra would fully recover, and if I let an innocent woman stay in jail one moment longer than she had to because of my feelings of guilt, Sandra would be the first to rake me over the coals when she woke up.

I signed. "Okay, but I'm putting my phone on vibrate. If there's any change in her condition, I want you to call me, got it?"

She patted my cheek. "You know we will," she said. "Now, go on and get out of here. If Sandra was awake, you know she'd say the same thing."

"Better listen to her, boy," Blood said. "You don't want to have all three of these women mad at you, do you?"

Charles Ray

Chapter Thirty-Three

My Volkswagen was in no condition to be driven, but Heather had thought of that. Instead of bringing her car, she'd rented a used Chevy Camaro, a dark blue that wouldn't draw any attention in Simpson's neighborhood. She was showing a lot of promise in field work. That's something I should've thought of, but hadn't. Maybe, I thought, I was getting too old for this line of work. Nah, I decided, I was just distracted.

I'm never completely comfortable being a passenger in someone else's car; kind of like a doctor being a patient, I'm always tense, and trying to drive the darn thing from the passenger side, which I know is distracting as all hell, so I leaned back in the seat and closed my eyes as Heather made her way from the hospital parking lot to Viers Mill Road. Fortunately, traffic at that time of night was light, and Heather's actually a pretty good driver, so I was only slightly tense by the time she found a parking spot four houses past Simpson's place.

We made our way to the back of the house by way

of the service road, both of us wearing black and more or less blending into the murky background. I wasn't equipped as I would usually be, because my plan had been to take Sandra shopping, and then back home where I would grab my night vision goggles, K-Bar knife, and whatever else I might need. Heather, in her black pullover and black stretch pants over black running shoes, looked like a model for an ad in *Soldier of Fortune*, but, this being her first night mission, carried nothing but a small penlight and her cell phone, both of which were clipped to the belt around her waist. As ill-equipped as we were, we still went in.

The back door was ajar, probably left that way since my last visit. The kitchen was still a mess, with dust motes glinting in the beam of Heather's light, which I hoped no one outside would notice. The smell of rancid oil and stale booze assaulted my nose. Heather made a sound somewhere between a gag and a wheeze.

"Good grief," she said in a stage whisper. "This place smells like a pig sty."

"I don't think Sydney Simpson was a very good housekeeper," I said. "Let's check the bedroom, and get the hell out of here."

We made our way across the kitchen, through the living room, which smelled even worse than the kitchen, and down the hall to the bedroom.

The closet door was still open, the shoes still lined up on the floor. The curtains over the single window were closed, but I resisted turning on the room light.

We moved to the closet, and I knelt. "Shine your light on the shoes," I said.

One by one, I picked up the shoes, examining them inside and out, and finding nothing. Just to be sure, I went back through the whole process. There was nothing inside Simpson's shoes other than the unmistakable odor of unwashed feet.

"Well, that's a dead end," I said.

Heather squatted next to me, idly playing her flashlight beam over the floorboards of the closet. "Maybe, what he really meant was *under* his shoes," she said.

It took a few seconds for that to penetrate the fog-enshrouded organ that was my brain. Of course. I shoved the shoes aside, and began tapping my knuckles against the floor. Near the left side of the closet, the sound changed from a dull 'thump,' to a hollow-sounding 'thoink.' There was a hollow space underneath the floor.

"Shine that light over here, Heather. Let me see if I can find something indicating a lid or hatch."

The cone of light from her penlight was small, so it took several minutes for me to notice that about two feet from the wall there was a microscopically wider space between two of the floorboards than any of the others. Without my handy K-Bar to pry into the space, with only my stubby fingers to use to claw at the boards, it took even longer to get enough of a grip to move the board, but I was finally successful, and a section of the floor came off. What lay beneath, even in the narrow beam of light, was enough to cause both of us to gasp.

First, there was a stack of legal-looking papers held together with a large rubber band. Beneath the papers, though, was what had really caused the gasps. Wrapped in clear plastic were stacks of hundred-dollar bills, four long and six across, and when we pulled the plastic bundle up, we discovered, five deep. The bills were still encircled by the straps or bands the banks put around them, one hundred bills in each band, or, doing quick math, one point two million dollars that Sydney had hidden under the floor in his closet. Not bad for 'walking around' money. It didn't even make a dent in what he'd bilked his victims of, but was a good start. I was willing to bet that in that stack of papers there would be documents identifying an offshore bank account or two.

Heather and I high-fived each other.

"Wow," she said. "Who would've ever thought to look here?"

"Certainly not the cops," I said. "But, then, they were investigating the guy's murder, not looking for hidden cash. You know, I'll bet even his partner, Devlin, didn't know about this."

"So, what do we do?"

I hadn't thought that far ahead. I suppose the best idea would've been to call the cops and tell them, but then, we'd have to explain how we knew, and I wasn't sure the county police would look too kindly upon our nocturnal exploration. On the other hand, we couldn't just leave it there. I felt like we'd gotten ourselves between a rock and a hard place.

Before I could worry further about it, though, I heard a squeaking sound coming from outside the bedroom. Someone was walking across the living room floor, and I didn't need a recorded message to tell me they were heading for our location.

"Someone's coming," I said.

"What do we do?" Heather whispered.

Chapter Thirty-Four

We didn't have a lot of choices. There were only two ways out of the bedroom; the door or the window. I didn't think we had the time to get the window open and get out without being spotted, so I did the next best thing; I grabbed Heather's arm and moved to stand beside the door, so that we'd be concealed for a brief period when it opened.

The sounds of footsteps came right up to the door, and then stopped. It seemed like forever before the door began to swing inward.

I felt Heather stiffen behind me. I turned my head and put a finger to my lips, then realized that she could barely see me, so I reached back and patted her shoulder. I could sense a body moving through the open door, and then it closed.

The bedroom was suddenly dimly illuminated when a flashlight came on at about waist level. I was close enough to the arm holding the light, that if I inhaled I would touch him—I could see from the dark outline that our visitor was a slightly built male—but, for some reason, he seemed unaware of our presence.

He walked farther into the room, playing the beam of the flashlight across the open closet door and the shoes I'd left scattered about.

"What the—" a voice said.

I stepped forward. "Hold it, friend, I have you covered," I said.

Now, most people entering a dark room, when they hear a voice telling them to 'hold it,' will freeze, or panic and run. This turkey did neither. He raised the flashlight, one of those two-foot-long industrial models with a baseball-bat-sized tube and a flared light, and swung as he turned.

That was a big mistake on his part.

Not, mind you, that I *knew* that he'd be stupid enough to try and attack me, but because I was trained to be prepared for anything, and his attack was one of those 'worst-case' scenarios you hear about. In this case, worst-case for him.

I blocked his swinging arm with a knife hand, which, given the force of his swing, had to hurt like hell. He made a squealing sound, and dropped the light. The bulb smashed upon contact with the floor, plunging the room into total darkness.

I'd been prepared for that. When the flashlight started to fall, I clenched my eyes shut, so, my pupils had that fraction of a second to widen from lack of light. I banked on the perp keeping his eyes open like most people would do, and being blinded by the sudden change from even that low level of light to darkness. When I opened my eyes, I could see shadows, sense movement, and feel the heat from two bodies, the perp in front of me, and Heather behind me. He'd thrown his hands up, groping blindly, and was making grunting noises.

I focused on the top of the shadow, his head, and sent a right jab across my raised left arm, feeling the immediate and satisfying crunch of bone as my fist slammed into his nose. His grunt turned into a loud squeak, and I felt the hot moistness of blood on my knuckles. Half turning, I grabbed with my left hand, felt and arm, and took hold, squeezing hard. I pulled him against my left side, close enough that I could vaguely make out features in the darkness. The ambient light reflected off his wide eyes.

"Wha-, who? Lemme go," he said.

I had a firm grip on his right arm. I turned him until I could grip that arm with my right hand, and then grabbed his left arm, pinning his arms against his body.

"Hold still," I said. "Or I'll hit you again, and it'll hurt even more next time." I'd been thinking about what to do about the documents and cash, but now, with the squirming body bumping against me as he struggled, my mind was made up. "Turn the lights on, Heather, and call 911. Let the cops know we've captured an intruder."

While I might have been able to explain away not reporting the money and papers right away, a live body would be a more complicated matter.

Heather moved past us, and reached for the light switch near the door. I blinked as the room was flooded with orange light. After my eyes adjusted to the increased light level, I looked down at my prisoner. I'd only ever gotten a brief description of David Devlin, but I was pretty sure that was who I had in my grip. Heather, too, recognized him.

"Well, well," she said. "We've been looking for Mr. Devlin, and here, he finds us."

He looked wide-eyed from me to her. "Who the hell are you people?" Then, his eyes narrowed as he looked back at me. "Hey, you're the dude who was here before."

"And," said I. "You're the shit heel who hit me over the head."

"Uh, hey, I'm sorry about that, man," he said, cringing. "I heard noise in the back when I come in, 'n

I just grabbed an empty whiskey bottle 'n when you come outta that hall, I swung it."

I released his arms and grabbed the front of his shirt, nearly lifting him from the floor.

"What were you doing here?"

He swallowed hard, looked from me to Heather to the closet, his eyes blinking rapidly. I knew he was framing a lie before he even opened his mouth.

"Uh, I had loaned some stuff to Sydney before he . . . died, and I was lookin' for it."

I decided to play the line out to see how far he'd take it.

"So, you come in the middle of the night?"

His gaze went back to the closet.

"You know, I wasn't sure the cops would let me in. What were *you* doing here?"

Now it was time to take a little of the slack out of the line, to start sinking the hook in.

"I was looking for the money your friend scammed from his clients," I said.

His eyes flickered and he looked again at the closet. The opening in the floor was clearly visible, but not its contents.

"I, uh, dunno what you're talkin' about."

"I think you do. You know, the millions the two of you snookered people out of in the little real estate pyramid scheme you were running."

The color drained from his face.

"What did he do?" Heather asked. "Cheat you out of your share?"

His Adam's apple began to do a little dance. His eyes bounced back and forth in their sockets, from me to Heather. The hook was biting in.

"H-how'd you . . . whaddya mean, pyramid scam?"

"Cut the crap, Devlin," I said. "We know all about the little scam you two had going. Now, where'd Simpson hide the money? There's less than two million in the closet."

"Two million, b-but, that can't be. We had more'n five times that."

Seemingly realizing that he'd just blown his story, he snapped his mouth shut.

"Yeah, we know that," Heather said. "He must've put the rest in an offshore account, keeping this for walking-around money, and it seems he cut you out of it."

The little man seemed to deflate with every word.

"You got that right," he said. "He said we were gonna share fifty-fifty, but he only gave me pocket change. He never even said he was keepin' money here in the house."

"So, what were you looking for?" I asked.

His face wrinkled up, his eyes half shut. He was thinking very hard. In the end, though, I think he realized that we had him cold.

"I was tryin' to find the papers for the bank account," he said. "He has one in the Cayman Islands. I figured he'd have the account number and password wrote down somewhere . . . he wasn't good at rememberin' shit like that. I was thinkin' I could get in touch and, you know, withdraw it."

"So, you go from your cut of the proceeds to the whole shebang, right?"

"Hey, I deserve it. I found the marks, found the landowners willin' to sell. All Sydney ever did was schmooze with the marks to con 'em out of their dough. He promised me half of what we made. Hell, the work I did, I deserve a bigger percentage. That son of a bitch, though, wasn't even giving me half like he promised."

"When did you last see your partner?" I asked.

"When I, uh, I don't remember. Maybe the second or third of the month. That's when I asked him for my share of the money, but he said he was waitin' for the money from that Ay-rab dude. I thought he should sell to Keith and his people, they were offerin' more, but

Sydney turned 'em down."

I almost missed the name, but fortunately, my brain processes information, often without me being conscious of it. "Keith? You wouldn't be talking about Keith Hodges, would you?"

"Yeah," he said. "Do you know him?"

"I know of him. Why did Simpson refuse his money? I would think as a con man he'd want to get as much money as possible."

Devlin made a snorting sound. "Said he didn't like Keith's politics. Can you believe that? He'll take money from an Ay-rab terrorist, but not from a true blue American. Anyway, that's what we fought about."

"You fought?"

He blinked. His mouth had been running without his brain being fully engaged, and he'd let slip a piece of information I don't think he wanted me to have. His face turned dark under the room lights, a reddish hue in the circles on his cheeks. But, before I pushed him on that, it was clear that he knew a bit about Keith Hodges, and I had a personal matter to take up with Hodges and his militia.

"You know that Hodges is head of a militia organization," I said.

"Yeah, so what." His face contorted into an ugly snarl. "Keith and his boys are all about protectin' America against foreign dangers, like this Omar dude and his raghead friends. They want to keep the Ay-rabs out of our country. I tried to explain that to Sydney, but he just wouldn't listen."

"You wanted to deal with this bunch of militant rednecks, and your partner disagreed, is that what I'm hearing?"

"Hey, Keith's a good guy. He's an ex-marine, force recon of some shit like that, and he's got some high-powered friends. I just couldn't get Sydney to see that, so I asked for my cut of the money, so I could make my own deal . . . but, he wouldn't listen. If he'd just listened to me, . . ."

A thought hit me. Talk about looking in the wrong places. "Did you kill Simpson?"

His eyes went wide. "Uh, I didn't mean to. I just wanted my money, but he wouldn't pony up."

"Kind of stupid killing him before you even knew where the money was," I said.

"Tell me about it," he said. "Any chance I can talk you into lettin' me go?"

I laughed. "Not a chance, buster, and not just because you hit me over the head."

"Hey, I could've killed you. Don't that count for something?"

Heather pushed between us before I could answer. "Police are on the way, Al," she said.

I looked at Devlin and shrugged. "Sorry, friend, you're out of luck. If it was just the land fraud, I might consider it, but you killed a man. I can't look the other way on that."

He gave me a funny look, which should've made me suspicious, but the sound of approaching sirens distracted me.

Charles Ray

Chapter Thirty-Five

Heather, when she called 911, must have told them we'd cornered a suspected criminal, because the Montgomery County police showed up in force. Two squad cars with two uniformed officers in each, blue lights flashing and sirens blaring, pulled into the driveway with screeching tires, followed closely by an unmarked sedan with two plainclothes detectives. Pushing Devlin in front of me, we went to the living room.

They knocked and were just about to kick the door in when Heather went opened it, to find herself facing four service weapons aimed at her body, and shouts of 'get down, hands where we can see them.' One of the plainclothes guys, who I recognized from the response to my being shot at, came in behind them, and when he saw me, ordered them to stand down. But, if I thought that meant he was disposed to be friendly toward me, he quickly scotched that.

"Mr. Pennyback, I certainly didn't expect to see you again so soon," he said. "Wasn't getting shot at enough for one evening."

I recognized him as the detective who'd been hanging around on the fringes while his partner took my statement at the hospital. He showed me his badge, and the photo of Detective Roger Thigpen was no friendlier looking than the man to whom the badge had been issued.

"I'm working on a case involving a land scam, detective," I said. "This house belonged to the main criminal running the scheme, Sydney Simpson. I was looking for evidence of it on behalf of a client, who was one of his victims."

"Simpson; that was the guy that got himself killed, right? You know that you could get in trouble for disturbing a crime scene, don't you?"

I was beginning to get an itchy feeling about Detective Thigpen. He was sounding like one of those 'by the book,' 'you're stepping on my jurisdiction' kind of cops. At least he hadn't threatened us with a breaking and entering charge, and I wasn't about to poke him in that direction.

"The crime scene tape was gone," I said. "So, I figured it would be okay. Anyway, while it wasn't what my partner and I came here for, we just happened to stumble across the guy who killed Simpson." I pointed at a cowering Devlin.

Thigpen looked skeptically at him. "That little weasel? He's the killer?"

"I am not," Devlin said in a whiny voice. "He's lying. I didn't kill nobody."

Thigpen's gaze returned to me. "Well, what do you have to say to that, Mr. Pennyback? You have any proof that he's the killer?"

"He confessed," I said.

"I did not," Devlin wailed. "He's makin' that up."

Thigpen looked from him to me. "Well, looks like we've got ourselves one of those 'he said, he said' situations. It's his word against yours, Pennyback. I don't know if that's enough for me to take him into custody."

Devlin smiled triumphantly. I felt like punching the smile off his face. I balled up my fists and stepped toward him.

Heather coughed. "Excuse me, gentlemen," she said. "But, It's not really a case of one person's word against another's." She held up her phone, one of the newer models with more bells and whistles than I could manage. "It's Mr. Devlin, video recorded here, with great color picture and sound, against the lies he's telling now."

Devlin's face fell. Thigpen smiled.

"And, you are?"

"I'm Heather Bunche, a partner in A.E. Pennyback, Confidential Enquiries," she said.

"And, you have a recording of Mr. Devlin here confessing to murder."

"I do." She pushed a button on the front of the phone.

Devlin appeared on the tiny screen, small but still recognizable. His voice, heard very clearly, told me all about his visit to the house, his argument with Simpson, and, most importantly, his killing him.

"Hey," Devlin said. "I didn't give permission to be recorded. That's not legal."

"Actually," Heather said, a smug smile on her face. "I was recording my boss, and he's given me permission to do so, so there's absolutely nothing illegal about this recording. You just happened to be talking to him as I was recording."

Thigpen laughed. "Afraid she's got you there, pardner." He turned to one of the uniforms. "Read Mr. Thigpen his rights, and take him to lockup. I'll follow you in. I have a lot of questions for him."

"Uh, I didn't mean to kill him," Devlin said, tears streaming down his face. "We got into an argument, and he came at me. I was defending myself."

Thigpen smiled wolfishly. "So, you did stab him,

though, right?"

Devlin looked down at his feet. "Well, yeah, but, it was like, self-defense, you know."

"Save it for the judge and jury." To the uniform, he said, "Get him booked in, suspicion of manslaughter . . . for now. I'll question him later."

After two uniformed cops hustled Devlin out, Thigpen turned his attention to Heather and me. He looked like he was about to deliver a lecture, so I decided to take the offensive.

"We also found something interesting in the closet in the bedroom," I said. "Follow me."

He trailed close behind as we returned to the bedroom. When he saw the stacks of hundreds beneath the floorboards, his eyes went wide and he whistled.

"Holy shit. That looks like a lot of money."

"I estimate about a million, two hundred thousand," Heather said.

"And, there might be more secreted in other hidey holes in the house," I said. "Simpson bilked his victims of more than ten million."

"Damn, looks like you two just solved two cases. The department owes you a vote of thanks. I guess the little matter of you not having permission to enter this house can be overlooked." He winked at Heather. "And, lucky for all of us, Devlin implicated himself to me. I don't think your recording is illegal, but it's better if we don't have to bring it up in court, you know. A good defense lawyer would really try and muddy the waters with it."

"We're glad we could be of help, detective," I said. "This will, I assume, clear my client, Ms. Loretta Palmer. She was accused of killing Simpson, and was recently arrested."

"Not a problem. As soon as I give the brass my report, they'll contact the county attorney. I imagine Ms. Palmer will be released by breakfast."

"She'll be happy to hear that."

"Now, why don't you two make yourselves scarce," he said. "I'll have to get the forensics team back in hear to rip this place apart. I'd rather not have to explain why you're here. You understand?"

I nodded and shook his hand. Of course, I understood. And, as far as the current case was concerned, we were done. We'd proved our client innocent, and having found Simpson's stash of cash, and possibly bank account documents, there was a chance of the victims eventually getting at least some of their money back.

I could go back to the hospital and see about Sandra. I would suggest that Heather go home and grab some shuteye, which I knew she'd probably not do. Once I checked on Sandra, though, I had another mission; and, this one was personal.

Chapter Thirty-Six

The sky was just beginning to turn gray when Heather and I pulled into the patient parking lot at Shady Grove Hospital. Just as I thought she would, when I told her to go home and get some sleep, she'd told me to 'screw off,' she was not going home until she knew how Sandra was doing. She dogged my steps across the parking lot, through the reception area, and across to the ICU, which was located in close proximity to the Emergency Room, for obvious reasons.

Blood was dozing on a chair in the corner, and a sleep-looking Elizabeth sat near the head of the bed. Sandra still looked so vulnerable, lying there with the thin hospital sheet pulled up to two inches below her chin, and with tubes and wires trailing away from her body and going into machines and contrivances that blinked and made soft beeping noises. She looked so pale and still.

Elizabeth looked up and smiled wanly as we entered the room.

"She's still unconscious," she said in a quiet voice. "But, the doctors say that her autonomic nervous system is responsive to stimuli, so it's pretty certain she'll pull through. Right now, she just needs to rest while her body's immune system gets its act together."

Like the hotshot lawyer that she is, she had anticipated what I would want to know, and had presented it succinctly, and in enough detail—minus too much medical jargon—to ease my mind.

"Do they have any idea when she'll be fully awake?" I asked.

"The doctor said it could be later today, or it could be tomorrow. He seemed pretty sure of himself." She looked hard at me. "You look like you've been through the wash and not hung properly to dry. Why don't you go home and get some sleep? I'll call you if there's any change."

I couldn't argue with her, and not just because she was making sense. Her tone of voice made it crystal clear that she wasn't making a request. That gave me the time to do what I had to do, though, so this was another one of those silver linings in every cloud situations.

"Okay. I'll have my mobile phone with me at all times. Call me the instant she wakes up."

"You got it. Now, get out of here, before you pass out. You too, Heather. I'm not going to ask what the two of you have been up to—at least, not now. But, girl, you and I are going to talk when things settle down."

Heather smiled and ducked her head.

"Okay," she said. "But, I'm the second person you call after Al when Sandra wakes up. Okay?"

"Okay. Now, the two of you, shoo!"

We beat a hasty retreat.

In the parking lot, standing near Heather's rental, and my beat-up Volkswagen, I grasped her shoulders and turned her to face me.

"Heather, I want you to go home and get some sleep. I'll call you when I need you back in the office."

She looked up into my eyes. Her gaze bored into me like a laser.

"And, just what the heck will you be doing while I'm resting?"

"I plan to kick back, too."

"Right, and I've got some cactus patches in Arizona I'll sell you. My BS meter is pinging all the way to the right on that statement. Now, level with me, Al; what are you planning to do?"

I saw no harm in telling her. "I have a little score to settle with the thug that shot Sandra," I said.

"You mean, *we*, don't you?"

"Uh-uh, kid. You don't get a ticket for this ride. This one's all mine."

She put her hands on her hips and cocked her head. "This is about the guys who shot at you, right?"

Right for the jugular. Hell, I should've known I couldn't hide anything from her. We'd been working together for too long. It' s like she can read my mind. So, I told her about the militia and Keith Hodges.

"Hodges? As in the other mystery buyer?" Her eyes went as round as little saucers.

"Yeah. For some reason these goons that I suspect are part of Hodges' militia group were following me around, then, they took a shot at me, and . . ."

"It missed, and hit Sandra." She gripped my upper arms. "Oh, Al, I'm so sorry. So, you're planning to make them pay for what they did?"

"Damn straight I am," I said. "But, you can't go with me on this one, kiddo. It's probably gonna be pretty nasty."

"I can handle nasty. I been around you long enough, you know."

"No, Heather. This is one I have to do. I need you to get some rest, and then start digging up whatever you can about Hodges and his group. That's not negotiable."

She shook her head. "I don't like it, Al, but if that's

what you want."

"It's what I want."

She gave my biceps a squeeze, and after one last pleading look, got into her car and drove away.

I should've gone home and gotten some shuteye myself, but I was too wound up for sleep. I did drive home, but just to change into more appropriate clothing; my black cargo pants and a long sleeved black nylon sweater with pockets on the sleeves. I strapped my K-Bar knife to my ankle.

Then, I called Buster.

"Hey, bro, I just heard about Sandra," he said. "I'll be droppin' by the hospital later. I hear she's gonna be okay. How you doin'?"

I told him. Basically, I was physically undamaged, but royally pissed. "I'm going after the shooters, Buster, and since I don't think they were freelancing, I think I might just go after their boss as well."

"Damn, dude, you got this thing about militia, don't you?"

"And, you don't?"

"You know I do," he said. "Especially after what they did to Sandra and Alma. But, this Hodges guy is a cut above the ones we've dealt with before. He's politically connected, and pretty smooth. He ain't gonna be easy to take down."

"You seem to know a lot about him."

"Well, the dude's smooth, but we got our suspicions. So do ATF and the FBI. He's under almost as much surveillance as the Russian embassy people."

A thought began forming in my mind. "So, that means you know where I can find him, right?"

I heard him clear his throat, his tell that he was about to let me in on something that I probably wasn't authorized to know. "Uh, well, as a matter of fact, I do. I know the guys in the precinct who have the duty to watch him when he's in the District. In three hours, he'll be meeting with Congressman Eric Boswell, a far-right wing gun nut from out west somewhere. Boswell is one of his angels on Capitol Hill. I can't get you close to him, but I can let you get eyes on him. Can you meet me at the entrance to the Rayburn House Office Building in two and a half hours?"

"I'll be there," I said, and hung up.

I changed into more appropriate clothing. It's never a good idea to be near a federal building dressed like a commando, but even worse to do it in the paranoid environment that descended upon the capital after 9/11. I changed into brown cargo pants with only two extra pockets, and a brown sweater with elbow patches, and instead of my black, canvas boots, I wore my brown hiking boots. My K-Bar knife went back on the shelf in the closet. I looked at myself in the mirror, and saw a middle-aged man with caramel colored skin and close-cropped hair that was going gray at the temples staring back at me. My six-foot frame is not as hard and defined as it was in my thirties, but, except for a bit of softness around the middle—one of the things you have to deal with as you age—still pretty fit. I looked like a constituent from a farming community coming to Washington to talk to his elected representative.

I took my time driving to Rockville. After parking in the commercial lot behind the county court building, I walked across to the Rockville Metro, and got on a Red Line train for the fifty-minute ride to Metro Center, where I went downstairs and hopped on an Orange Line train to Capitol South station, which is one block south of the beginning of the House Office buildings. I walked up onto the marble entrance plaza at 9:30.

Buster, standing near a group of gawking tourists taking pictures of each other with the wide glass entrance doors in the background, was already there. He waved me over.

"Every visitor has to come through here," he said. "We'll catch sight of Hodges when he gets here."

You'd think two dudes our size hanging around in front of a public building would attract attention, but you'd be wrong. People hang around the government building entrances all the time in DC; even the White House, albeit a secure fence, sensors, and uniformed Secret Service officers with dogs keep them a good distance away; it's part of the beauty of the nation's capital, and, even with all the post-9/11 paranoia, Washington, DC is still one of the most open national capitals in the world.

We moved to the side, with the white marble walls to our backs and large shrubbery to our right sides. A group of teens, led by a harried-looking woman in a gray pants suit, gathered to our left, and began a chatter that made it all but impossible to hear anything beyond them. It did, though, effectively screen us from the rest of the crowd on the plaza, while enabling us to see over the heads of the giggling teens.

Buster nudged me in the side just as two black Chevy Suburbans with tinted windows pulled to the curb in front of the building.

The driver of the first vehicle stayed in place, his hands resting on the top of the steering wheel, and three young, beefy, military-looking goons, wearing dull green military-style uniforms got out. One positioned himself at the back, facing the street, while the other two mounted the sidewalk, facing the plaza, scanning the crowd on the plaza. They didn't appear to be armed, which, considering DC's strict gun control laws, was probably wise, but looked like they could handle themselves.

The curbside doors of the second vehicle opened, and, like the first vehicle, three men emerged, leaving the driver, his head moving from side to side, and his hands resting on the steering wheel.

I didn't need to be told which of the three was Keith Hodges. He stood out like a pimple on prom night.

While the five men surrounding him on the sidewalk looked like clones of military action figures, with their broad shoulders, narrow waists, hair cut high and tight in military style, and bulging muscles apparent under their military-style uniforms, Hodges, who was six-inches shorter than their six-foot height, and slighter of build, and wore a similar uniform that had obviously been tailored to fit still commanded attention. His blond hair, short, but not cut in military style, was slicked back over an oval skull, not a strand out of place, and his eyes, glacial blue under heavy light brown brows, surveyed the scene like a general reviewing his assembled troops. He walked with the confident gait of someone accustomed to command.

He and his five-man escort mounted the marble steps and headed for the center glass door, behind which stood four Capitol policemen who screened people entering the building, looking for weapons, explosives, or other dangerous objects.

I moved to stand behind Buster, just in case one of Hodges' escorts, or Hodges himself, might recognize me, but they hardly even looked in our direction.

We waited until the doors had swung shut behind them, and then entered the building through the door nearest us, and got into the security line on the end, keeping them in sight as they lined up to go through the metal detector.

I couldn't hear what they were saying, but Hodges chatted with the policemen as he emptied his pockets and walked through the detector, followed by his five escorts. Buster and I walked through the detector at our end and turned left to stand near the wall, waiting to see which way they would go.

They walked toward the bank of elevators beyond the security checkpoint, where a tall, patrician-looking man in a gray suit, his thin blond hair in a combover to hide a rapidly receding hairline and a scowl on his florid face, waited for them. As they approached, gray suit began waving his arms. His scowl deepened.

His words weren't clear. I only heard "You shouldn't be here, Keith." Hodges held his hands up in a placating gesture. He spoke so softly, I couldn't hear the words, but whatever it was, it didn't make the older man any happier.

"I told you not to come," he said.

Hodges said something else and put a hand on the man's shoulder. He jerked his shoulder away.

"Look," he said. "I have a meeting now, but I can come to your place in two hours. So, go back, and I'll see you there."

Now, Hodges was frowning, and his five guards pressed in closer. Next to me, Buster was tense.

"Don't look like they're gettin' along too well," he said.

A couple of the Capitol's own, their hands resting on the butts of their weapons, were also watching the group closely.

Before anyone could react, though, Hodges, smiled and patted the gray-haired man's shoulder. He turned, and with a jerk of his head, directed his men to follow him. They headed for the exit, and the gray-haired man went to the elevator marked for 'Members Only,' and stabbed a button. The doors opened immediately, and he stepped inside.

My attention, however, was on Hodges and his entourage, who were leaving the building through the left exit.

Let's follow them," I said, nudging Buster.

We went out through the right exit, just as they reached the edge of the sidewalk. One of the men with Hodges pulled out a phone, hit a button, and put the phone to his mouth. The two Suburbans came around the corner two blocks down before he'd even put the phone back into his pocket. They pulled up quickly and stopped. The driver of the second vehicle got out and ran around to open the door. I recognized the big galoot who'd shot at me.

"That's him," I said. "That's the guy that shot at Sandra and me. Let's get him."

We started moving toward them, but before we'd reached the sidewalk, Hodges was inside the Suburban, and both vehicles sped away with a squeal of tires.

"Dammit, we have to go after them," I said, slamming my hands against my thighs.

"You sure that was the guy?" Buster asked. "I mean, you one hundred percent sure?"

"I smacked him at Simpson's office, and was looking right into his eyes when he shot through my car window. You're damn right I'm sure. Now, let's go after them."

"My car's too far away. They'll be long gone before we can get to it. But, not to worry, bro. I know where they live."

Charles Ray

Chapter Thirty-Seven

Hodges group, The True Sons of America, known informally as TSA, were well-known to local and federal law enforcement. Suspected of involvement in several gun-running, drug smuggling, and several robberies in four states on the eastern seaboard, nothing had ever been proven, but not for lack of trying. What had been achieved, though, was an unprecedented level of police cooperation. The result was that their main headquarters location was well known. None of the agencies had ever been able to get inside the place because of the inability to demonstrate enough probable cause to get a search warrant, but it was kept under surveillance, which was how Buster had come to know that Hodges would be in the District that morning.

With me being able to ID the man who'd shot at me, and again having seen him with Hodges in front of the congressional building, Buster felt there was now that 'probable cause,' that would allow the police to get past the TSA compound's front gate. So, he asked me to go home and wait. He would call his FBI and

Montgomery County contacts and ask one of them to get a warrant to search the place, and let me know when or if an arrest was made.

Like hell. I wanted to be there to see that they were good and got.

"I should be there," I said. "If all you have is my description, there's a danger you won't get the right guy. You saw 'em, man. These guys all look like clones of each other. If I'm there to finger him, though, they won't be able to pull a fast one."

He didn't look to happy about it, but finally agreed.

"Okay, but just remember, this is likely to be a joint federal-state operation. Even I'll just be along for the ride, since these guys are out in western Montgomery County where I don't have jurisdiction."

I promised to be on my best behavior. Buster assured me that I had time to go home, because it would take more than an hour to get a warrant. He wasn't far wrong. I'd just gotten home and changed into my black outfit, complete with K=Bar knife strapped to my ankle under my pants' leg, when he called and told me to meet him at the CVS drug store at the corner of Route 28 and Quince Orchard Road. That location had been selected because the TSA compound was just west of Route 28, near the little town of Beallsville.

Buster, dressed in a black S.W.A.T. uniform, complete with armored vest, was there with four county cops, similarly dressed, when I arrived.

"I feel underdressed," I said as I walked to the black Ford van with a county police logo on the door.

Thigpen, who I hadn't recognized at first, because of the uniform, laughed. "You won't need anything, Mr. Pennyback," he said. "You're staying in the vehicle until the place is secure."

"Got it," I said, smiling. "I'm ready to go."

He frowned. "We have to wait for the feds. They insist on being involved."

"Yeah, but this was just a shooting, how does that involve federal authorities?"

"The shooting doesn't," he said. "But, this is the first chance ATF and the FBI have had to get inside that compound. They're hoping they'll see something that'll give 'em probable cause to make another visit."

It was ten minutes of impatient waiting until a black Suburban with government plates and no other markings pulled in next to us. Four guys in black coveralls, wearing black baseball caps and black leather combat boots got out. Two of them had FBI in big white letters on their backs, and in smaller letters over their left breast, while the other two had ATF. This was truly a joint operation. One of the FBI agents, a guy about my size with gray at his temples like me, all craggy faced and square jawed, came over and stuck his hand out to Thigpen.

"I'm Special Agent Harvey Lake," he said. "You, I assume, are Detective Thigpen?"

"Yeah, and these are officers Jackson, Carter, and Weinberg from the county police." He pointed to each of the county cops. "The big fella here is Detective Buster Mayweather from DC Metro, and the civilian is Mr. Al Pennyback."

Lake frowned at me. "We weren't told there'd be a civilian on this operation. Are you sure that's wise?"

"Agent Lake, we're executing a search warrant to find the suspect in a shooting that happened not far from here a few days ago. Mr. Pennyback was an eye witness, and can identify the perpetrator, so that makes him an essential part of this operation."

I knew that Thigpen had objected to my inclusion, but in the face of apparent federal objection, he was now my biggest fan. It was good to see that some things hadn't changed. Joint threats be damned, local and federal cops are like oil and water, they just don't mix well.

Lake was unhappy with the situation, but for once

the feds didn't have the lead. The county was doing them a favor by letting them tag along, so he had no choice but to go along with it. If looks could kill, though, I would've dropped dead on the spot.

"Well, I guess I should introduce my team," Lake said, with a petulant tone in his voice. "This is Special Agent Lee Holmes, and ATF Special Agents Jack Moore and Leland Oldfield."

The three other feds inclined their heads in acknowledgement. They didn't look any happier with the situation than Lake. Buster and Thigpen shared a look that clearly said, 'suck it!' I kept a neutral expression on my face, but I was smiling inside.

"Let's saddle up," Thigpen said. "Time to move out."

Chapter Thirty-Eight

From the Quince Orchard area, Route 28 goes through an area of farms, horse ranches, and small towns. A complete change from the more urbanized environment near I-270, it usually shocks people from the District the first time they drive through it. While there are some very prosperous farms and mansions, for the most part, it looks like some of the lower middle class rural areas in other parts of the south, and make no mistake about it, Maryland *is* a southern state. When the Civil War broke out, the only thing that kept Maryland in the Union was the fact that federal troops were dispatched to the state house in Annapolis, and surrounded it, not allowing the legislators to leave until they'd voted to remain a part of the United States. Even so, Maryland supplied units to both sides in the ensuing conflict, and it was in Maryland that John Wilkes Booth and his co-conspirators hatched the plot to assassinate Abraham Lincoln. Except for Annapolis, Baltimore, and the suburban areas around DC, Maryland is about as south as it gets.

The FBI had the lead in keeping tabs on TSA, and

knew precisely where his compound was, so Agent Lake's vehicle took the lead. Thigpen was quick to remind him, though, that once they approached the entrance to the compound, the Montgomery County vehicle would move into the lead, because he was the official who was technically serving the warrant. The federal agents were to keep quiet and follow his lead. Lake rather brusquely said that they were there mainly to observe, and if they saw anything to justify a federal warrant, they would return to DC and obtain it. He pointedly made no mention of whether or not he would invite the County to participate in serving *his* warrant. Thigpen didn't give Buster and me the 'keep out of the way' lecture, but his expression said it all. We were to stay in the background. He was, I was sure, only doing it that way to nettle Lake.

I had a right-side window seat in the back, and had nothing do during the thirty-minute ride but watch the scenery scroll by. I love nature, but I'm not a good passenger, as I've already mentioned. And, with nothing to do but sit and look, even the scenic vistas through which we drove turned incredibly boring after the first five miles. I breathed a huge sigh of relief when the federal vehicle, made a left turn and pulled over and stopped.

Weinberg, who was driving our vehicle, pulled alongside, stopped and Thigpen, who was riding shotgun, rolled his window down.

"Okay, the compound is seven miles ahead," he said. "Keep close, but leave yourself room to turn around if things go south."

Lake, riding shotgun in his vehicle, leaned forward. "Got it, thanks."

Thigpen patted Weinberg's arm. "Move out, Jacob, but keep it at the speed limit. We don't want to approach the gate so fast they think it's a raid."

With a nod, Weinberg pressed the gas, and the van lurched forward, throwing up a cloud of dust that coated the Suburban. I looked back through the rear window to see arms flailing as the Suburban pulled in behind us. Apparently, we'd taken off before they'd had a chance to get their window up, and were batting at clouds of fine, red dust. The smiles that Thigpen and Weinberg shared confirmed my suspicion.

The dirt road we were on bore no markers from the highway, so it could've easily been missed if you didn't know the turn. But, once on it, the TSA compound was impossible to miss. There were no crossroads for a full seven miles, and both sides of the road were lined with fairly thick forest for the first six miles. After that, a five-strand steel mesh fence, topped with coiled barbed wire, lined both sides, with signs warning, NO ADMITTANCE. TRESPASSERS WILL BE PROSECUTED. TSA. They certainly left no doubt that visitors were not welcome.

If the signs didn't turn strangers off, the fifty-gallon drums blocking half the road, backed up by concrete and corrugated iron guard posts flanking the road, with a drop bar between them, and two six-foot, scowling, muscle men in cammies with AR-15s at port arms probably would.

Weinstein slowed to a sedate five miles per hour as we approached the guard post, stopping six feet from the line of drums.

One of the guards approached the driver's side of our vehicle, making signals for Weinstein to lower the window.

"You lost, friend?" he said, more statement than question. "This is a private road, so turn it around and go on back to 28."

Thigpen pulled a document from his jacket and held it up, along with his badge.

"No, *friend,* we are not lost," he said. "We're here to serve a warrant on Mr. Keith Hodges, so lift the bar and let us through."

With a confused look, the guard turned to his

companion. "Willie, this dude's a cop, says he's got a warrant for the boss. Better call up and ask 'em what they want us to do." He turned back to Thigpen. "You gotta wait here until we get clearance to let you enter."

"Don't take too long, or I might just think you're trying to obstruct an officer of the law in the execution of his duties."

That caused a look of even deeper confusion.

The other guard, after speaking into the phone in the guard booth for a few seconds, hung it up and came out.

"Boss said we can let 'em in," he said.

The confused-looking one stepped away from the vehicle. "Go up yonder and turn right at the end of the hedge. Park in front of the day room; that's the big one-story building."

Frowning at us, he waved us past as the other guard raised the barrier. Through the rear window, I saw the two of them staring after us.

A six-foot hedge blocked the view from the dirt road on the right. On the left, a large grass-covered field stretched out toward a pine forest. We turned right at the end of the hedge, as instructed, and there before us were four buildings, a large, block-like one-story building of gray concrete with a green roof of metal slate, and three two-story wood-frame buildings that looked like the barracks I remembered from my army basic training days. The four buildings were surrounded by gravel surfaces. A blacktop parking area was in front of the large building. There were fifteen vehicles there; the two black Suburbans with Maryland plates we'd seen in DC, a gold Buick Park Avenue with DC plates and a congressional parking sticker in the window, two old olive drab army jeeps with the official markings painted over and bearing West Virginia plates, and ten pickups of assorted makes and colors, with Maryland, Virginia, West Virginia, Pennsylvania, Idaho, Colorado, Texas, and

Wyoming plates. Ast the far end, I saw the car from which we'd been shot at. I nudged Buster.

"See that one on the end," I said. "That's the one they were driving when they shot at us."

He nodded.

"Good," Thigpen said. "I don't mean, good that you were shot at, but good that you recognize the vehicle. That probably means that the perps on site. Stay alert. These TSA guys have never been in a shootout with the police, but there's a first time for everything."

Weinstein pulled the van up directly in front of the entrance to the large building. The fed's pulled their Suburban in on our right.

A muscle-bound, blond with a crew cut, tight green cargo pants, and an olive drab tee shirt that was so tight it looked painted on, stood in the open door. We all got out, and followed Thigpen who stood in front of crew cut, who stared at him with an expression of belligerence.

Thigpen showed his badge and the warrant. "We're here to see Keith Hodges," he said in a no-nonsense tone.

With only the slightest change in expression, crew cut stepped aside, and motioned for us to enter. "The colonel's in the training room," he said.

We entered a small anteroom containing a desk and chair, walls bare except for a bulletin board covered with bulletins and notices. There were two doors opposite the entrance. The one on the right had a sign that read, 'Day Room/Training Room -Step into Greatness,' while the sign on the left-hand door read, 'Commandant.' Between the two doors was a table, with a cardboard sign that read, "Mail.' On the table was a distribution box, five rows of six slots, each with a white adhesive strip with names written in black ink. Crew cut stepped behind the desk and sat, ignoring us. Thigpen pulled the right-hand door open and we stepped through.

The space we entered was huge, bigger than a high school gymnasium. The right side had a lectern, with three rows of ten chairs each arranged in front of it, and a large chalkboard behind. On the left side of the room was a pool table, a ping pong table, a large screen TV, and several cushioned chairs scattered about. Large, three-shelf book cases against the left-hand wall were filled with paperbacks and magazines.

Keith Hodges stood near the pool table. Flanking him were several of his 'soldiers,' dressed like the blond who'd met us at the door. At the back of the group, Congressman Boswell, dressed in jeans and a brown sweater over a plaid shirt, tried to make himself look small.

Hodges stepped forward as we entered.

"So many officers, and from so many different agencies, just to serve a simple warrant," he said. "I feel honored."

Chapter Thirty-Nine

Up close, Keith Hodges looked older than he had in front of the Rayburn Building. He had crows' feet at the corner of his eyes, and I could see strands of gray in his slicked-back blond hair.

He took the warrant from Thigpen and took his time reading it. He then handed it back.

"This is a rather unusual warrant," he said. "It says that you're here to search for an individual believed to be associated with this organization, in connection with a shooting recently, but you only identify the individual as a white male, approximately six feet in height, weighing two hundred pounds, age twenty-five to thirty years old. That's not very specific." He waved his hands at the group of men who stood around, their expressions alert, as if waiting for orders. "It could apply to more than half the men in this room at the moment. I'm not sure you have the authority to initiate such a nonspecific search."

"I assure you, we have the means to identify the specific individual," Thigpen said. He pointed at me. "Mr. Al Pennyback here got a good look at the individual we're looking for."

"I think I should have an attorney review this warrant before I consent to the search." Hodges turned to Boswell. "Congressman Boswell is a lawyer. What do you say congressman? Is this legal?"

Red-faced, Boswell edged forward. "Uh, on the face of it, I'd have to say it's a bit of overreach, detective," he said. "A warrant should state specifically what you are looking for."

Lake stepped up beside Thigpen. "Hello, congressman. I'm a bit surprised to find you here. Mr. Hodges is not one of your constituents. Are you now representing him?"

Boswell puffed his chest out and glared at the FBI man. "My reason for being here is of no concern to you, or your agency, sir. I happen to be a member of the bar in Maryland, Virginia, and the District, as well as my home state, and I was asked for legal advice, which I am entitled to give. I might ask you why the FBI is interested in a local crime."

Before Lake could respond, Thigpen held a hand up. "I appreciate your concern, congressman, but rest assured, Agent Lake is here merely as an observer, and this warrant was signed by a judge, who was convinced that this search as outlined in the document is legal." To Hodges, he said, "Are you refusing to allow the search, Mr. Hodges? Before you answer, keep in mind, your refusal could be taken as an indication of guilt."

Cowed, Boswell stepped back. Hodges merely smiled. "Of course not, detective. I was just expressing my unease at this blatant act of intimidation on the part of law enforcement. I take it that you wish to have Mr. Pennyback take a look at my men to see if he recognizes the person you seek?"

"That's correct. Now, if you men would all line up, we can get this over with."

"Do as what the man says, boys," Hodges said. "It's

their time if they wish to waste it."

With military precision, the men arranged themselves into two rows, twelve in front and thirteen in the back. They stood loosely at parade rest, their eyes on Hodges, and slight smiles on their faces. As for Hodges, he had a smug, condescending look on his face as he turned to Thigpen.

"Very well, detective," he said. "Do your job, and leave us in peace."

There was something about their demeanor that bothered me, as if they knew something that we didn't. Then, it hit me.

"Okay, Mr. Pennyback," Thigpen said. "Take a close look, and tell me if you see the man who shot at you."

"I don't have to," I said. "He's not here."

Thigpen's face fell.

"What? But, you said—"

"I know what I said, and I stand by it. But, the shooter, and probably the man driving the vehicle, are not in this group."

I watched Hodges. His smile was wider now.

"Like I said, detective, you're wasting your time."

With a disgusted look on his face, Thigpen started to turn away, but I put a hand on his arm.

"Not really," I said. "There are two men missing from this group."

I saw a flicker of doubt cross Hodges' face, but it was only momentary. "Of course," he said. "I have two men on sentry duty. You have to have seen them when you arrived."

"Oh, I'm including them. But, you have thirty marked mail slots outside, and even including the two sentries, that only makes twenty-eight. Where are the other two men?"

Thigpen's look of disgust morphed into a triumphant smile. "Damn, I didn't even notice that." He turned back to Hodges. "Do you have two men unaccounted for, Mr. Hodges?"

"All of my men are present and accounted for. You can search the barracks if that'll make you feel better." I detected a slight tremor in his voice, and noticed that Boswell had started sweating.

His offer was too easy. I was pretty sure we would find the barracks empty. Then, I noticed a door in the back of the room, between the training and recreation areas. The sign said, 'Supply Room.'

Out of the corner of my eye, I saw beads of sweat appear on Hodges' forehead. His eyes drifted toward the door I was looking at, and then quickly cut back to me. Thank you, body language, I thought. He probably wasn't even aware of what he'd done, but, that's the beauty of the body's automatic reflexes, unless you're really paying attention, they'll always give you away.

"I don't think looking in the barracks is worth the effort," I said. "I believe the men we're looking for are not very far from us at this very moment."

Hodges' face was immobile, but his eyes darted toward that door again.

"And, just where do you think they might be?" he asked. There was that tiny tremor in his voice again. I don't think anyone else in the room noticed it, but I've spent a lifetime observing people.

I walked to the door and put my hand on the knob. His eyes widened, and he pressed his lips so tightly, the skin around his mouth paled.

"I think they're inside here," I said.

I tried the door. It was locked.

"That's our supply room," Hodges said. "We keep it locked to keep the supplies secure."

"How about unlocking it and letting us take a look," Thigpen said.

"Your warrant says you're looking for people, not *things*. The supply room is not a part of your search."

Hodges tried to put steel in his voice, but it came out more like tin, and everyone knows how tin bends. He was putting on a good show, but I could tell that he was nervous.

"If there's no one inside the room," I said. "You have nothing to worry about. Like you said, the warrant only pertains to people."

"He's right, Keith," Boswell said. "Whatever he sees in there is off limits as far as their warrant's concerned."

Hodges shot a warning look at the congressman. Whatever else might be inside that room was irrelevant—except that if the feds got a gander, they'd have what they needed to get another warrant to come back. Of course, I wasn't about to bring that up.

"So," I said. "How about letting us take a peek. It should be easy to see if there's anyone inside or not."

I saw defeat in Hodges' eyes. He pointed at one of the military clones standing in line, still waiting. "Okay, Jerry, open the damn door."

Jerry, one of the dudes in the back row, walked over to the door, pulling a chain from beneath his tee shirt, at the end of which was a big, brass skeleton key. He inserted it in the lock and turned, but hesitated about opening the door.

"Open it," Thigpen said in a commanding voice.

Jerry looked at Hodges, and Hodges nodded. He pulled the door open.

Chapter Forty

The thing that makes it easy for the cops to catch most crooks is that crooks are, for the most part, stupid.

The two men hiding in the supply room had been standing at the door, probably trying to hear what was going on. They looked like two deer caught in headlights when the door swung open.

The goon who had shot at me and hit Sandra instead, his face still showing some discoloration from his first encounter with me, was standing in front, with another, similar looking, similarly clad goon right behind him.

I was about four feet from the door, directly in front of him. I lifted my hand and pointed. "That's the shit heel who shot at me," I said.

When confronted with a crisis, the average person experiences a 'fight or flight' reaction, usually immobile for several seconds while their brain processes what's happening. The man in the rear did neither. He dropped to his knees and put his hands up. The shooter, like most stupid crooks do when confronted by the law, went into immediate flight mode. I've never understood the rationale behind that action. With several armed cops in the immediate vicinity, fleeing is like an admission of guilt, and unless you're a world-class sprinter with tons of resources behind you, you're bound to get caught.

But, they run anyway. That's exactly what he did.

He exploded through the door, his arms pumping, and headed for the exit.

With eight cops between him and the door, he had a snowball's chance in hell of making it. But, there was an even more dangerous obstacle in his path. His flight took him within two feet of me, and in a split second I decided that the cops could have him when I'd finished with him.

I brought my right hand back, and then shot it out, knuckles leading, and caught him on the point of the nose. The laws of physics did the rest.

I felt a satisfying crunch as my fist, toughened from hours of work on a *makiwa* board, pushed his nose flat against his face, shattering the bones, and causing a spray of blood over his lips and cheeks. He made a 'urgh' sound as the forward momentum of his head met the forward, and much faster, momentum of my fist. His body continued forward, but his head snapped back. The force of that backward movement of the head pulled his body back, and he landed on his butt, his hands going to his mangled and mashed nose, and his eyes clenched shut.

Two of the county cops rushed past him to slap cuffs on his wide-eyed partner, still kneeling in the supply room, while Thigpen and the other cop moved to stand beside me.

"Good stop, Pennyback," Thigpen said. "I'll bet that felt good." He smiled as he leaned over and pulled the injured goon to a sitting position. To the cop, he said, "Cuff 'em, and read 'em their rights."

All eyes in the room were on the two men being pulled to their feet by the cops. I heard the thump of boots on the hardwood floor. Turning, I saw Hodges heading for the exit. Buster whirled to chase him.

"No," I said. "He's mine."

He was going through the door when I started after him. By the time I got to the door, he was already exiting the building, in a dead run toward the parking lot. He, it turned out, was a stupid as the shooter. Trying to run when there was nowhere to run.

Thanks to my morning runs about four days a week, and despite my advanced years, I can get up a good head of steam. Before he'd gone ten feet across the parking lot, in the direction of the parked vehicles, I was out the door and closing.

He made the mistake of looking over his shoulder, causing him to lose some speed, and allowed me to close the gap between us in four swift strides.

What I did next wasn't strictly necessary, but my instincts took over. I could've just closed in and grabbed his collar, which would've been the kind thing to do. But, at that moment, I wasn't feeling particularly kind toward Keith Hodges and his ilk. While most Americans are obsessed with foreign terrorists, I was well aware that our own home-grown terrorists, in the guise of patriotism, were more dangerous. Thriving on hate and conspiracy theories they get from right-wing politicians and media, and believing that religious and ethnic minorities are their enemy, they kill and injure more people than the foreign radicals do. Under the misguided belief that they are in a fight to save America, the more than 300 extremist groups who hide behind the first and second Amendments, deal in guns, drugs, and death, and most Americans are blithely unaware of their existence. No, collaring this guy was not on my menu.

I tensed my muscles, and took a running jump, pulling my legs up, and then shooting my left leg out. My boot caught him between the shoulder blades, sending him forward at an angle, causing his face to hit the hard surface of the parking lot. He slid forward on his chin and chest a couple of feet, and lay unmoving.

Buster came up behind me.

"Damn, bro, that was harsh," he said. "I hope you

didn't kill him."

His hand moved, and he made a wet, groaning sound.

"He's not dead," I said. "But, I think he might be in need of a little reconstructive surgery on his face."

"Oh, that's okay, then. I didn't like that smug look of his anyway."

He stepped forward and grasped Hodges by the shoulder, and turned him over. His face was covered with blood, and little patches of skin hung loosely from his forehead and chin. His lips were bloodied, and I saw a tooth embedded in the hard scrabble. He swayed as Buster pulled him to his feet and began guiding him back toward the building, none too gently shoving him in the back.

His smug look was gone.

Chapter Forty-One

The TSA compound became a beehive of activity over the next three hours. While Thigpen and his men were securing the three prisoners, Lake had phoned and requested a federal strike team come in to secure the compound. In the chaos of arresting Hodges and the two men who'd been hiding in the supply room, the two ATF agents had gone into the room, under the pretext of making sure that no one else was hiding there.

The first vehicles, FBI Suburbans with light racks, and four prisoner transport vans, arrived within forty minutes, leading me to suspect that the federal dudes had prepositioned them not far from our departure point. Sneaky devils.

While Thigpen and his guys did the preliminary questioning of Hodges and his two goons, Harley Munson, the guy who shot at us, and Edward Cates, who drove the vehicle, about the attempt on my life and the wounding of Sandra, the ATF agents were scrambling over boxes of copier tonier cartridges and copy paper, while the FBI contingent stood in the door and watched them.

One of the ATF agents pulled a large cardboard box aside, and shouted, "Holy shit. You're not gonna believe what I just found."

"What is it?" Lake asked.

The agent held up a tube, which I recognized as an older model of the Soviet SA-7 shoulder-fired rocket launcher. Looking like one of the old World War II bazookas—essentially a stovepipe with a flared end—with a machine gun trigger assembly on the bottom, the approximately five-foot long launcher with a missile weighs a bit over 30 pounds, and can fit into a duffel bag. Developed by the Soviets in the late 60s, the missiles use an infrared tracking system to home in on a target's heat source, the engines, and from a range of two miles can hit a target flying at an altitude of 12,000 feet. One man can set up, acquire a target, and fire a missile six to ten seconds.

"There's four crates of these things back here," the ATF guy said. "Along with a bunch of Uzis and AKs. Looks like these guys were preparing for a pretty big battle against someone."

Someone with aircraft, I thought.

"Okay, I'm activating Operation Pandora," Lake said. "Forensics and EOD will be here in an hour."

Thigpen stopped his interrogation of Cates, as Munson and Hodges were still groggy and incoherent, and glared up at Lake. "What the hell is Operation Pandora?" he asked.

Lake looked a little sheepish. "Uh, well, just on the off chance we'd see something that required immediate action, and you have to admit, portable ground to air missiles are pretty immediate, we had a contingency in place. We have an agent sitting in a federal judge's office in DC with a warrant ready to be signed, giving us authority to take this place apart, and, as you heard, forensics and EOD guys on standby back in Gaithersburg." He pointed at the other agent, who was putting his mobile phone back into his pocket.

"They're rolling now."

Thigpen didn't look happy at having been kept in the dark, but Lake didn't look like he was about to apologize. I understood it, though. Need to know. The feds wanted to make sure they could respond to whatever developed, and minimize the danger of their operation being exposed.

"Just so you know, these three belong to me," Thigpen said.

"Not a problem," Lake said, smiling expansively. "We can always get 'em after you're done with 'em." He turned to Boswell, who was ashen-faced and looking at the exit. "In the meantime, congressman, I have a few questions for you."

"L-look," Boswell said. "I had no idea they had those weapons here. I would never—"

"Save it, congressman," Lake said. "You'll still need to explain your relationship with a group that's been on the FBI and ATF watchlists for five years."

Boswell's face fell. "I have nothing to say without my attorney present," he said.

"Too bad, but, that's probably wise." Lake turned his attention back to the supply room, a smug smile on his face.

Buster and I were forgotten in all the excitement. So, we sat on the rim of the pool table and watched the hubbub.

I'd thought the process of six cops arresting thirty-one suspects, and the reaction to finding illicit arms in the supply room had been chaotic, but when the forensics and explosive demolition specialists arrived, I learned what chaos really means, albeit a kind of controlled chaos.

The men and women of the six-person forensics team wore white coveralls, booties, and surgical gloves, and immediately began checking, measuring, and photographing every inch of the compound, including the vehicles, while the EOD guys, in their bulky protective suits and plexiglass masks, commandeered the supply room, and began the slow, laborious process of unpacking and checking the ordnance, which, along with the SA-7s and firearms, also included several crates of Simtex, a powerful plastic explosive from eastern Europe that's a favorite of terrorists, and crates of detcord and detonators, enough firepower to start a small war, or do a lot of damage.

I'd done what I came to do, seen to it that the thug who'd shot Sandra, as well as his boss, were led away in handcuffs, complete with the bruises I'd administered to Hanson and Hodges, and Buster, who was out of his jurisdiction, had no role to play in what was going on. But, since no one had told us to leave, and we were curious, we both hung around the pool table, watching, and picking up fragments of conversation about what the investigators were finding, and what I heard gave me chills, and turned my stomach.

When they took Hodges' office apart, they found a treasure trove of information. Like many would-be dictators and tyrants, Hodges kept meticulous records, and his written rants were classic.

His main bone of contention was, in his words, the invasion of America by immigrants from shithole countries, who were debasing the culture and taking jobs from 'real' Americans. But, he also wrote at length about the standard supremacist topics, the Jewish conspiracy, African-American crime and laziness, women destroying the family structure with their feminist nonsense, and the threat of radical Islam.

Unlike many of the skinhead neo-Nazi gangbangers, though, Hodges had a carefully crafted plan to deal with all these evils. And, that's where Sydney Simpson, et al, came in.

Unhappy with their current compound, Hodges had been seeking an easily secured area that was nearer a major transportation artery. He saw the perfect opportunity when he learned of Simpson's plans to sell farmland adjacent to I-270, within fifty miles of DC. Not only would it be easier for TSA to smuggle arms and drugs, but it would facilitate the organization's political agenda. Which is where Boswell came in.

In a separate folder, Hodges had dozens of Boswell's speeches and PR releases. The freshman representative was an ardent opponent of immigration, welfare, and any restrictions on arms ownership. The documents had been marked up in many places with Hodges' own views, or with praise for Boswell's stance on issues. In this folder was also a letter from Boswell, thanking Hodges for his support during the former's election campaign. Most damning, though, was a recently dated letter informing Hodges of Boswell's plans to run for president in 2007, and ensuring him that if he was elected, his administration would implement the programs they had discussed. Unfortunately, no details were given of those programs. One sentence, in particular, was strange. It read, 'Hopefully, we will not have to implement Operation Armageddon, but you must remain at the ready.'

"What the hell is Operation Armageddon?" Buster asked.

Lake frowned at him, but he too seemed shocked by the letter. "I have no idea, but whatever it is, it's not good."

"Guess that's gon' make it hard for the congressman to deny knowin' what Hodges and his boys were up to."

"Not necessarily." Lake shook his head. "This establishes that they knew each other, and had similar views, but doesn't prove that Boswell knew the details of Hodges' operation. It's gonna complicate the hell out of his plans to run for president, though."

"Too bad it won't affect his election to congress," I

said.

"Yeah, that's the problem with a lot of these congressional districts, especially some of the ones out west. Everybody's related to everybody else, and as long as their guy thinks and acts their way, they get reelected." Lake's face had a sour look. "Actually, it's pretty much the same all over. There was even one congressman who was reelected while he was sitting in a jail cell. Go figure that one, right."

I had to nod in agreement. Democracy is a messy, inefficient form of government, but it's better than all the other kinds. The thing, though, is that I wondered if what we had could still be considered a democracy, considering some of the people who were getting elected, and how they were going about it.

"Oh well, better half a loaf than none at all," I said. "At least you're getting these TSA goons off the street."

"Yeah, there is that."

He should've been happy, but he had a troubled expression. I was pretty sure this Operation Armageddon had a lot to do with that.

It was no longer my problem, though. I'd helped put Hodges and TSA out of business. Boswell and his political machinations, along with Operation Armageddon was not my headache. I planned to leave that to Lake and the rest of the feds.

Chapter Forty-Two

It's never that simple, though. First, Thigpen, after getting his three prisoners bundled into a county transport vehicle that arrived behind a convoy of assorted federal agency vehicles, he insisted on getting a quick statement from me regarding the shooting.

"I want to make sure I've got this guy nailed down tight," he said.

I couldn't disagree with that, so I walked him through the incident. Only when he was satisfied that he had everything he needed did he close his notebook and put it away.

"What's the word on Loretta Palmer getting released?" I asked.

"Oh, yeah, in all the excitement, I forgot," he said. "She was released this morning."

Well, thanks for telling me, I thought. Not that I could really blame him. I'd been so focused on getting a lick or two in on Hodges and his thugs, I'd forgotten to ask.

"Good to hear," I said.

"That's not all. In with that haul of cash you found

in the closet, we found documents to all of Simpson's offshore bank accounts, and get this, the guy had his passwords written on the statements. The Treasury guys said we should be able to repatriate every penny." He smiled. "Your client and her friends should eventually get every penny of their money back."

That would probably make my client happier than getting out of jail. I called Heather and passed the information along. She promised to call the client and let her know.

Another case closed. Another satisfied client.

Chapter Forty-Three

I was just putting my phone back into my pocket when Lake walked up and tapped me on the shoulder.

"Pennyback, before you go, I just wanted to thank you on behalf of the bureau and ATF," he said. "Thanks to you, we'll finally be able to put Hodges and his crew away, and stop a major arms and drug smuggling operation."

"Glad to help. I'm a firm supporter of the Constitution, but the way these guys exploit it, especially the Second Amendment, is just plain wrong."

Suddenly, Lake looked tired, like a man who has just trekked forty kilometers through triple canopy jungle carrying an eighty-pound ruck. "Yeah, and when elected officials like Boswell get in bed with these guys it's a real clusterfuck. They make it hard to file indictments, get wiretap warrants, the whole shebang, all in the quest for votes."

"You don't think some of these politicians don't believe in all this crap?"

His laugh lacked humor. "I couldn't tell you *what* the hell they believe in." He seemed to be deep in thought. His head turned, taking in me, Buster, and Thigpen. "Look, I'm about to go out on a limb here, so I'm gonna have to trust you guys. What I'm about to tell you is not to ever be repeated, not even on your death bed."

Thigpen and Buster both looked surprised. I understood that. The FBI, according to Buster, is stingy as hell with information, insisting that local cops share all, but seldom reciprocating in kind. If Lake was about to tell us something that he wouldn't normally share, it had to be pretty damn bad.

"I can't speak for these guys," I said. "But, I was in the army long enough to know how to keep a confidence."

The other two nodded.

"Okay," Lake said. "This would normally be on a strict need-to-know basis, but you guys have already been exposed to some of it, and in order to impress upon you the importance of keeping it mum, I'll tell you what I know."

"Don't tell me these dirt bags were planning to steal the nuclear codes or something," Buster said. "Or maybe, blow up the Pentagon?"

"No, nothing quite that dramatic. But, we found documents in Hodges' office showing plans for a new TSA compound just north of Germantown, Maryland, a sprawling area that would accommodate over two thousand men."

"Did he have that many men in his organization?" I asked.

"As far as we know, the current membership in TSA is about five hundred. But, Hodges had plans to recruit more. The place in Germantown was to be the training base and headquarters for the larger organization. There was a problem, though, when Sydney Simpson changed his mind about selling it."

"Yeah, I got that from Devlin, but I'm not clear on it. Hodges was offering more for the land than the other buyer."

Lake chuckled. "Well, despite his line of work, apparently, Simpson had a line he wouldn't cross. According to some email back and forth between them, it seems the con man wasn't sympathetic to TSA's aims, at least Simpson wasn't. There were a couple of emails between Hodges and Devlin that indicate Devlin was."

"I wonder if *that* might've been what caused the confrontation when Devlin killed his partner?" It actually made more sense than a deadly argument over bank accounts.

"You can be sure we'll be asking Mr. Devlin about that," Thigpen said.

"I'd appreciate that," Lake said. "Especially anything Devlin might know about Hodges' plans for the land."

"Anything in particular?"

"Try and find out what Devlin knows about Hodges' plans for the land. For example, on a rough sketch of the proposed new compound, there are several points on hills in the western sector marked as FP. See if he knows what they're for."

Thigpen took out his notebook and made notes. I didn't need to. I knew what an FP was, and when I thought back to the SA-7 missiles in the supply room, I shuddered. FP in military parlance stands for 'firing point.' From an FP on an elevated piece of land, a gunner has a pretty clear shot at low-flying aircraft. Helicopters are easy targets, but, low-flying jets, or commercial airliners on landing approach can also be taken down. My first thought was that this gave Hodges and his crew shots at planes coming in for landings at Dulles International Airport, just south of the Potomac River. The ones coming in from the north are pretty low by the time they're over Germantown.

"You think they'd go after an airliner?" I asked.

Lake looked grave. "I wouldn't put it past 'em.

Maybe that's what this Operation Armageddon is all about. Think about it. If an airliner was shot down this close to the capital, the first thought on everyone's mind would be terrorists. We'd be looking for someone to hit back at. And, if it could be shown that an SA-7 was used, it would have international implications."

"Holy shit," Thigpen said. "This just got a bit more complicated than a simple murder. You think the congressman's involved in this?"

"I don't know, but Mr. Boswell will have some pretty serious questions to answer."

"I guess that shoots his run for president down," Thigpen said. "No pun intended."

All I could think was, thank goodness for that. The politicians we get are bad enough, but if a militia-supporter became president, we'd be up a deep creek in a leaky boat.

"I hope when you question him, you stick it in deep and twist it," I said.

Lake shook his head. "I wish I could. Unfortunately, he's a sitting congressman, so we'll have to treat him with kid gloves unless we get some hard evidence. But, I promise you this, I'm gonna make that son of a bitch sweat as much as I can. Now, I remind all of you. You never heard any of this."

The three of us made zipping motions across our mouths. I, for one, was planning to try and put the whole thing out of my mind as much as possible. Hodges was good for a long time in a federal pen, and Boswell would be busy trying to cover his tracks. Crisis avoided—this time.

I had my own problem to deal with.

Chapter Forty-Four

Most of the color had come back into Sandra's face, and they'd removed all the tubes and wires from her body. She was sitting up in bed, with the thin blanket down to her waist, eating a red gelatin dessert. She looked up and smiled when I walked through the door. Blood was still asleep in a chair in the corner, and Elizabeth was nodding off in a chair at bedside with her back to the door.

"Hey, stranger," I said. "You're looking good. How do you feel?"

"Like I've been shot," she said. "Now, come here and kiss me."

I braced myself on the edge of the hard mattress and kissed her gently on the forehead. She grabbed my head and pulled me down until our lips met, and kissed me deeply.

"Take it easy, babe. Don't want to open your stitches." I pulled back, albeit reluctantly.

"I'm not that fragile," she said. "I bend, but I don't break."

I searched her eyes for any sign of emotional

distress. Post traumatic stress can hit at any time, and when it does, it often hits hard. Getting shot is a truly traumatic experience, physically and mentally. Hell, being near someone who gets shot is traumatic. I'd been in that situation often enough that I'd learned to cope with it. Sandra, on the other hand, hadn't really. So, I was primed to help her through whatever came. Her gaze, though, was clear.

"I know you're a tough cookie, but sometimes, the emotional reaction to an incident like this strike long after the fact."

"How well I know that. You forget, Al; I work in a high school in one of DC's most depressed areas. With drug overdoses, gang fights, and drive-by shootings, I've seen enough death to know how it affects people." She pinched my cheek. "And, by the way, this is not the first time danger has knocked on my door since I met you."

That last stung, because she was right. But, I'd also forgotten that she *had* seen violence up close and personal for a long time—probably more than most soldiers—and, she understood fully how it could affect someone.

"I know, babe," I said. "I . . . I just want you to know, I'm here if you need me."

"I know that, honey." She lay her head against my shoulder.

Elizabeth, who had gone from nodding to full sleep by the time I'd crossed the room, snapped awake with a snort and a little grunt.

"Oh, I'm sorry," she said, as her head jerked up. "I must've fallen asleep."

She had dark circles under her bloodshot eyes.

"Good grief, you look like you haven't slept," I said.

"I wanted to be awake when Sandra came around," she said. She shook her head. "Looks like I blew a simple job."

Sandra reached across and patted her hand. "Don't

beat yourself up, Elizabeth. When I came around, there was a nurse here. You and Carlton were sleeping so peacefully, we didn't have the heart to wake you up."

"But, I was supposed to call Al to let him know you were awake." She looked on the verge of crying.

I walked around to her side of the bed and put my arm around her shoulder. "Hey, Elizabeth, you're only human," I said. "Don't worry about it. Sandra's fine now, and I'm grateful for you guys for watching over her for me."

She looked up at me, her eyes glistening, but with a determined, steely look. "Did you find the son of a bitch who did this?"

"Yeah," Sandra said. "I meant to ask that, too."

"Yup, I found him, and when he gets out of the hospital, he'll be going straight to a jail cell, along with the dirt bag who gave him his orders."

They both looked at me with questions in their eyes. "Hey, I'll tell you all about it later. Right now, I'd just like to sit here and look at my lady. Why don't you and Blood go on home and get some rest."

"You look like you could use some rest yourself," Sandra said. "Why don't you all go get some rest. You can come back later."

"If they don't mind waiting," a deep voice with a sing-song British accent said from behind me. "You can take her with you, and you can all get some rest."

I turned to see a tall, dark-skinned man with a hooked nose, dark, almost black eyes, and slicked-back black hair, wearing green scrubs with a stethoscope around his neck. The white tag over his left breast read, Singar.

"You're releasing me?" Sandra's eyes were round and her smile lit up her face like a thousand-watt bulb.

"Just as soon as the discharge paperwork is done," Singar said. He applied the stethoscope to her back and the center of her chest, between the swell of her breasts. Then, he thumbed back her eyelid and checked her eyes. "Your wound is healing well, and the internal damage was minimal. You will, of course, have to let that arm rest for ten days or so, but I don't foresee any long-term consequences to worry about. You were extremely fortunate that the bullet didn't hit any major blood vessels or bones. It tore some muscle, but they'll regenerate. You'll have scars from the entry and exit wounds, which can be removed by plastic surgery if you wish. Other than that, you're good to go. Any questions?"

She just sat there, her mouth open, shaking her head.

"Thanks, doc," I said.

"You're welcome. Now, you will experience some residual pain at the site of the injury. I'll be prescribing some pain medication, but honestly, I would suggest trying to work through the pain without medication."

He didn't have to tell either of us that. We'd both seen people become addicted to pain pills, and that was a road neither of wanted to travel.

"Don't worry, doc," I said. "I'm a fan of Oriental holistic methods."

"And," said Sandra. "I don't like taking pills anyway."

He patted her uninjured shoulder. "That's good to hear. I'll prescribe anyway, just in case the pain becomes too much, but I think your approach is better."

After examining the dressings over her wounds, he shook my hand and left.

"We'll stick around and help you get your things to the car," Elizabeth said.

"No, you will not," Sandra shot back. "You wake Carlton up, and get him home. You can come by the house tomorrow, and we'll catch up."

"You sure?"

"She's sure," I said. "I got this."

Smiling wanly, she rose and went to the corner to shake Blood awake. He grumbled at first, but then, his eyes snapped open, and he smiled at Sandra and me.

"Hey, little girl, I see you're awake, and you're looking pretty good," he said.

"Fit as a fiddle," Sandra said. "In fact, I'm busting out of this place in a few minutes."

"Well, maybe more than a few," I said. "The doctor said they're preparing the discharge papers."

"Whatever. I'm getting out today, that's what counts. Now, Carlton, you and Elizabeth get out of here and get some rest."

He started to protest, but Elizabeth grabbed his hand.

"Not to worry, sweetheart. We can drop in on them tonight. I think Al wants some time alone with her."

He waggled his eyebrows. "Yes, I suppose you're right. Okay, kids, see you tonight."

"Great," I said. "I'll prepare something special, and we can have a homecoming dinner."

After they were gone, I turned back to the bed and took Sandra's hand. There was so much I wanted to say to her at that moment, but my voice refused to cooperate, so I just sat there looking at her with my mouth gaped open.

"You have something on your mind, Al Pennyback," she said, stroking my hand. "What is it?"

I snapped my mouth shut and swallowed hard.

"I, I was afraid I would lose you, babe."

She squeezed my hand. "But, you didn't. I'm still here, and I'm not going anywhere anytime soon."

"I don't want you to go anywhere ever."

"What? Why would you think I'd be going anywhere?"

I have no idea where the thought came from, or when, but, sometime since that bullet bored through my car window and hit her, I'd been thinking of what my life was like before she came into it, and what it would be like if she left. And, I didn't like the thought.

"No, it's not like that, I mean—" I am not a very talkative person, but I don't normally have so much trouble expressing myself. "Look, Sandra, I have something, I mean, there's something we need to talk about."

Her brow furrowed as she frowned.

"Al, what is it? You're worrying me. Is there something wrong?"

"No, babe, nothing's wrong," I said. I took a deep breath, reaching deep inside for the calm I needed for what I was about to say. "You're okay, and we're going home. Everything's fine."

She cocked her head to the side.

"If everything's all right, why do you look like you're standing in front of a large crowd, and have just realized that your fly's open?"

"Is it that obvious? Wow, I thought about this all the way here, but I didn't think it'd be this hard."

"Al Pennyback, the martial arts expert who goes up against armed militia men with nothing but his wits and bare hands, is intimidated by something? I never thought I'd see that day." She laughed.

I knew what she was doing. She was poking to get me just upset enough that whatever it was that was bothering me wouldn't seem so daunting anymore. It worked—sort of.

"You're right. This shouldn't be that hard."

"Then, spill it."

"Okay, here it is. Sandra, I think we should get married."

Her mouth opened in a little 'o'. Her eyes went wide. She tightened her grip on my hand.

"Are you asking me to marry you?"

"Well, yeah."

Then, she smiled.

"It's not the romantic proposal I expected, but I guess it'll have to do."

"Does that mean you will?"

"Isn't that what I just said?"

She rested her head against my shoulder, and I pulled her close. Suddenly, I didn't feel so nervous anymore.

Charles Ray

Books by this author:

Al Pennyback mysteries

Color Me Dead
Memorial to the Dead
Deadline
Dead, White, and Blue
A Good Day to Die
The Day the Music Died
Die, Sinner
Deadly Intentions
Death by Design
Till Death Do Us Part
Deadly Dose
Dead Man's Cove
Dead Men Don't Answer
Deadly Paradise
Kiss of Death
Death in White Satin
Death and Taxis
Deadbeat
A Deadly Wind Blows
Death Wish
Deadly Vendetta
A Time to Kill, A Time to Die
Dead Ringer
Death of Innocence
Dead Reckoning
Murder on the Menu
Over My Dead Body
Bad Girls Don't Die
A Deal to Die For

Ed Lazenby mysteries

Butterfly Effect
Coriolis Effect
The Cat in the Hatbox
Negative Side Effects
Murder is as Easy as ABC

Buffalo Soldier series

Buffalo Soldier: Trial by Fire
Buffalo Soldier: Homecoming
Buffalo Soldier: Incident at Cactus Junction
Buffalo Soldier: Peacekeepers
Buffalo Soldier: Renegade
Buffalo Soldier: Escort Duty
Buffalo Soldier: Battle at Dead Man's Gulch
Buffalo Soldier: Yosemite
Buffalo Soldier: Comanchero
Buffalo Soldier: Range War
Buffalo Soldier: Mob Justice
Buffalo Soldier: Chasing Ghosts
Buffalo Soldier: The Piano
Buffalo Soldier: Family Feud
Buffalo Soldier: The Lost Expedition

Other fiction

Angel on His Shoulder
She's No Angel
Child of the Flame
Pip's Revenge
Wallace in Underland
Further Adventures of Wallace in Underland

Dead Letter and Other Tales
The White Dragons
The Dragon's Lair
Dragon Slayer
The Last Gunfighters
The Culling
Frontier Justice: Bass Reeves, Deputy
  U.S. Marshal
Angel on His Shoulder-Revised Edition
Battle at the Galactic Junkyard
Mountain Man
Devil's Lake
Vixen
Wagons West: Daniel's Journey
Wagons West: Trinity
Awakening
Fatal Encounters: The Adventures of Bass
  Reeves, Deputy U.S. Marshal

Nonfiction

Things I Learned from My Grandmother About
  Leadership and Life
Taking Charge: Effective Leadership for the
  Twenty-first Century
Grab the Brass ring
African Places: A Photographic Journey
  Through Zimbabwe and southern Africa
A Portrait of Africa
There's Always a Plan B
In the Line of Fire: American Diplomats in
  the Trenches
Advice for the Insecure Writer
Looking at Life Through My Lens

Ethical Dilemmas and the Practice of Diplomacy
Making America Grate Again
DC Street Art
Dead Letters and Other Tales: Revised edition

Children's books

The Yak and the Yeti
Samantha and the Bully
Molly Learns to Share
Where is Teddy?
Catie and Mister Hop-Hop
Tommy Learns to Count
Catie Goes to School

About the Author

Charles Ray has been writing fiction since his teens. He won a Sunday school magazine writing contest when he was thirteen, and having his byline on a short story published in a national publication forever hooked him on writing. During his time in the army (1962-1982) he often moonlighted as a newspaper or magazine journalist, and was the editorial cartoonist for the Spring Lake (NC) News, a weekly newspaper, during the 1970s. In addition to his writing, he was an artist/cartoonist and photographer for a number of publications, including Ebony, Eagle and Swan, and Essence, and had a monthly cartoon feature and did several covers for Buffalo, a now-defunct magazine that was dedicated to showcasing the contributions of African-Americans to the country's military history.

After retiring from the army, he joined the U.S. Foreign Service, and served as a diplomat in posts in Asia and Africa until his retirement in 2012. He has worked and traveled throughout the world (Antarctica is the only continent he hasn't visited), and now, as a full-time writer, continues to globetrot looking for interesting things to write about, draw, or take pictures of.

A native of Texas, he now calls Maryland home. For more on his writing and other projects, check one of the following Web sites:

http://charlesaray.blogspot.com

http://charlieray45.wordpress.com
http://www.twitter.com/charlieray45
http://www.facebook.com/charlieray45
http://www.flickr.com/photos/charlesray45/
http://www.viewbug.com/member/charlesray

You can also order some of my books through my author's website: http://charlesray-author.com/

Authors write to be read, and that can only happen when readers are made aware of the books available. Reviews are one way this happens. If you liked this book, please leave a review, even if only a few words, on Amazon or Goodreads.

www.ingramcontent.com/pod-product-compliance
Lightning Source LLC
Chambersburg PA
CBHW071450170626
46811CB00007B/2533